under

NEWEST

eyes

under NEWEST *eyes*

STORIES FROM NEWEST REVIEW

edited by

PAUL DENHAM & GAIL YOUNGBERG

Thistledown Press

Canadian Cataloguing in Publication Data
Main entry under title:

Under NeWest eyes: stories from NeWest review

Includes bibliographic references and index.
ISBN 1-895449-55-3

1. Short stories, Canadian (English) - Prairie
Provinces.* 2. Canadian fiction (English) - 20th
century.* I. Denham, Paul, 1941- II. Youngberg,
Gail. III. NeWest review

PS8329.5.P7U53 1996   C813'.01089712   C96-920020-X
PR9197.32.U53 1996

Book design by A.M. Forrie
Cover design and illustration by Dik Campbell
Set in 10pt Carmina Lt by Thistledown Press

Printed and Bound in Canada by
Veilleux Printing
Boucherville, Quebec

Thistledown Press Ltd.
633 Main Street
Saskatoon, Saskatchewan, S7H 0J8

This book has been published with the assistance of a special grant from
the Saskatchewan Arts Board.

Thistledown Press gratefully acknowledges the continued support of The Canada Council
and the Saskatchewan Arts Board.

Saskatchewan
Arts Board

EDNA ALFORD. "The Garden of Eloise Loon" was originally published in *NeWest Review* (September 1981) and subsequently in *The Garden of Eloise Loon* (Oolichan Books, 1986). It is reprinted here by permission of Oolichan Books.

SANDRA BIRDSELL. "The Wild Plum Tree" was originally published in *NeWest Review* (October 1982) and subsequently in *Agassiz Stories* (Turnstone Press, 1987). It is reprinted here by permission of Turnstone Press.

PER K. BRASK. "The Sign" was originally published in *NeWest Review* (September 1983) and is reprinted here by permission of the author.

ELIZABETH BREWSTER. "Well-Meant Advice" was originally published in *NeWest Review* (October 1987) and subsequently in *Visitation* (Oberon Press, 1987). It is reprinted here by permission of Oberon Press.

BONNIE BURNARD. "Music Lessons" was originally published in *NeWest Review* (April 1984) and subsequently in *Women of Influence* (Coteau Books, 1988). It is reprinted here by permission of Coteau Books.

SHARON BUTALA. "Belle in Winter" was originally published in *NeWest Review* (October 1983) and subsequently in *Queen of the Heartaches* (Coteau Books, 1985). It is reprinted here by permission of Coteau Books.

RICHARD CUMYN. "The Sound He Made" was originally published in *NeWest Review* (August/September 1993) and subsequently in *The Limit of Delta Y Over Delta X* (Goose Lane Editions, 1994). It is reprinted here by permission of Goose Lane Editions.

BETH GOOBIE. "The Detachable Appendage" was originally published in *NeWest Review* (August/September 1991) and subsequently in *Could I Have My Body Back Now, Please?* (NeWest Press, 1991). It is reprinted here by permission of NeWest Press.

FRANCES ITANI. "Iron Wheels" was originally published in *NeWest Review* (March 1977) and is reprinted here by permission of the author.

TONJA GUNVALDSEN KLAASSEN. "Fall River" was originally published in *NeWest Review* (August/September 1994) and is reprinted here by permission of the author.

ED KLEIMAN. "The Wedding I Never Attended" was originally published in *NeWest Review* (December/January 1994/5) and is reprinted here by permission of the author.

JAKE MACDONALD. "Becoming" was originally published in *NeWest Review* (February 1982) and subsequently in *Two Tickets to Paradise* (Oberon Press, 1990). It is reprinted here by permission of Oberon Press.

SHARON MACFARLANE. "Stains" was originally published in *NeWest Review* (November 1985) and is reprinted here by permission of the author.

KEN MITCHELL. "You Better Not Pout" was originally published in *NeWest Review* (December 1976) and is reprinted here by permission of the author.

ROSEMARY NIXON. "The Cock's Egg" was originally published in *NeWest Review* (April/May 1994) and subsequently in *The Cock's Egg* (NeWest Press, 1994). It is reprinted here by permission of NeWest Press.

HELEN ROSTA. "Hunting Season" was originally published in *NeWest Review* (February 1977) and is reprinted here by permission of the author.

DIANE SCHOEMPERLEN. "This Town" was originally published in *NeWest Review* (February 1981) and subsequently in *Hockey Night in Canada* (Quarry Press, 1987). It is reprinted here by permission of Quarry Press.

LOIS SIMMIE. "Mick and I and Hong Kong Heaven" was originally published in *NeWest Review* (January 1984) and is reprinted here by permission of the author.

GUY VANDERHAEGHE. "Café Society" was originally published in *NeWest Review* (November 1980) and subsequently in *The Trouble with Heroes* (Borealis Press, 2nd edition, 1986). It is reprinted here by permission of Borealis Press.

RUDY WIEBE. "Home for Night" was originally published in *NeWest Review* (April 1976) and is reprinted here by permission of the author.

CONTENTS

INTRODUCTION   *Paul Denham and Gail Youngberg*   /9

HOME FOR NIGHT   *Rudy Wiebe*   /13

YOU BETTER NOT POUT   *Ken Mitchell*   /20

HUNTING SEASON   *Helen Rosta*   /27

IRON WHEELS   *Frances Itani*   /35

CAFÉ SOCIETY   *Guy Vanderhaeghe*   /42

THIS TOWN   *Diane Schoemperlen*   /50

THE GARDEN OF ELOISE LOON   *Edna Alford*   /58

BECOMING   *Jake MacDonald*   /67

THE WILD PLUM TREE   *Sandra Birdsell*   /83

THE SIGN   *Per K. Brask*   /96

BELLE IN WINTER   *Sharon Butala*   /102

MICK AND I AND HONG KONG HEAVEN   *Lois Simmie*   /114

MUSIC LESSONS   *Bonnie Burnard*   /127

STAINS   *Sharon MacFarlane*   /134

WELL-MEANT ADVICE   *Elizabeth Brewster*   /137

THE DETACHABLE APPENDAGE   *Beth Goobie*   /150

THE SOUND HE MADE   *Richard Cumyn*   /158

THE COCK'S EGG   *Rosemary Nixon*   /171

FALL RIVER   *Tonja Gunvaldsen Klaassen*   /183

THE WEDDING I NEVER ATTENDED   *Ed Kleiman*   /190

NOTES ON CONTRIBUTORS   /204

Introduction

E dmonton, June 1975: George Melnyk got out the first issue of
NeWest Review, with the close help of his wife Julia Berry and
the assistance of friends Samuel Gerszonowicz and Deloris Russell.
Then a tabloid, the eight-page paper had the homely air of '70s desktop
publishing — ragged right columns hammered out on an IBM Selectric,
Letraset headlines.

It was a modest appearance for a publication intended to start a
cultural revolution. *NeWest* was launched to provide a forum for
western Canadians to talk to each other about themselves, about
their culture, in the broadest sense. Melnyk's concern was to develop
the indigenous voice of the prairies. What vehicles there were for the
exchange of ideas were mostly narrowly focused — on "news", as
defined by a variety of editorial perspectives, on politics, on business,
on agriculture, on literature. None saw "culture" from the all-en-
compassing perspective that Melnyk was developing in his work on
regionalism. Contributors to that first issue included George Woodcock,
Maria Campbell, Rudy Wiebe, Sid Marty, Laurence Ricou, Henry
Kriesel, Joe Fafard, names that are now synonymous with the voice
of western Canada. Ken Mitchell wrote to say that he "immediately
recognized it as something long overdue . . . There are many of us,
writers and critics both, in Saskatchewan who are beginning to feel
a strong regional identification, and *NeWest* is just what is needed."

Two years after it was launched, *NeWest* received its first govern-ment grant —$500 from Alberta Culture to pay contributors. The editor noted that "This amounts to $50 per issue or approximately $5 per contributor." While *NeWest* is grateful for the continuing support of the Canada Council and currently the Saskatchewan Arts Board, it is only recently that a wider understanding of "culture" — one that looks beyond the support of fiction, poetry, and the performing arts — has been apparent in the ruminations of our granting agencies. Lately there have been signs of an understanding that even the political behaviour of a nation, or a region, may be related to the prevailing cultural assumptions, and that the stories we tell one another about ourselves arise from the same rich and complex nexus.

In selecting stories to represent two decades of fiction writing in *NeWest Review*, we had riches to choose from, and the present collection is only one among many possibilities which might have taken form. Various commentators have noted that the short story seems to be particularly strong in Canada, and its flexibility and variety are pecu-liarly suited to the small magazines on which so much of this coun-try's literary and cultural life depends. It seems appropriate, therefore, to mark our coming-of-age with a collection of stories.

The initial selection, of course, was the work of previous editors. By 1978, three years after George Melnyk established the magazine, Reg Silvester (September 1978 – June 1980) became the first volunteer to begin the endless and rewarding process of fishing in the steady stream of fiction directed our way. He was followed by Greg Holling-shead (October 1980 – June 1981, David Carpenter (September 1981 – February 1987), Lorna Crozier (March 1987 – Summer 1987), Lew Horne (September 1987 – August/September 1991), Elizabeth Brewster (October/November 1991 – December/January 1992), and Bill Bar-tley (February/March 1993 – October/November 1995). Bill Bartley actually began the process of review and selection for this anthology, and contributed greatly to the final choices, before handing over his title to Nancy Taylor (December/January 1995/96), who is the current fiction editor for the magazine.

In making our selection for *Under NeWest Eyes*, we have avoided theoretical, ideological and even regional commitments in favour of as much variety as possible. The result is that, although *NeWest* is a regional magazine devoted to the prairie region, several of our writers are from elsewhere and the subject matter is often derived from other regions, other societies. This is not a book of prairie stories. Still, we might provisionally assert a post-colonial significance to this effort; the Canadian prairies, though still a resource-based hinterland of empires variously defined, has a more mature culture than it did a generation ago. Sarah Binks is dead. Our writers are finding an audience here, and writers from elsewhere are interested in reaching an audience represented by our readers.

Some of these writers had already established reputations by the time they published in *NeWest*; others, such as Guy Vanderhaeghe, Sandra Birdsell, Bonnie Burnard and Edna Alford, were little known when they appeared in our pages but have gone on to make national and even international names for themselves. Others may at present not be as well known, but it seems likely that at least some of these will find a wider readership in the future. The small magazine is a place where writers can try things out, get reactions, find their voices and their audience. *Under NeWest Eyes* is a partial record of that living culture. We have arranged the stories chronologically, in the order in which they appeared in the magazine.

Paul Denham and Gail Youngberg
Saskatoon, April 1996

Home for Night

Rudy Wiebe

When he came forward, quickly, the stewardess was alone in first class, contemplating the flawless face reflected in her nightcase mirror. He swung into the right seats. Already the plane had edged up to the river lying north and south here but in the distance bending in a long curve back, east, and further ahead there was the tiny blackish spiderwork of trees arranged by loops upon river loops into a wider valley — that had to be the Red Deer — it was all so fast, too fast. He slid across to the left seats — that deep cut angling southwest must be the South Saskatchewan. He pressed his forehead against the window; six miles below, between white prairie and white river, the brownish fringes of cliffs crumpled back up ravines until the river gradually straightened as if drawn free-hand into the far blue mist of land barely yellow and grey in the white. He pushed harder, but directly below the incredible raw valley was steadily drawing away behind them — that stupid pilot was flying dead-centre over the point, he would need a bomb-bay to see exactly where the two rivers joined their ice . . . had needed, it was already inevitably past, and he had not even a memory to —

"It looks so cold down there, doesn't it!" The perfect face of the stewardess tilted on the seatback, smiling her perfectly trained exclamation. He stared at her.

Rudy Wiebe

"The Old Man River is always . . . " she began after a moment, and stopped.

"Then what's the river below now," he said.

"The Waterton?"

He was past her legs, unflawed nylon marble; back in his own seat. Stupid. Strong plastic trayback, strong plastic window. The Red Deer River looped back and forth across its shallow drift, again and again swinging almost back to touch itself in shadows carved by the winter sun. The window hardened his face with cold, gradually hardened, straightened the river out of curls into curves, then simply bent lines among the grey-white mushrooms and straightened egg-cups of bad-lands.

Soon that too had vanished in a long valley northwest, but he had a memory to lay on the white ordered land outlined by faint webs of fences, by squares and oblongs of texture. The memory of a little man, on a summer day, white sleeves looped by gold links, a hand passing over his face like a kiss and suddenly holding . . . holding an unbe-lievable curve of teeth, teeth which have just emerged out of the man's head. He must have seen that standing, he remembered now, carefully, in front of the cabin where he was born, on the spot where his mother stood once when a greyish picture was taken, she small in an apron like a white yoke against the greys of mudded logs, the even smaller figures of his two sisters already whitely aproned on her right, and himself a tiny greyish bump smudged against her other side. In front of the door, the screen door where in summer he had often stood fearfully, waiting to hear the cowbells return from the free-range stretching forever west of their homestead, knowing his mother would surely bring the cows if she could find them in the mosquito-whining bush, knowing if she went too far she would have to find them to guide her back home, the smudge-smoke waiting too, a blue flat cloud caught above the corral in a motionless net of poplars. He had stared, rigid, at the teeth cut with such inhuman precision out of, what he had thought till then, a living face. The man's blurred voice asked

14

him if he could take his out too, and he could not so much as shake his head when he had never thought it possible to try.

And his mother leaning beyond the sheen of screen door, not laughing like the grey man when with a sudden jolt of terror he clawed inside his own mouth, tearing at his tiny, o blessed be Lord Jesus, immoveable teeth.

"That's not for us, Bengelchi," she said reaching out, nubbling his head. "We're not that advanced yet."

But she was soon advanced enough, the first in the family, after she wrenched her left arm out of its socket falling between the split poles of the hayrack and after two years of sporadic paralysis finally getting to a doctor who told her she should have been sewn together immediately when it happened, that she would never heal properly now, and that her teeth were broken pipes draining poison into her body. Her teeth then no more than grey or black stumps destroyed systematically by chewing salt whenever their unending pain became more unbearable than the sharper, but briefer, agony of killing them.

The Bow River in a greyish crevasse; his tongue slid around his own teeth capped, filled, so solid and strong the dentists always said, all those turnips and boiled cabbage grown in Alberta bush that had destroyed his mother's . . . she was younger then than he was now. His body shuddered in the foam seat; he tried to somehow comprehend that. She had always seemed so . . . ancient . . . was that the word? Bits of pictures, touches, words would be falling on him like rain as long as he lived and how would he ever recapture her, the feeling he understood when her eyes were still level with his and she would say a word to him, her hand now soft as weathered cloth then firm, unshaky in his own. *"Die letzte Nacht im Eltern Haus."*

In English that sounded merely sentimental, perhaps it was her rhythm of saying *Eltern* that made the equivalent "parents" so bony: words she first said when he first left and almost every time he returned, even for a day, even the short day he brought his wife through the door, married in a ceremony across an ocean and for which she could do no more than airmail a poem he never knew where she found. The poem was

Rudy Wiebe

doddery, stale to him snoring lyric Rilke daily under his breath, though the feelings were right, for her; he could hear her voice sounding the words as her hand slowly moved copying them, perhaps out of her head: *"Wohl dir, du hast es gut . . . "*

The Calgary airport was khaki metal walls and fans blowing through heaters hung from exposed pipes; after an L10-11, the plane south barely a basket. He folded himself in with some others, it quivered like a Model A., though the airvents and window were plastic. And the white mountains, the Bow and Old Man Rivers sifted him out of his jet-lag, out of the staggering weariness of walking momentarily on cement. Among the trees of these valleys — the plane seemed in them rather than over them — buffalo had wintered with the Blackfeet, bedded in those folds. The voice of the long distance operator trying to hammer him awake, to make him understand. How had they found him at the Montreal hotel?

The memory had to be wrong, they would never have carried the tub up those pole stairs, leave alone the hot kettle, yet he always remembered her bending across the tub in the angle of the rafters under which he slept at night curled into wool on a straw sack, the house logs cracking fearfully in the cold when he rammed himself out of a bad dream, the stovepipe standing straight up into darkness at the edge of his bed. In that memory she leaned forever at the angle of the rafters, clawing at the kettle from which his older sister poured boiling water into the tin tub and thoughtlessly onto his younger sister — her thigh — squatting to bathe in the tepid water he had just left: that scream must have echoed in the kitchen below, and his mother's too, the kettle now in her hand with his older sister suddenly rigid in the soft steam of her pouring, her mouth fallen open and her hands still up, crooked as if still holding the blackened kettle. That might not have happened in winter, any more than it happened in the sleeping loft; it might have been the summer when the gigantic bull stalked out of free-range, roared about the yard all afternoon so that none of them dared open the door, not even his mother, and he prayed if only his father would appear, oh help him to come, now from wherever he is, somewhere,

16

help him to come home early for Sunday, help, and then there he was, coming steadily down the wagon tracks with a thick green stick in his hand and going to the bull pawing dust over himself, head down and roaring, and had thumped him across the nose and jammed the stick into the bull's ring and led him west out of the yard; had broken the poplar on the bull's swiftly retreating rump.

He could not have been thinking in English then — how could he have thought? In the Low German she still spoke to him, that he screamed into the telephone to make her understand he would come, yoh, yoh he was coming! Her removable teeth perfect and even as though carved from marble filling her mouth, moving her jaw down out of the folds of face to shape her strong chin again, the uneasy evenness of her sudden smile which no longer depended only on her eyes, her cheekfolds.

There was no language necessary, only pictures. She stood with her left arm crooked against the belly of a shaved, decapitated pig hung from a beam between two poplars in snow, the long knife in her hand ready to slice down that belly and spill the guts into the waiting kettle; guts she would clean and stuff with ground meat and boil in the bubbling fat cauldron that winter evening; where he would stand stirring with a long pole, waiting not for the sausage but for the short chopped ribs to be crisp, stuffing wood under to keep the fire leaping. She herded chicks across the grass mat of farmyard to their log shelter, away from the night coyotes. She tramped manure into the clay mud of a shallow pit and smeared that between and over the crooked logs of the house. And once when their dog Carlo had torn the neighbor's dog apart and she had had to accept all that neighbor's obscenities because his father was not there — he was never there, always away from home, somewhere, working like an animal for someone who would give him a dollar a day not to think for himself, just give him orders to work like a beast — Carlo lying complacent, his red tongue lolling — why can't you ever be home like other husbands, work here like you work for others; and his father stood so easily, his arms hung motionless at his sides, the sobs of a wife far easier to manage than that

17

a neighbour think him less a fine fellow. And Carlo panting in the corner shade of logs, the black fur still perfect at his throat for almost one more year.

World War Two hangars and brown sheds intact at Lethbridge Airport, shingled together now into one U-Drive office available with two cars. White mountains and, as always, wind. Almost too much to climb home against at right angles on a bicycle, singing in the nostrils with silvers of a February spring. The elevators still stood, grew larger, centered in the highway.

She lay sleeping. Her face held between her hands, mouth bunched like delicate, weathered rags.

Despite his all-day coming he had to lean against the curtained doorway; she was still here, suddenly. As if half his lifetime had never been so much as a sound swallowed in an empty room. The sound of her songs, sad as he always thought them, then, offering a faith used as it seemed for nothing but to long for a "the Home over there", though there were always edges of happiness in her voice as she cooked berries for winter, sweat running down her uncreased cheeks, her left arm bent against her side while the other moved swiftly for both, her high clear voice glistening like cobweb in the summer heat gathered black with thunder over the spruce. His stare must wake her: if she lay like this when he pounded on the door, shouted her name in the kitchen as he came around into the living room, what could not walk into the house when she slept? Alone like this, just the tiny shape halfcurled towards him, barely breathing.

He turned suddenly, past the empty bed in the corner of the living room, out again. Backed the car away.

"He was so old, he really wanted to . . . go," his sister said, unable to say the word in her house. "And such a look, of peace, just all of a sudden." She faced him, her legs folded sideways, crossed at the ankles. "Always, even when he was sleeping with the pills, you know he breathed so loud, like gasping, his face all — but there was this look, as if something just beautiful . . . as if he saw it all, all of a sudden, really beautiful . . . "

For the first and only time he felt tears prickle along his nose and behind his eyes. His sister leaning forward on her chrome kitchen table, her warm voice talking and tears sliding on her cheeks she did not shift her hands to wipe away. It was not there again, not even when he came through the door and his mother was tight against him, when after a moment he let her go so he could bend down and kiss her, he did not feel that. Past her cheek he saw her gray hair pulled into the same bun she made when she combed it out and he knew that either visitors were coming or they were going somewhere, otherwise she would never have time to comb.

He was bent forward so awkwardly, his back kinked by the plane anyway, as if trying to kiss a child without either lifting it in his arms or hunkering down —he could not do that to bring his face level with his mother's but she pulled back and his hands caught on her two shoulders, her bones there fragile as willows.

"For a whole year he lay in that bed, in the corner," she said. "And I took care of him."

She was looking up into his eyes. Her teeth clacked and he wanted to pull her close, against himself; out of sight and sound to make her feel only, I really love, I have always, always . . .

"I haven't cried for three years, the heavenly Father has taken my tears away. Even now. I cried too much then, you know, yoh?"

He pulled her tight, floundering for the murmurs of understanding, the indiscriminate sounds of whatever language to get past her wavering right arm.

"Mom . . . Mama . . . I wanted to . . . I really . . . "

"Don't," she said, thin and dry against his chest. "Don't lie. Not today."

You Better Not Pout

Ken Mitchell

At nine, I believed without question in Santa Claus, the kindly saint of the Coca-Cola ads. His red nose and shining grin glowed from the back covers of *Maclean's* and *Saturday Evening Post*. He beamed from a halo of poinsettia and mistletoe, toasting us with a bottle of his favourite beverage as he paused for refreshment among the elves and paint-pots.

Every year, my parents and I left a bottle of pop under the Christmas tree for him, along with some shortbread cookies and a list of requests from the Eaton's catalogue. And every year he left a polite reply, sometimes bragging about his bountiful contribution, sometimes apologizing for what he did not have. This note was documentary proof of his reality, supplemented by the white crumbs and the filigree of dried cola he left in the glass.

My faith had stood firm longer than my friends'. At school I endured gross slanders about Santa Claus. Some said that he did not exist at all. They said their fathers donned Santa disguises and prowled the house at midnight. The biggest liars claimed to have seen them. My loyalty remained firm until the year I turned ten, the year of the cufflinks.

The annual Rebekahs' Lodge Christmas Concert was held every year in the Oddfellows' Hall, two Saturdays before Christmas. I had never gone before —my mother was the protective sort —but when I learned that Santa Claus arrived there in a kind of pre-Christmas performance, handing out gifts, I begged her to let me go.

"You wouldn't like it," she said. "There will be rowdies." The concert was also a charity for immigrant children in Moose Jaw and she feared contamination by lice.

I won my invitation by agreeing to stand in front of the assembled throng and deliver four choruses of "Santa Claus is Coming to Town."

> *He sees you when you're sleeping,*
> *He knows when you're awake,*
> *He knows when you've been bad or good,*
> *So be good for Goodness' sake!*

The chorus went:

> *Oooh, you better not pout!*
> *You better not cry!*
> *Better not shout,*
> *I'm telling you why:*
> *Santa Claus is coming — to town!*

I performed this in the centre of the Rebekahs' meeting room in the basement of the lodge, in front of five rows of children and mothers. I was nineteenth on the program, between a piano duet of "Silent Night" by Kelly Forbes and his mother, and a baton-twirling exhibition by Marilee Pavelochenko.

After two hours of such entertainment, lunch finally came. This was supervised by Mrs. Goranson, another folk hero of my childhood. In her home she maintained an astounding pantry, laden with choke-cherry jelly and crabapple butter. She baked bread, and any kid in town could wander past her back door and receive — without even asking — a thick slice of hot bread slathered with the sweet red jelly of his choice. Our mothers tried to suppress this custom, which was practised on our way home from school — but Mrs. Goranson was a devout Samaritan and we were greedy little beggars prepared to lie in our jam-stained teeth.

The Rebekahs had asked her to cater the Christmas extravaganza, apparently hoping it would exhaust her generosity. It took forever for her to tour the hall with her aged assistants, handing each of us a salmon sandwich, a cup of orange crush, some unbearably delicious fruitcake, and a Jap orange. The Rebekahs began to shuffle their feet and fill the air with cigarette smoke, but we understood and were patient.

However, a tension built as she progressed around the room and finally disappeared back into the kitchen. The chatter died into silence. The older kids stopped peeling their orange sections and raised their heads, as if listening to some far-away sound of music, beyond the double doors at the far end of the hall.

Then I heard it — a faint tinkle in the distance. The kid next to me went rigid, staring at me with wild eyes as the sound of jingling bells grew clearer. "It's Sannaaa!" he shrieked.

The bells jingled louder, and a thin reedy voice drifted through the doors. "Ho-oooo, ho-oooo, ho-oooo!"

This asthmatic wheeze, sounding like a forlorn cry for help, was my first live communication from Santa Claus. Something in it made me shiver, but our excitement swelled as the older kids slipped off their chairs and stood peering toward the door. The handle rattled and the door swung open. There was a general surge and cheer. I climbed on the seat, the better to see the happy old saint, flourishing a bottle of Coca-Cola. I had a moment of delirious vision in which every material thing I had ever desired flashed through my consciousness. This ecstasy passed. My eyes cleared.

A skinny little dwarf stood in the doorway. I thought for a minute he was one of Santa's elves scouting the hall, until I saw the lumpy potato sack he was lugging on his back. It was Him, but he looked beaten and starved. His red suit was tattered and full of moth holes. His stomach didn't shake like a bowl of jelly at all, but hung like an empty dishrag. His boots, the big, polished black leather boots, had become scuffy old rubbers which barely covered his ankles. His pants bagged out everywhere.

But the worst was not the costume. For some crazy reason, he had covered his beaming face with a putrid-looking mask the colour of stale bologna. I thought maybe he was suffering from frostbite.

"Ho-oooo," he gasped, "Ho-oooo, ho-oooo . . . " His voice screeched like a fingernail on a blackboard. I froze, not knowing what to expect next.

He shuffled toward the Christmas tree, which stood in a blaze of coloured lights at the far end of the hall. He stopped and dipped one skinny claw into the sack, withdrawing a small square package. A voice quavered behind the mask, "Da-an-ny Ritco!"

Danny Ritco's mother propelled him from his seat and across the room. Danny sidled up to the dwarf, snatched the parcel from his hand and ran back, ripping the paper off. We all strained to see his gift. He lifted a couple of brass things from the box and stared at them.

"Cufflinks!" Santa wheezed in explanation.

Cufflinks? I'd never met a kid who owned a shirt with anything but buttons. It was a cruel hoax. And when Kelly Forbes and then Bruce Fitzwald got cufflinks too, the extent of the fraud became clear. One by one, we all trooped up and received our cufflinks, identical ones, engraved with the Rebekah Lodge symbol. The girls received barrettes, similarly decorated.

Every few minutes, the old swindler would pause in his shoddy handout and whine, "Ho-ooo, ho-ooo, ho-ooo," shaking his sleigh bells like some palsied reindeer. We sat back in the arena of seats and glared at him, his gifts lying at our feet like garbage.

When the last cufflinks were disposed of, he began shuffling his feet, unsure what might happen next. He seemed, for one embarrassing minute, to be waiting for applause. In the silence, we slid off our chairs and began edging toward him. The Rebekahs smiled at one another, pleased by our childish innocence. Santa lifted his arm to shake the bells in a last farewell, and his sleeve slid down to reveal a forearm that looked like a piece of chalk.

"Ho-oooo," he said, "ho . . . " The laugh died in his throat. His feet stopped.

"He's *ascairt*!" a child cried.

Santa shook his head as if in disbelief, then turned and hobbled toward the door. A low moan followed him. He broke into a trot, the empty seat of his baggy red pants flapping behind like a bad joke. There was a massive howl like the yodel of wolves, and Santa took off on a dead gallop. The chase was on.

Santa reached the oak doors and fumbled with the handles, trying to wrench them open. The pack leaders almost caught him at that point, but he threw the empty sack at us and slipped into the foyer, slamming the door in our teeth. A few younger kids started tearing the sack apart, but the rest were already shoving through the heavy doors.

"This way! This way!" From the foyer, a staircase ascended to the Oddfellows' Hall ballroom on the second floor. We rampaged up the stairs, stopping at the first landing only to check the ladies' washrooms. The front-runners dashed in and out, slamming cubicle doors, while others followed behind, flipping the toilet seats up and down and checking to make sure. He was not in the ladies' washroom.

"Up the stairs!" we roared. "Up the stairs!"

The herd pounded up another flight and surged into the dance hall. A small patrol split off to check the men's. The rest skidded to a stop on the waxed floor of the ballroom.

At the far end of the enormous hall was a stage with heavy green curtains drawn across it. The room was empty, echoing with our squeaks and whispers. "Ssshhhht!" everyone whispered at once. We strained to hear a sound. Nothing. On the left side of the stage was a door which led to the wings. It was open, but as I watched, it slowly closed itself with a sharp click.

"There he is!" I shrieked. With a roar, the mob flung itself the length of the ballroom, hitting the door in a wave. It was locked. No one said a word, but there was a deep, swelling sigh and a distinct heave against the door. The third heave popped it out of its frame like a Christmas cracker, and we poured through.

But old Saint Nick had disappeared. We stood on the empty stage, confused.He wasn't in the wings; he wasn't hiding in any backstage closets. The backdrop scene in some medieval woodland full of dark trees, and gloomy castles in the distance —a bewitched forest, the home of a vanishing dwarf. Someone, Bruce Fitzwald perhaps, gave a cry of rage and punched a hole through the canvas with his fist. The whole flat would have been kicked to shreds in the instant, if one of the little toddlers had not suddenly screamed and fallen through a trap door in the centre of the stage.

There was a few seconds of milling panic as her screams echoed beneath us in the gloom. Then Danny Ritco and I saw the hole in the floor and peered in. It was about two feet deep, and the little girl lay at the bottom, covered in dust to her neck and yelling her head off.

"Shuttup!" Danny said, and she did. We pulled her out, and climbed in. In the darkness, we could see a trail through the dust leading from the trap door to the rear of the stage. On a splintered board in front of our eyes was a scrap of red cloth from Santa's jacket.

Smacking our skulls against the stage beams and cursing like grown-ups, Danny and I groped our way through the dark billowing dust until we ran into a wall. Danny found a door which opened into a staircase, and we could suddenly stand up, although we still couldn't see.

The stairs might have descended straight into Hell for all we knew, but there was no turning back. The horde pushing behind allowed no pause for breath. Down the stairs we stumbled, gasping for air in the dusty tomb until we ran into another wall, a half-turn in the stairs. Far away at the bottom we could see light. Rolling and tumbling, we pelted down the stairs and poured out a door —into the kitchen of the Rebekahs' Hall.

Against the far wall, a group of old ladies recoiled in horror from this nightmare invasion of begrimed trolls spewing out of some long-forgotten closet.

"Where's Sanna Claus?" snarled one small black face.

They shook their heads, appalled. Two kids started pounding the kitchen walls, looking for a secret panel. Others raged through the cupboards. Danny Ritco watched the old women clutching each other. He waved his arm for silence.

"I know," he said. "He's in the games room."

The games room was an adult sanctuary. Behind its closed door, Oddfellows played snooker and card games in a fog of cigar smoke. We charged down the corridor and burst through the door, not caring how many men were inside; they couldn't have stopped us.

We found Santa huddled under the billiard table, his red suit trasnformed to a bundle of black rags. He cringed, wheezing for breath through the cloth mask twisted sideways on his face.

From the circle of children surrounding the table, Danny suddenly darted forward and plucked the mask away, flinging it clear across the room. We stared, sick with fascination.

It was Mrs. Goranson, the sweet old lady who gave out bread and jam every day from her back door. She crouched before us like an unmasked Judas. Her gold-framed spectacles sat awry on her round, unblinking eyes, glinting with light as she trembled. She tried to smile —a withered horrible smile, as if she'd just caught herself raiding her own cookie jar.

For a whole minute, no one moved. Then we turned in silence and stomped back to the meeting hall, snapping at each other and body-checking the little kids into the walls.

Hunting Season

Helen J. Rosta

S he saw the footprints early one morning, directly below her cabin in the soft muck around the beaver dam, first one, and then a few yards farther on, another. She followed them until they disappeared on the hard ground that led into the trees. Then she turned back, and straddling one of the prints, stood for a long time looking at it. It was sunk deeply into the mud, a large oval heel and five toes, the big toe nearly the size of her hand, as if, during the night, a giant had walked across her field. She wondered what they had used to make it.

She heard the putt-putt of his truck and looked up just as it was rising over the brow of the hill. For a moment she thought of moving into the shadow of trees and waiting . . .

She could imagine him with his ear close to the cabin door listening to the sound of his knocking reverberate through the two rooms, and when he was satisfied that she wasn't there, turning away, his hand shading his eyes, slowly scanning the countryside for a sight of her . . . then sauntering, heavy-footed, to the corral where Star would whinny to him, stopping to pet her, whistling softly through his gap teeth . . . continuing on to the barn, peering into the stalls, climbing the stairs to the hayloft . . . down again . . . and over to the garage, which was locked, and windowless . . .

He got out of the truck. She could hear the tinny sound as the door slammed shut. When his back was toward her, she started away from the trees at a dead run, circling the hill so that when he saw her he wouldn't know where she had come from. He was still pounding on the door when she walked up behind him.

"There's nobody in there," she said.

He turned and a smile spread over his long, sun-reddened face. "Some people are up and about early."

The cabin was warm inside. She stirred the fire and set the coffee pot on the stove. He pulled up a chair to the table, took off his red hunter's cap, placed it on his knee and clasped his hands around it. His hands were large and square, the fingernails flat and rimmed with grease.

"When hunting season starts you shouldn't wander around without something red on," he told her.

"My land's posted," she said.

"They don't always pay attention to that . . . there's lots of game hiding out in this bush."

"But it is my land."

"Doesn't matter whose land it is . . . during hunting season you wear something red." He smiled, showing big, gap teeth and then covered his mouth with his hand, speaking from behind it. "They say this year maybe they'll bag the old maid over on the Coulter place."

"It's not the Coulter place anymore," she said and then added, "Nobody's going to bag anything on my land."

"Now don't go getting mad. You know how people talk." He took his hand away from his mouth.

"I just don't want them tramping all over the place." She thought of the tracks down by the beaver pond and for a moment considered taking him down and showing them to him but then the image of the hand covering his smile came to her . . . probably he knew about the footprints already, had helped plot them, and was waiting for her to say something so that he could go back and tell his buddies. Maybe he had been one of them, skulking about her place in the dead of night.

"I came to help you trim the mare's feet," he said.

"But you've been here nearly every day doing something for me."
Every day, every day . . . and he's the only one. "I can do them."

"I came to help," he said. He stood up, smoothed his hair and set
the red cap on his head.

She led the way out to the corral. "You're doing too much for me,"
she continued. "I appreciate it, but you have your own work." He
whistled and Star whirled about, ran toward them, and then stood
stock-still, ears pricked, watching their approach.

"Trimmers still in the barn?" He started toward it. He knows where
everything is, she thought. She climbed over the railing into the corral
and put an arm around the mare's neck. She could feel a quiver moving
like a ripple under the skin. He emerged from the barn, watched for a
moment, then unfastened the gate and came into the corral, the hoof
trimmers in one hand.

"You hang onto the halter," he said. "I'll take care of the feet." He
ran his hand over the horse's neck and shoulder, bent down, slid his
hand along the leg, straddled it, and grabbing the fetlock pulled the leg
back toward him. The horse reared up, jerking the halter from her hand
and knocking him to the ground. He swore, picked himself up, and
lunged for the halter.

"Don't!" She grabbed his sleeve. "Leave it for now. She's trembling . . . something's frightened her." They did, prowling around.

"Shouldn't let her get away like that. She'll try it next time." He
seemed undecided, standing, slightly stooped, the hoof trimmers still
in his hand.

"She's too nervous."

"Shouldn't let her get away."

"Something's frightened her," she repeated. "Do you have any idea
what it might have been?"

"Horses spook easy . . . maybe one of those wild animals you've
been harbouring scared her."

She saw the beginnings of the smile, turned her back and walked
ahead of him. "It is my land. I don't have to let them hunt it."

"They've always hunted this land." He paused and gazed toward the dark line of trees behind the beaver dam. "You know how they are."

"No," she said, "I don't know how they are. I never see any of them."

"They're kind of shy," he said, "that is the bachelors are shy, and the married ones . . . " The hand went over his mouth. "Course being a widower, none of that applies to me . . . " He looked away, letting the words hang in the air. "And the women . . . people don't like what they don't understand."

"What don't they understand?"

"They wonder what's a woman doing out here all alone."

"I've got as much right to be here as anyone."

"Oh, it isn't a question of right. They wonder, that's all."

"How do they feel about your coming here?"

"Oh, I get teased but I can take a joke."

"I imagine," she said, "that everyone around here really loves . . . a good joke."

He waved his hand toward the craggy, sombre hills covered with dense clumps of trees. "To survive in this country, you've got to have a sense of humour."

After he left, she rushed down to the beaver dam and inspected the tracks, again following them to where they disappeared, pausing on the margin of the trees, peering into the shadows, listening, turning back . . . They must have gone to a lot of trouble to make the footprints, she thought, and how could they be sure she'd even find them . . . unless they were watching her . . . knew her habits, the walk by the beaver dam in the early mornings, the rides along the fencelines.

Two days later she found her mailbox, still attached to its post, lying in the ditch beside the road. The side with her name on it was shoved in, the lid ajar. She dragged the box up to the roadbed, reached inside and felt for the letter which she had placed there the previous evening. She found the envelope. It was covered with black smudges and one end had been slit. The letter was gone. She held the envelope gingerly by one corner and studied it. They've left fingerprints, she thought. She was standing beside the road, the envelope still in her hand when he drove up. He stopped the truck beside her, jumped out, and started to throw tools from the back.

"Aren't you lucky," he said, "that I've been carting around all this fencing stuff."

She didn't move. "How did you know it was torn down?"

"Didn't. Just happened to be going by and saw you standing here. Like I said, you're lucky." He got a hammer from his tool kit and started to tap out the side of the box. "Guess you'll have to do without mail today."

"If I had any, the mailman could have brought it to me."

"Maybe when he saw the box gone, he figured that you didn't want any." He gave the box a final tap with the hammer, stood up and rubbed his hands on his trousers. "Good as new. Now all we have to do is dig another hole and set it up again." He picked up the post-hole auger, leaned his weight on it, and began to move rhythmically in a circular motion.

"This time they've gone too far." She shoved the envelope under his nose. "They've stolen my letter and that's a criminal offence."

"I wouldn't go making a fuss about it . . . it's nothing serious."

"Serious! They could go to jail for this." She waved the envelope at him. "Fingerprints all over. Look at it."

He snatched the envelope from her, wadded it up and stuffed it in his pocket. "When I get the box up, you can send another letter easy enough." He lifted the auger out of the hole and emptied the dirt from it. "Ground's moist. It won't take any time at all to get that thing standing." He set the auger back in the ground.

"They stole my letter!"

He gave a violent twist to the auger, stopped and looked straight at her. "Was there anything in that letter you wouldn't want people to see?"

She kicked the ground angrily. "It's nobody's business what's in my letters."

He reached into his pocket, extracted the envelope and smoothed it out on the auger handle. When he had finished examining it, he put it back in his pocket and smiled at her. "That looks like a business letter to me. I've been to Edmonton. Think I've even been in that store."

"I was ordering a gun."

He started working again. "Any money in that letter?"

"No . . . but it's stealing anyway . . . it's a federal offence to tamper with the mail."

"A gun won't do you any good," he said.

"What do you mean?"

"Can't hunt on your own land if it's posted."

"I wasn't going to hunt."

"Then what do you want a gun for?"

"Target practice."

"You don't need practice to hit a target," he said, "as long as it isn't moving."

He set up the mailbox in silence. She helped him tamp dirt and gravel around its base and carry the tools back to the truck.

"They could go to jail."

He started to load the tools into the truck as if he hadn't heard her. When he had finished, he said, "You know, maybe you should get yourself a gun after all." He paused and gazed in the direction of her cabin. "Seems like they've noticed some kind of funny tracks leading onto your land."

"What kind of tracks?"

"You noticed anything?"

"What kind of tracks?" she asked again.

He shrugged. "I don't know . . . funny tracks . . . maybe you should take a look for them."

"Why are they doing this to me?"

"Nobody's doing anything to you." He gestured toward the mailbox. "That's nothing."

"They've done other things."

"A few jokes . . . "

"My letter was no joke."

He climbed into the truck, started the engine, then rolled down the window and leaned out. "You didn't thank me," he said.

"I'm thanking you, but as far as I'm concerned, the rest of them should go to jail."

He started to roll up the window and his words drifted back to her over the roar of the engine. "Hunting season starts tomorrow."

That afternoon, she saddled Star and rode around the fence lines. South of the beaver dam, she found a dead tree lying across the wire.

She dismounted, tied the horse to a sapling and, thinking that they had pushed the tree onto the fence, examined the ground for footprints. She found none. She grasped the trunk and tried to swing the tree off the wire. It moved slowly in an arc, its limbs catching in the branches of the trees surrounding it. She struggled with it, her breath coming in short, quick gasps. Star snorted and pawed impatiently. Suddenly, the tree broke loose and crashed to the ground. The mare reared back, nostrils flaring. She approached the horse, speaking softly, "Whoa, Star . . . easy girl . . . take it easy." She ran her hand along the quivering side. All at once, the mare became rigid, head up, ears forward. She turned slowly, following the mare's gaze.

It didn't move, just stood, looking at her, its hairy body towering among the trees, hands resting at its sides, its eyes a pale translucent amber, large, luminous, and full of fear.

The horse, as if she'd finally caught an alien scent, snorted and plunged. The creature stepped back, turned, and with huge strides, vanished into the shadows like an apparition.

Early next morning, the shots started. The first one was faint, far to the north-east. The next was louder, and the next. By dawn, they were sounding in a steady, staccato rhythm, closer, closer, one after the other. By nightfall, she imagined that they had advanced to the borders of her property.

That evening when she heard his truck, she waited silently behind the closed curtains, listening to the sound of his fist on the door. After a time, she heard him move away from the door, around the cabin, in front of the window, pause, then on . . . She thought she heard Star whinny softly and the thin sound of whistling. Finally, she heard the truck door slam and the roar of his engine as he drove away.

She listened to the roar fading in the distance, then opened the door and peered out. The moon was high, a large silver disc in the black sky. Below the cabin, the beaver pond gleamed like a pale circle of light. Behind it, the trees lay in impenetrable darkness. She thought of the creature crouching among the trees, its long arms resting on its knees, hands motionless, eyes large and luminous as the moon, staring into darkness.

Shortly after midnight, she heard the trucks. The sound cut through the cold air like the thud of wings. She ran to the window and looked out. The trucks came slowly up the road, gleaming shapes, lights extinguished, moving like a caravan. One by one they stopped outside the cabin and the dark figures alighted. At first she thought he wasn't with them, but then she saw his truck, saw him step down.

He joined the others, and they all walked together, their long, black shadows moving ahead of them.

Iron Wheels

Frances Itani

The trains, always the trains to remind me. The Pacific Great Eastern. Mother and my brother Masao beside me. Our two mattresses the only things we have been able to bring. There is dust and dryness in my mouth, my tears, my throat. The sensations numb as I cling to Mother — first on the boat from the Island, then to Hastings Park, finally on the train to Littleneck where our fractured lives become suspended like fluff hanging from a web, during the next three years of the war.

But Father. Father has missed the train. In the dream the engine is blasting its warning, the cars pulling out. The last coach seems to falter, disconnect somehow, rolls back to wait for him. He is running between the tracks, loaded down with sacks of rice, sugar, dried fish, noodles. Far more than one man can carry. He drops to his knees under the load as the coach suddenly reverses, speeds and links up to the moving train. Father is left behind; perspiration turns to dust as it streams down his rough cheeks. Mother does not turn to look back. Masao puts his arms around me. His face seems to crack in the dryness. He has no tears. There are no tears for anyone. Only the new fear that we are learning to live with.

But it was not only a dream, taking that train. I remember trying to reach the elusive height of the first step —higher than the mountie's knees; I remember the scrubbrush feeling of the seat's bristles; the strong scent of varnish from the woodwork panelling (then later trying to inhale this very scent, which was preferable to the stench and sourness of the spittoons). And always, the odour of urine, everywhere. I remember the white cloth rectangles buttoned to the tops of the seats —these removed by the conductor and the mountie when we were herded into the coaches. I remember . . .

"Where is Father?" asks Masao.

"Hush. He has gone to collect food. He must have missed the train."

Mother whispers, thinking I am asleep. My eyes are closed but I hear, "Thank God he has been registered —his card is stamped. He will find us."

But when I fall asleep, Father is between the tracks again, on his knees, his face turning to dust. Grains of rice spill out of the sacks and are scattered across the ties and buried beneath the cinders. And the man. The shadow of the man, is huge behind him.

It is March when we are brought to Hastings Park. Mother keeps the stall scrubbed clean with rags and disinfectant that have been given to her. The water swishes through the troughs, giving birth to a little song as it circles the arena. When someone washes in a stall farther up, the soapsuds drift by and bubbles rise gracefully to adhere to the framework that surrounds us. Blankets are strung between our stall and those on either side, ensuring a small degree of privacy. But at night, it is coats we wrap around us to keep out the rawness of March.

Uncle Tad and Uncle Yoshio are here, in a separate building. Uncle Tad has a pass to get in and out of the grounds. He can stay out until the seven o'clock curfew but he has not yet found anyone who knows where Father is. Perhaps he was picked up near the boat when he went to look for Nishi-san. Nishi-san is dead. His boat was found drifting near the U.S. side. The men say that blood was splattered everywhere in the cabin. As for our boat, it has been impounded like the rest.

We are on our way to Littleneck —the first group to leave Hastings Park. Our two mattresses have been loaded onto the train. Masao and I have helped to carry the food. Mrs. Nishi was brought here from the Island and will stay with us in Littleneck. She was permitted to go to our house to bring clothing, and Mother's big basket. Mother has our kettle and our rice pot, too, and even a few rice bowls. Everything else had to be left behind — Mother's sewing machine, my wooden doll with the topknot, everything.

"Don't cry," Mother says. "If other children see you they will cry too."

But in the dream I cry. I cry for mothers; I cry for children who cling to coattails; I cry for the silent conformance to these hastily put-together laws. The wind stings my legs through my high brown socks. I feel it even through the woollen bloomers Mother has knit for me. I feel it even through my dreams.

Uncle Tad and Uncle Yoshio are not allowed to come to say goodbye when we climb aboard. I have only memories of them, standing in their aprons in the doorway of the big kitchen where they work, serving food to hundreds, thousands, like us.

The countryside flows sluggishly, distorted by the thick glass of the train windows. When the windows are open, we breathe fine black cinder dust that blocks our nostrils. The dream begins again. It is night. The train's iron wheels grow and grow, becoming gnarled and twisted. They leave the tracks, rumble across the fields, approach the sea. The boats are chained together, listless in the harbour, evanescent, suddenly eclipsed by the shadows of the train. Quickly then, the train swings directly toward our house as though it will surely demolish it. But the wheels only skim by, crushing the tiny garden beneath my window. The green shoots are pushed back into the earth. Our house is safe.

※

For two nights we sleep on the motionless train. Mother sits with her feet propped on our huge yellow basket made of willow, smooth and highly polished. It contains all that is left of our home — and the wooden rice paddle that Uncle Tad gave us before we left. Masao and I stretch out on the seats to sleep. The police bring food — fried fish and macaroni that is not very tasty.

There have been conferences and speeches and men from the town walking up and down the platform talking to the mounties. We know that another trainload of people has been sent farther up the valley. There is no place for them yet so they will have to live in tents. We are lucky because here there is plenty of drinking water and we shall be living in houses. We will even have a room for a school. Four of the older girls have been assigned to teach us and were given a course in Hastings Park before we left.

Finally the men from the town go away from the platform. It is whispered throughout the coach that this is where we'll stay. This will be our home. The mountie reads out our names at the beginning of the list. Mother, Mrs. Nishi, Masao and I are to have a room on the top floor of a three-storey wooden house. The kitchen will be shared with three other families.

Masao and I follow Mother along the street next to the tracks. But it is not the house, it is the man on the roof we first see. There are charcoal streaks running through him but he is mostly green — metal — all different shades, the way copper turns. He is dressed in a long overcoat and holds a briefcase, which seems to have been pressed from a mould. A fedora juts low over his forehead. He is taller than one storey of our house, and he sways up there, bending and cracking over a corner of the roof. There is neither word nor slogan beneath him. We climb the stairs to our room, look out of the window and up, and see that his shadowy profile menaces directly overhead. The train, farther along the track, gathers itself together and puffs away.

In our house there are eleven families. The walls of our room do not reach to the ceiling and we hear every sound from the Takamoris on the other side. It is the same along the hall — footsteps in and out, up and down the stairs all day. Some of the men have made a table and chairs from crates, scrap lumber, wooden pegs. Every night they sit out there in the hall, playing cards, long after we are in bed.

And every night after dark, a train passes by. I lie on my bed and watch for the beam of light that begins as a small circle on my wall, then balloons out, larger, larger, exploding finally in a dazzling vortex as the train roars past. The man on the roof bends with the roar and the house shudders in the wake of the train.

There has been no word from Father but we know that our house has been sold. It has been taken over by the "Custodian of Enemy Alien Property." Uncle Tad wrote to tell us before he and Uncle Yoshio were sent to Ontario. They are in the camp now and must wear red targets on the backs of their jackets so they will not try to escape. The adults here in Littleneck say we are lucky we have no typhoid; there have been outbreaks in some of the other camps where the drinking water is brought in by truck.

At night I listen for the train rumbling from far away. The train comes every night. As the pinpoint of light grows slowly on the wall, the man on the roof begins to shake. Masao and Mother and Mrs. Nishi seem to be asleep. Am I dreaming? Father's face is there in that speck of light. He is running along the tracks and the circle on his back is as crimson as blood. The light of the train flashes as the train thunders behind, overtaking him. He tries to reach the house but he stumbles and slips beneath the wheels. The target on his back splits open; sand streams out of the fissure in his jacket. The train passes over him in silence, then on into the distance.

Rain lashes the windows. Rain seeps through the ceiling and runs down the wall in rivulets. Mother and Mrs. Nishi take turns emptying the basin beneath the drip. Mrs. Nishi has been weaving scraps of cloth into the oval footwear that will be our slippers. There are arguments in the kitchen: so little space on the stove; the women cannot prepare meals at the same time. It is not often that we hear the hum hum of our mother stirring rice in the pot. Perhaps it is the rain and the dampness that make everyone so irritable. Even Masao pushes me away when I show him my printing in my new exercise book. If Father were here, our lives would be different. It has been months since we have seen him.

Mother sends me to bed early, long before the train is due. The wind moans, circling. On the roof the man curves as though he will swoop down upon us; the rain splatters him like beads rolling on tin. I lie on my bed listening to the sharpness of the small Japanese cards as the men on the other side of the wall crack them down against the crate. We know nothing of the war here; only the long wait until it will be over.

I force my eyes to stay open. The man on the roof heaves and cracks as he is battered first from one side, then the other. An army of feet charges across the roof, outrunning the wind. The train will soon be here.

The speck of light appears above me, dancing from spot to spot on the wall. The iron wheels turn. There is a sudden loud explosion as the light bursts and drops from my wall, vanishes at the same moment that the man, in a shudder of metal, plunges past my window, down, down . . . his final descent.

But Father, it was you, wasn't it? On that train, ready to jump as it flew past the fugitive lights of Littleneck? How were we to know that you'd been in the roadcamps, that you'd found our names on the lists? That you'd surrendered your life insurance policy and had with you the little cash you'd been paid.

Was it only a dream that the man fell from the roof, that the men in the hall heard the crash and left their cards to investigate, that when they ran down into the rain, you were both lying there? If it was only a dream, Father, why then, does the train never go away?

Café Society

Guy Vanderhaeghe

They made an odd trio, the three men seated around a zinc-topped table at a sidewalk café in the Avenue de Marigny. George Demanche, editor of *La revue française de l'exploration,* was a spare, pale man who always wore his journalist's face with great seriousness. That afternoon he had chosen to top it off with an imposing silk hat, a magnificent, gleaming (yet sober) cylinder that his fragile neck appeared incapable of supporting.

The other two men gave off an air of greater solidity than did Demanche, though the impression of substantiality each one produced was of a different order. Robert Bataille, speaking forcefully at that moment, was red and beefy and loud, a gentlemen with a stake in things, a proper bourgeois.

The other man, listening to him closely with a patient, if uncomprehending expression on his face, was of a different type. He sat with quiet dignity; thick, rough fingers curled laxly around his glass of beer. His cheap black coat hung awkwardly on his heavy shoulders and his beard was ragged and badly needed trimming. The man was dark too, so dark and so obviously foreign that in the year of the great Paris Exposition of 1889 with so many colonial peoples decorating the Esplanade des Invalides on the fair grounds, he could easily be mistaken for an Arab, perhaps an Algerian.

"What you gentlemen are proposing is out of the question," said Bataille, shaking his ponderous head, "especially now with the Americans here in Paris."

"I suggested it might not be wise when he and Riboulet wrote me from Quebec," explained Demanche. "He had ample warning." He turned to the dark man. "When was it . . . two years ago, Gabriel?"

"December of '87."

"These things cannot be mounted on such short notice," said Bataille complacently. He lifted his glass and drained it. He already had an impressive stack of saucers by his elbow.

"Yes," agreed Demanche, "perhaps you are right. In any case, I, myself, would prefer to be associated with something more educational and dignified than a Wild West Show. Lectures might be the thing. After all, it is the centennial of the Revolution . . . Liberty, Equality, Fraternity, etc. This man *is* a patriot *and* a revolutionist. What could be more topical, I ask you? There may be something in that side of him."

"They invited me to make a speech at Holyoake, Massachusetts, and once I spoke to 500 people at Woodcrest," volunteered the subject of their conversation. "In New York City I talked and they gave me a silver medal." He reached into his jacket pocket and displayed to the men at the table the bright disc shrunk to insignificance in his large, brown palm.

"Lectures mean renting a hall and publicity," said Bataille, ignoring the medal and directing his attention wholly to Demanche, "and *he* has no money for a hall. As you told me yourself, your friend is broke and living in that filthy Ternes district."

"But you see, Monsieur Bataille," said Demanche, "that is why we have come to you. We assumed that *you*, as a *distinguished* theatrical producer, would raise the necessary capital for a share in the profits."

"What profits?" exclaimed Bataille. "He doesn't even have a company."

"He can provide Indian chiefs and other supernumeraries from Canada on a moment's notice. This man has connections. He's respected among his own people."

43

Guy Vanderhaeghe

"But even if he can deliver, it will be too late for the Exposition crowds, and by the time he gets his friends over here, everyone will have had his fill of savages. That American, Buffalo Bill Cody, is packing them in right now on the west side of the city." Bataille paused. "But Paris tires easily," he noted indifferently, "and by autumn, paint and feathers will be passé."

"This gentleman appeared with Cody," said Demanche, unwilling to give up. "He was a principal performer; he is a man of wide experience in ventures of this type."

"I performed with the Wild West Show in Philadelphia and on Staten Island," said the dark man. He laughed quietly to himself. "Son of a bitch, I rode around, shooting glass balls thrown in the air. A man feels like a fool." He shrugged. "But then again a man has to eat."

"Now that's not the sort of thing for Paris," commented Demanche, "shooting glass balls out of the air. What's needed is something more refined, something historical and educational, even allegorical in nature. Liberty trampled by Tyranny might be a motif. Something more to French taste."

"That American serves French taste well enough," commented Bataille. "He was certainly a hit with the illustrious President of the Republic himself, Monsieur Carnot. Cody's carnival of mock heroics has been a stunning success with all the fashionable crowd, and he," said Bataille, pointing, "is not the kind to steal Cody's thunder. No golden locks. In any case, that's what Paris is really interested in this season." His finger stabbed at the Paris skyline. "That and Edison's phonographs in the Palais des machines. Things, Demanche, not people. Bring me attractions like those and we can talk business."

Demanche blinked at the sight which Bataille had indicated, the new Eiffel Tower, completed that May for the opening of the Exposition. The gaunt iron skeleton thrust its pinnacle at the blue underbelly of the sky. "That sort of drawing card we can't provide you with, I'm sorry to say," he said with a sigh but Bataille wasn't listening. "From the moment it opened to the public this spring," he said, "it has been a hit. What a little money maker! They've all been riding up and down it —

44

Edison, the Prince of Wales, the Shah of Persia, the Grand Duke Vladimir of Russia, even the midget Tom Thumb. There are crowds of people lined up every day for two hours to gain admittance. Paying money to scramble on that pile of scrap iron. Incredible!"

The Arabic-looking man stared intently at the tower. It had puzzled him for some time now. Perhaps Bataille, who was so authoritative in all his judgements, would know. Most people only laughed and shook their heads uncomprehendingly when he asked them about it. "Monsieur Bataille," he inquired, "what's that tower thing for?"

"For?" said Bataille, taken aback.

"I mean what is its purpose?" asked his questioner earnestly. "What I mean to say is, why was it built?"

Bataille studied the man closely for a moment to assure himself this character wasn't pulling his leg. Also, if the truth be known, he needed time to think. "Why my dear fellow," he said finally, with a sly wink and a flash of his teeth, "it's there for young ladies of fashion to fly gas balloons from with their addresses attached — it's rumoured they've received answers from as far away as Switzerland! It's there to provide a restaurant in an amusing place, a situation where the nobs can eat soup and display their moustaches. It's also there for swarms of dirty little workers and their sluts to climb on for an afternoon so they can forget the miserable lives they live. In a word," he concluded, "it exists for the reason all things exist — to make money!"

His questioner considered this explanation. "Someone," he said at last, "told me it was built to look out for the Germans coming. It's not a bad idea."

Bataille threw back his head, hooted with laughter, and thumped the table until the glasses jumped. "The mind of a bandit!" he shouted. "You've brought me an original, Demanche!"

Demanche squirmed in his chair. He felt compelled to correct the mercenary interpretation which Bataille offered for the construction of the tower.

"Really, Monsieur Dumont," he said, addressing the man across from him by his surname for the first time, "Robert is trying to be witty. The tower is not merely an amusement but a triumph of engineering Science, a symbol of man's ingenuity in treading the path of Progress." Demanche regarded the tower for a moment with evident satisfaction. "Three hundred metres high," he said. "Higher than the tallest structure ever erected by man! One hundred and seventy-five metres taller than Chartres Cathedral! A colossus! You see, Monsieur Gabriel Dumont," he said confidentially, "you are privileged to catch a glimpse of the future in that tower. It is, quite simply, a signpost for the generations to come. An achievement which they will be compelled, by example, to strive to excel."

"Ah, I see," said Dumont nodding uneasily. It was plain he didn't see.

Bataille clapped him on the shoulder and shouted, "Don't let Demanche fool you with his romantic twaddle. That jumble of iron was piled up for money and nothing else! And the idiots are paying through the nose right this minute for the privilege of gawking off it!" He stopped to consider. "Still, I'll wager you've never seen the like, not on your godforsaken Canadian plains at any rate." Bataille was growing drunk and a shade belligerent. "It takes a Frenchman to build something like that," he said, as if defying Dumont to contradict him.

Dumont closed his eyes momentarily against the sight of the black needle supported on four squat, crouching limbs. He didn't understand any of this talk. He gathered, however, that he was wrong in supposing it a lookout. It appeared it wasn't really anything.

Nothing done by these damn people, the French, made any sense. They were as bad as the English, who were always at you to stop wandering, to knock together a hut to crawl into, and to scrabble in a vegetable or barley patch. And when you obliged them, then they decided you'd settled down on the wrong piece of land. Why it was the wrong piece of land was never clear, especially since there was unoccupied dirt wherever you looked. And so the upshot of it all was they made a war, burned your barn, chased you to Montana, and the police confiscated your billiard table which had been shipped all those expensive miles from Ontario. It was crazy.

And now this bunch, building their Tower of Babel to prove they were something out of the ordinary. At least they had put their tower in the right place, so when God scotched it (as he was sure to) nothing decent would come to harm. Just this accursed city where the meat tasted of everything but meat, rum was hard to find, the river stunk, there were no fiddlers worth a damn, and nobody believed your stories.

Take his fellow lodgers in the grimy block of flats in Ternes. When he had told them (as it was only polite to do after listening to their stories about women and gambling) of the big fight with the Sioux on the Grand Coteau in '51, the fools in blue denim workmen's smocks had only snickered and winked and poked their calloused thumbs in one another's ribs.

That had spoiled the story. For every man's story deserves respect if he does his best to tell it truthfully, and it will die on his lips when it is mocked. And Dumont had wanted to get it right for them, every detail, so in this strange place, far away from the broken, rolling country where it had happened, they would feel how it had been on that glorious day.

He had wanted them to see the two hundred Métis carts drawn wheel to wheel, his friends in the shallow rifle pits loading and firing and calling to the Mother of God in their fear, their rifle barrels grown too hot to touch. He had wanted them to see Father Lafleche in his dirty, rusty black robes parading with a crucifix held boldly to the sky, thrust, so to speak, into the very face of God, demanding protection for his Métis children.

The rattle of musketry; plunging, screaming horses sprouting the shafts of the arrows of Teton Sioux; a sky bleached white with heat; women crying and saying their beads; the Sioux dying in the grass and chanting their death songs; the old Métis hunters who had sworn they could smell the blood rising from the earth like a rich, sweet mist.

A good fight! And there had been others. Duck Lake, Fish Creek, even ones that had been lost, like Batoche.

"No," said Bataille emphatically, interrupting Dumont's thoughts, "you must understand, Demanche, that I'm not in the least interested despite your pleading the gentleman's case. And I've said it for the last time. After all, who is he? What's he done that the public would care about him?"

"For the love of God," said Demanche, reddening with embarrassment.

"Oh, I'm sure he's a good fellow," conceded Bataille, jovially drunk. "Eh, you're a good fellow aren't you?" he asked, addressing Dumont. "But what did you ever do?" He fumbled for a memory. "Why was it that Cody had you in his show? Tell me again."

"I fought Crozier and the police at Duck Lake," Dumont replied shyly, staring at the back of his hands, "and the English general at . . ."

Bataille drunkenly interrupted him. "Yes, yes," he said, "you shot some policemen. You know what that makes you, don't you? An anarchist!" He roared at his own joke. "An anarchist!"

"I don't know what that means," said Dumont gravely, "anarchist."

"It means that commercially speaking you are a nonentity. Nothing."

"Nothing?" said Dumont bewildered.

"There you have it," said Bataille getting to his feet. "I didn't mean to put it to you so strongly, but I'm an honest man." He looked to Demanche. "Are you coming, George?"

"Yes," replied Demanche, who wanted to flee the sight of the miserable figure in his ill-fitting coat, looking at him for all the world as if he, Demanche, were Judas.

"No hard feelings, eh?" said Bataille heartily. "And in any case, if things get really tough you may be able to sign on with the American as an extra. In the meantime, let me buy you a drink! A real drink, not that slop in your glass." He beckoned to a waiter. "Hey! Bring this man an absinthe!" He rang some coins down on the table top in a grand, careless gesture and turned on his heel. Demanche tipped his hat to Dumont, smiled apologetically and thinly and hurried off to catch up with his companion. Dumont watched them make their way down the bustling pavements.

As he watched them go he thought about the tower. He amused himself with the notion that with a thing like that at his disposal he could have enjoyed the pleasure of watching fat old Middleton, his red-coated militia men, and the straggling line of cracking freight wagons hump it all the way from Humboldt to Batoche. From such a height and equipped with a good spy glass, he speculated he might have been able to pass the time counting the brass buttons on the General's coat. Maybe even the beads of sweat strung on his quivering jowls. It was, after all, a good idea to always keep the enemy in sight.

When Bataille and Demanche reached the curb at the corner they paused to let a landau pass before crossing the Avenue de Marigny. Bataille took the opportunity provided by this halt to say to Demanche, "I must implore you not to bring your strays around to see me anymore. I haven't the time."

"I tried to dissuade him when he wrote from Canada, but he came anyway. What was I to do? And the British have treated him very badly. I do have some sympathy for him."

"I save all my sympathy for primitives who wriggle," said Bataille, "like the Javanese and Tahitian dancers at the Exposition. I suggest you do the same."

Despite himself, Demanche broke into laughter. Bataille was vulgar, but there was no denying he was a real card. The two men linked arms in a comradely way and strode across the Avenue de Marigny. When they reached the other side of the street, Dumont saw them hesitate for a moment. They appeared undecided as to which way to go. Then they turned toward the Eiffel Tower as if it were a terrestrial lighthouse, a beacon by which they could unerringly steer their course down the boulevards.

The eyes of the hunter eventually lost sight of them, even after he had got to his feet, in an unfamiliar forest of brave silk hats and a bright cloud of fashionable parasols.

This Town

Diane Schoemperlen

GENERAL INFORMATION:

A lot of the people in this town have come here from other places. There is always someone new in town, there is always someone just arriving (see POPULATION).

When you meet a new person in this town, the first questions are always the same.

"Where are you from?"

"How long have you been here?"

Some people will become friends on the basis of the answer to these and other questions.

Some people will say they were just passing through on their summer holidays and they had such a good time in this town that they just never left.

"That was two years ago last summer."

Because these people didn't come to this town on purpose, they never lose that sense of just passing through and so they are always talking about leaving.

Some of these people were on their way to the coast and now they are always talking about going there for the next long weekend. Some other people were on their way to California and now they always go there for their two-week vacation in the summer. They come back with furious suntans and colour slides of the ocean.

In this town someone is always talking about leaving. Some of them do leave, but some of them don't. Most of those who do, come back in two months. Sometimes it is only when these people come back that the other people in this town notice they've been gone.

CLIMATE:

The standard saying in this town is: "If you don't like the weather, wait five minutes, it'll change." Living in this town means never knowing what to wear when you get up in the morning and then having to change your clothes four times a day anyway. This generates a lot of washing (see LAUNDROMAT). It is considered overly optimistic to go out without a jacket in July.

POPULATION:

There is room in this town for everyone. Someone is always arriving (coming to this town is easier than leaving it) but this town never gets any bigger and it never gets any smaller either.

Every other year they put a new number on the green sign on the highway. No one can ever remember what the last number was so no one ever knows if this town is gaining or losing ground.

Lorraine said, "We don't need to know anyway. Those signs are for tourists. They like to know these things" (see TOURISM).

PUBLIC HEALTH:

In this town someone always has or is just getting over a twenty-four hour bug. All such recurring afflictions are credited to the water, which is regularly infected by some kind of parasite that comes down off the mountains with the spring runoff.

All other afflictions are credited to the altitude and the thin mountain air.

Kevin said, "We are all suffering from chronic lack of oxygen."

This can be used to explain or excuse a number of things, including the milder forms of insanity and unhappiness.

Someone in this town always has a cold (see CLIMATE) or a virus.

ACCOMMODATION:

Most of the people in this town live in rented apartments or houses. These are very hard to come by. Everybody is always complaining that their rent is too high and so they are always moving to a smaller, cheaper place. Someone is always saying, "If you hear of anything coming up for rent, let me know." A lot of people, even families with children, keep renting because they are planning to leave in the spring (see GENERAL INFORMATION).

Some couples buy a lot in the new subdivision, which is the only part of town where the streets are paved. They like to build their own houses. This keeps them very busy. They are always working hard to make the mortgage payments which are usually higher than they bargained on. They are always planning patios, babies, and vegetable gardens.

The power of a nice new $100,000 house is never underestimated. Andy and Mary said together, "Once we move in, we'll be so happy."

TOURISM:

In this town it is standard summer practice to go out for a walk on Sunday afternoon with or without the dog which you may or may not own (see PETS). You will be stopped on the average of five times and asked for directions.

Most of these tourists will want to know how to get back to the highway. Before beginning your walk, it is important to know how to get to: the golf course, the liquor store, a fast food place (there isn't one), a bathroom, a campground with hookups (it's full).

One Sunday a man in sunglasses in a big blue Buick said to Barb: "This is such a quaint little town. But what do all you people *do* here?"

ENTERTAINMENT:

In this town all roads lead to the bar. There might also be one road which leads to the pool hall. The pool hall is a recreational distraction. The bar, on the other hand, is a serious place where serious business occurs.

Connie said, "We were in the bar when Kevin told me he was leaving town and moving to the coast (see GENERAL INFORMATION). I was crying but nobody noticed and the beer kept coming. Pretty soon the whole table was covered with empty bottles. Leon kept lying them down on their sides and calling them dead soldiers. He was comforting me (see LOVE)."

In this town there is a dance once every two months. Most of the people in this town love to dance so everybody goes and nobody ever dances with the person they came with. This is important because of course everybody needs to feel free. The small town version of freedom means flirting with your best friend's husband or lover or both. It is likely that you will end up at the same table with three old lovers and one or two new lovers. Most of the people in this town are very civilized.

Most people in this town harbour a disproportionate fear of going home alone (see LOVE). This fear becomes especially prevalent on Saturday night.

Barb said, "I hate eating breakfast alone on Sunday. If a man is with me I make bacon and eggs and biscuits. Sometimes, if it's a special occasion or I think we might be in love, I make strawberry crepes. If I'm alone I have three cups of coffee and five or six cigarettes. I know that's unhealthy."

HOBBIES:

A lot of people in this town are always having dinner parties. In the summer they are always having barbecues.

Lorraine said, "I enjoy taking care of people. Everyone likes to eat, everyone tells me I'm a good cook. Maybe someday I'll become a chef. I'm happy when I'm watching someone eat."

Marshall, who is Lorraine's husband and also a realist, said, "You just like showing off. Life isn't a dinner party, Lorraine."

Lorraine and Marshall are always talking about leaving this town (see GENERAL INFORMATION) or getting a divorce (see MARRIAGE).

Most of the people in this town have, at one time or another taken up macramé, weaving, baking bread, gardening, running, and photography. Some people still do some or all of these things. Everybody owns a 35mm camera with multiple interchangeable lenses. Most of the people in this town do not collect stamps or coins or salt and pepper shakers. Some people collect postcards or comic books.

PETS:

Everyone in this town loves animals. If you have a dog, it will be a German Shepherd, a Siberian Husky, or an Alaskan Malamute. If you don't have a dog, it will be because your landlady doesn't allow pets or because you are planning to leave town in the spring (see GENERAL INFORMATION) and you don't want to get tied down (see LOVE).

Some people have cats. Most people have more than one.

Barb said, "I'd be lost without them."

Someone in this town is always giving away kittens or puppies.

CHILDREN:

This town is very fertile. Someone is always pregnant. There is always someone wanting to buy your old baby carriage and your bassinette. Everybody believes in cloth diapers and breast-feeding and making your own baby food in the blender.

When the baby cries in a restaurant, the parents are embarrassed but they smile proudly.

Everybody is thankful for the Day Care Center which has just been established in town. The young mothers talk about how their children will grow up and be friends and go to school together.

LAUNDROMAT:

Almost none of the people in this town own a washer and dryer. Everybody goes to the laundromat, which is always full. Some of the washing machines are always breaking down. Most people go down the street to the bar while their clothes are drying (see ENTERTAINMENT).

Mary said, "If Indians are supposed to be dirty, my mother always said they were dirty, then why do they spend so much time in the laundromat?"

LOVE:

Some of the people in this town are congenitally reluctant to form attachments because they don't want to get tied down (see PETS). Most of these people have been hurt before in some other town and now they are afraid of meaningful relationships. These things, however, do not stop most people from devoting a lot of time to looking for love (see ENTERTAINMENT), even though they don't seem to know what they will do with it when they find it. They just don't like going home alone.

A lot of people think that having sex with a person is the only way to get to know them and to decide whether love is likely or not. It is educational to drive around this town early on a Saturday morning and see whose car is parked in front of (or behind, depending on the complexities of the situation) whose house.

Kevin said, "I call it the Lending Library."

When a couple breaks up, there is always some friend waiting to comfort the wounded party.

Leon said, "There's always some woman in the bar who needs to forget her troubles (see ENTERTAINMENT). I try not to miss these opportunities to be understanding."

When an unhealthy relationship finally ends, friends are relieved and they say, "I wanted to tell you before but I didn't."

Sex, if not love, is easy to come by in this town. Barb slept with six different men in a month and a half. This was immediately after her break-up with Bill, a carpenter she'd loved fiercely for two years and four months.

Barb's friends were all worried about her and they said:

"You'll get a reputation."

"You'll get a disease."

"You'll get hurt."

"You'll get pregnant."

"You'll get bitter and cynical."

"It's time to get serious."

MARRIAGE:

Most of the married people in this town are unhappy. Some of these unhappily married people are still giving dinner parties (see HOBBIES) and pretending to be happy.

At a dinner party at Lorraine and Marshall's house, Lorraine asked Mary, "How are you?"

Mary said, "I'm so happy it seems unnatural."

Lorraine said, "Have some more guacamole."

Some of these unhappily married people aren't pretending anymore and they are always talking to anybody who will listen about their marital problems and the merits of a trial separation.

At a dinner party at Andy and Mary's house, Mary asked Lorraine, "How are you?"

Lorraine said, "I'm miserable."

Marshall said, "I want a divorce."

Mary said, "Have some more guacamole."

There are wedding parties and sometimes there are divorce parties. Everybody always gets drunk at parties.

At wedding parties, some of the guests are talking about when their divorce date is coming up. At one wedding party, the bride said, "If we get divorced, I won't ask for a thing." Hugging her, the groom said, "That's my girl."

At divorce parties, some people are always talking about how important it is to stay friends.

DEATH:

Susan said, "When I was a child one day my father was in the basement trying to kill himself. Of course I was too young to understand how someone I loved could be that upset. After I unloaded the gun, I called the doctor. After the doctor left, my father went upstairs to his bedroom and rested. For five years my father didn't speak to me. After five years, I asked my mother to tell me why. She said it was because he thought that I thought he was crazy."

Ed said, "Well, of course he was crazy."

Three years ago, Ed tried to kill himself with pills, not a gun. In this town one death has nothing to do with another.

The Garden of Eloise Loon

Edna Alford

She wasn't one of them. She didn't belong here. She was not what they thought she was nor was she part of any other people. She nodded in the sun on the makeshift step, four large gallon ketchup cans supporting two grey planks, a spike driven through each of them into the tins for good measure. The stoop of the shack faced south and she nodded toward the sun as if to say yes. Whatever it wanted to do with her, it could. Melt down the body, even the moving mound in her round belly, render the fat, make soap, dry the withered hide of her and peg it to the ground, stretch it flat and smooth, scrape it free of all the filaments of flesh. Evaporate the water from the blood and scatter the rusted powder of her seed in the fields, wheresoever it should please. There was nothing left but the beginning of summer.

She hadn't seen Earl since two weeks ago last Friday. Sometimes he went up to work in the bush, but usually he said if he was going. This time he took his cheque, left without a word, and she hadn't seen him since. Nor had she any idea when she would see him again. She had no way of knowing. She had come to the point of not caring either. To fretting, she preferred moving her feet in small spiralling circles in the dirt in front of her, making smooth furrowed patterns in the grey dust, watching a film of dirt powder slowly accumulate over her feet, her ankles, her shins. She had eaten nothing for two days.

The sun made her dizzy. She leaned her head back and watched the leaves on the poplar trees flutter in the wind. Poplars and spruce surrounded the shack. The leaves were round and green and looked like they were spinning, spinning green, almost lime, they were so new. Her belly was hard now, no longer high. The baby dropped three or four days ago, dropped closer to the hole through which it would make its way, like a worm. She cursed the lump. "Shit," she would say, circling the mound with her arms, laughing and crying at the same time. "Shit, shit, shit." And she rocked back and forth to the rhythm of the curse.

She closed her eyes. The lids flooded orange, then red, like thin hot blood. The red was all over her and warm as if it circled inside her brain and coated every cell with warmth the colour of a red rain. Now there were small black dots beginning to appear scattered over the clear warm red in her head. They expanded and grew, black and grey and elongated, like the worms. Finally they overlaid the red and she shivered and opened her eyes and blinked.

From the stoop she could see two other shacks through the bush. One straight ahead, one off to the right. Both were patched with cardboard and tarpaper. Eloise Loon was hanging out her clothes, grey and dripping, from a tin tub. She was silent and the flies buzzed round her head. There were chickens in her yard, all colours, chickens with ragged heads and one, almost pecked to death late one night, staggered with maggots near the outhouse.

The other house off to the right was grey as a grown over grave, silent in the heat. Usually there were many children. She didn't know how many; she had never figured that out except she knew there were a lot of them. All ages. Ragged little diapered ones and ones with fine new store-bought clothes and some with running noses, some with faces brown and alive and shining round as the round round sun. But today, not one. Someone had driven up in a van a couple of days ago and now there were none.

She stretched her arms out. She wore a checkered blue smock from the Mission rummage, slid the sleeves up for more sun, her skin already a mass of freckles. Her hair was red and thin and she hadn't combed it since the day Earl left. There were freckles on the skin of her face, all over except for the eyelids and the mouth which was now a round black hole, agape a yawn.

She felt the first on her foot, looked down, batted off a long black worm with pale yellow ovals along the ridge of its back. But mostly black. The worms were mostly black. They were not really worms, she knew. They were tent caterpillars, by rights, but everybody called them worms.

Last year they layered the bush in a black mass, writhing over the walls of the shack, solid black and moving over the window panes, turning the inside black at the same time as the outside. She stayed outside, batted them off her ankles and her shins. Sometimes they fell from the roof in a clump and landed in her hair, began to move there over her scalp and she would fly from the stoop and scream and run around in circles till Eloise Loon would look up from her garden and laugh. But last year there was food in the house, at least.

And Earl was here. And sometimes he took her down to the lake where she swam. The worms covered the sand but they couldn't really swim. Only once had she seen a fleet, undulating, black, carried over the lake by the wind. Only once had she seen them land and writhe toward the high shore and the bush. They devoured everything in their path. Earl once said they were a lot like people that way. They ate everything in sight and had no natural enemies. But he said they carried their own parasite inside, sooner or later would do themselves in, and the cycle would end. The birds would have nothing to do with them. Even Eloise Loon's starving hens wouldn't eat them. Earl said a man from Chicago had brought a single pair over from Europe years ago. He figured he could make a fortune selling silk.

She remembered the night Earl rode out of the bush wearing a hood and shrouded in the white gauze of the worms, his horse lathered white, the calf a ghost of spun white. But as he drew near, she could see the worms, dropped from trees, black and writhing over the three, the man, the horse, the calf. When the worms were finished with the bush, there was nothing left on the trees but bones and the skeleton branches reached up toward the summer sun which bleached them clean and thin and white against the sky.

But this year, there wasn't even food for worms much less her. Much less the baby inside. There wasn't even Earl. There would be no eating off her this year, she thought, and coughed a small high-pitched laugh, spat toward the sun.

Last year the worms came into the shack too. There were gaps in the floors, knotholes in the walls, a ring of sky around the stovepipe hole. The worms used all of those last year. So let them come, she thought, and shifted on the stoop. And let it come, the little one.

She wondered if maybe she shouldn't go across to the shack of Eloise Loon and ask for scraps. But the air was too warm, too thick, seemed solid between her and the shack of the brown old woman. And Eloise Loon would laugh. She always laughed, her fat heaving in round brown wrinkles, her eyes winking one, then the other, as if she had a tick, these flip-flop eyes. No, she wouldn't go over for a while yet. Maybe Earl would come back tonight.

She reached and batted two worms from her legs. One had climbed as high as her thigh, one only near the ankle bone on her right foot. She reached over and around the mound of her bellied child and picked a stick up out of the dirt and began to hurt the worms, first one and then the other, squashing out their jelly, green, a kind of green, not lime, but poplar, like the leaves they had devoured. Like the leaves, she thought and smiled, upside down, her thin lips twisted in a small half circle, like a pale young branch bent by wet snow.

Earl in winter found her in the snow, half buried, wearing a ragged old coat. She had taken the bus from the city where there were banks and brokers, lights and water, pimps and grocers, singing in the bars. And other darker things, of course. But now, as the sun burned low, shattered black by the branches of the spruce, she thought especially of light, the many flickered city light. She could only half remember the rest. Then the city a ring in her nose, a noose around her neck. She had thought that nothing could be worse, cursed the cracks in the sidewalks, broke her mother's back a million times. But she was wrong.

When she got off the bus at Trestle, she began to walk, stopping from time to time to talk to herself, to ask herself where she thought she was going with one cardboard suitcase and open-toed shoes, the snow blowing up her skirt, the cold obscenely creeping into the crotch of her pantyhose. The noise, the whining wind, instead of dying, rose and covered her head with the sound of something white, all white and smothering and warm, a swarm of white, like cats in her head, a thousand white and mewling cats. Then howling, bitter ripping cats. Then no cats. Then no white. Then no sound. Only a lying down and a feeling of every round and silent moving thing surrounding her, taking her place, talking with her breath. Oh please. Oh shit, oh shit, and a feeling of rocking. Of rocking herself to sleep in a soft white drift.

Then Earl. In a truck. Earl had stopped and picked her up. Picked her up and put her in the truck and that led to heat and something to eat and fucking.

He took her to the reserve. And for a while things worked out all right. She made him supper, peeled potatoes, roasted meat, everything ready every night when he came home from wherever it was that he had been.

She missed no one, none of the other girls who preened in the can at the Queen's every night. None of the Johns, not one. She picked berries all day, strawberries and chokecherries and pincherries and blueberries and gooseberries and dewberries and red currants and black currants and lowbush cranberries and saskatoons, blue. Blue, her fingers blue, dyed blue and red and purple all through the summer into fall when great wedges of geese fell out of the sky and cried for the summer inside the hope, cried for the sun inside the north, the days the sun was dying south.

The winter was spent in the mouth of a long black stove. Shove, shove in the wood, split the wood, carry the wood. Then shove, shove, the sparks on the floor of the shack, the smoke, the long black pipe, a ring of winter silver sky around the stovepipe hole. Then no more wood. Then no more coal. The cold. Everywhere the cold.

For water she melted snow while Earl was in town running around wherever he could find a woman white enough. Every day she hauled her tubs out of the house and into the yard. She filled them full with a spade, the snow sometimes dry like sand, sometimes crusted, sometimes so heavy her hands ached for hours inside the shack where she sat and watched the stove and waited for the snow to melt in the round tin tub. Sometimes she saw Eloise Loon in the yard with a tub and a spade, heaving and hoisting too, laughing and cursing both the sun and the moon.

Sometimes she hid from Earl when he came home and the headlights of the truck shone through the shack window. Sometimes she hid under the bed. But he found her and grabbed her by her thin red hair and banged her head and banged her head on the cold grey floor, till her nose bled and her ears rang with the roar of the stove and white of the storm. He swore and dragged her all over the shack backwards until he got tired and fell on the bed and began to snore.

The second summer came the worms, the walls of worms, the grey floor crawling black. She squashed them and gathered them in the stove. She laughed. The summer passed and the poplar branches, stripped clean, began to leaf again, grow green. Earl went up to the bush. There were no berries because of the worms. She sat on the stoop and looked over at the shacks across the yard, watched Eloise Loon hang out her clothes, tend her garden, weed and hoe and reap in the fall under the sun and the call of the great wedges falling through the sky around the curve, the round wound of the world.

The white of the following winter, a narrow hole, a silver needle with the dark of a hundred icy nights, back to back. The air flecked silver like glitter on glue. She peeled the potatoes and tended the stove, heaped wood in the box till the flue glowed dusty red as powdered blood. In the morning she walked in the bush, clumps of white powdered snow falling from the spruce, sometimes falling on her head, spreading a crown of crystal on her hair, spraying from there down the neck of her coat, down her spine, a thin line of white lumps under white skin, white as the skin of a cutworm in the garden of Eloise Loon.

Edna Alford

And the wind blew. Earl returned for two weeks, nailed her to the bed two, three, one day seven times, the long hard line of his own fishing swallowed by her hole, the jigging ungentle, mortal, full of milk, full of resin, full of slime. There was a time in the middle when she could no longer tell the winter day from the winter night. And somewhere in the time of the winter worm, on the bed in the corner of the small dark room, the child began.

Now in the summer sun she sat rocking the round wound, circling the mound with her arms, laughing and crying at the same time, cursing both the sun and the moon. Finally the sun went down and she rose and opened the screen door, flack flack behind, stuttering the present into past, the past into the dark future, into the shack. As soon as she was inside she saw the worms begin to move across the floor.

She lay on the bed and regarded the pain from the distance of stars, the moon through the window welding arcs of shimmied light against the wall of the shack, her back a rigid arc, a wall of ache. The hole of the night narrow in her throat, the skin on her bloated belly shiny, white as the face of the moon and tight, too tight, the skin splintered with the silverfish of too much light inside, as if she would explode if ever there were another long hard night of arcing time.

In the morning she sat on the edge of the bed with the bloody child. The sun rose red. In the morning she took a rag out to the rain barrel and dipped it in and pulled it out dripping. She carried it back to the shack and wrung it out over the grey scum in the basin on the washstand. Then she began to clean the child which did not utter sound. But moved. Moved a little, flinching like an open wound. When she had him clean, she leaned over him and sang a song with no words, a song which found its own articulation in her throat, a curve of sound drawing honey from the bush and from the lake and from the wild and cunning throat of Eloise Loon. She wrapped the child and held him to her close.

Most of the morning she sat on the edge of the bed and suckled the child which clung to her breast like the rest of men do to the world. And she thought of the thing that she could do, deliver the child to

Eloise Loon and beg for scraps. That was the thing that she could do. And then she wondered if the van might come and she could talk to the man who drove the van and deliver the baby to him. She smiled; her smile was thin.

Finally she took the child acradle on her arm and she went out of the shack to sit on the stoop where it was warm. With the sun today had come the worms, in swarms, hanging from the eaves in clumps, their gauze in all the branches of the trees. The black of millions lying on the leaves, eating, eating quietly. She saw them moving over the ground, around the stoop, a black mass thick and round on the rain barrel, layered velvet bobbing on the water in the barrel. Over the way the garden of Eloise Loon, once green and full of bloom, now was black, undulated toward the stoop of her shack, looped over her clothesline, onto her roof.

And still there was no sign of Earl. Earl, if only he would come, could take her to the lake where she could swim in the wide water, water full of silver and no worms. But by late afternoon, Earl still had not come and she sat on the stoop, suckling the child and drumming the fingers of her right hand on the grey plank and wondering what she could do.

Watching the worms move, she grew sleepy, the lids of her eyes lying low. The clump of worms fallen from the eave onto her hair began moving now, moving slow across her brow, curling round her ears, up into her nostrils, flowing down her neck, down the white line of lumps marking her spine through the thin white shirt. She looked up at the sun and closed her eyes. For a moment she saw the shadow of Eloise Loon against the lids which flooded orange, then red, like thin hot blood. The red was all over her and warm as if it circled inside her brain and coated every cell with warmth the colour of a red rain.

Now there were small black dots beginning to appear scattered over the clear warm red. They expanded in her head and grew, black and grey elongated. Finally she brushed them away from her eyes and raised the child in her arms, held him out toward the sun, stood up still holding him high, sighting along him as if he were a barrel of a gun, sighting the poplar and the spruce and the wide wide water. She left the stoop and began to run toward the garden of Eloise Loon. There she laid him down among the worms. As many as she could gather in her arms, she heaped high in a black and moving mound which began to spin a canopy, a shroud, delivered him to the dark, surrounded by her own laughter and the high arc of the only sky.

Becoming

Jake MacDonald

T he blizzard hit at mid-afternoon.

Later in the day, with darkness descending on the city, Nimitz realized he wasn't going to get away clean. It was just before supper time and he had turned off all the lights in his apartment; he heard footsteps coming in the outside hall. They were heavy footsteps, creaking, stealthy, and he was into the broom closet, peering through the crack, when they kicked the apartment door in.

One of them was a heavyset, bleary-eyed man. The other was a woman, mid-twenties, attractive, carrying a microphone in her hand and a tape recorder in her right. Her lips were moving as she held the mike. The big man stepped past the splintered door jamb and beckoned for the young woman to follow. He gestured for absolute quiet. They moved down the hall towards the bedroom and out of Nimitz's line of sight.

His heart pounded in his ears. He was torn between anger, pure rage that they would barge into his apartment like this, and an intense embarrassment that at any moment he would be discovered. Then suddenly they were coming.

They walked right up Nimitz's cluttered hall and stood in front of the broom closet. The fat man planted his hands on his hips, and shook his head in disgust as he looked around. "I don't know what to tell you ma'am. The crazy guy, he could be anywhere."

The big man was Nimitz's landlord. He always paid his rent on time but nonetheless the landlord seemed to hate him. It was not unheard of for the landlord to go around kicking doors in. He was a self-made man, a rumoured millionaire, and often declared that he hadn't worked his ass off all his life so that people could tell him what he could or couldn't do.

The young woman, carrying the tape recorder in the crook of her arm, moved down the hall and studied the big color posters that he'd taped to the walls. Nimitz watched. She paused in front of the beautiful Kodachrome blowup of the fan coral, his favorite too.

"He certainly does like the sea, doesn't he."

The landlord tossed a hand. "Aw, summabitch. He's a nutcase, eh? All I know is, he says he's going to the ocean to be a fish, he should have given me 30 days' notice."

The landlord fingered a rip in the wall-paper where Nimitz had tacked large photo of a hammerhead shark. The hall window ticked, betraying a windblown gust of sleet. Nimitz's luggage was still piled in the hall, where he'd hurriedly abandoned it after hearing their approach. The young woman, who in her black leather coat, tightly pinned hair and red lips looked vaguely feline and untrustworthy to Nimitz, eyed the luggage and glanced casually at the broom closet door, slight ajar. "Well I'd certainly like to talk to him, anyway," she sighed. "I, uh . . . don't want to disturb this young man's privacy but I think he has a most interesting idea . . . a very clever advertising gimmick. Don't you think so? I mean, with these awful prairie winters . . . what a promotion scheme!"

Nimitz was gritting his teeth, jammed into the closet, standing on one leg. Curses, he thought to himself, I never should have rented that billboard. Now I've even got reporters after me.

With the last dregs of his bank account he'd commissioned a billboard at the corner of Stradbrook and Main, showing him in his fish outfit, bidding Winnipeg adieu with a lifted fin. SO LONG WINNIPEG — the caption read — I'M OFF TO THE OCEAN TO BECOME A FISH! And he'd signed his name. This public statement, which he'd intended strictly as a sincere farewell, had backfired horribly. The billboard company, after charging him $400, erected the message a day ahead of schedule and caught Nimitz unprepared. He'd hoped to be well under way, jetting his way south to the Caribbean by the time the billboard went public, but the phone had started ringing by early afternoon and hadn't stopped. He'd been besieged by relatives, family, employer, neighbours — each demanding, no doubt, an explanation. But each time he'd taken to the broom closet. So far it had worked.

His landlord ground coins in his pocket, impatient. The lady reporter kept exploring the apartment, lifting, poking, spinning the fat papier mâché fish that hung on threads from the ceiling. "I gotta get back to my hockey game," said the landlord. "Well thank you very much for showing me his apartment," the young woman said. "I hope he's not out wandering around in this blizzard tonight . . . " She glanced at the broom closet. "The weather is so bad that they've cancelled all the flights at the airport. Perhaps I'll leave my card, in case he decides to contact me." She smoothed the leather coat over her hips and walked to the broom closet. Her eyes were unfocused, abstract, her lips parted as she wedged the card in the door jamb, her face perhaps six inches away. This woman, Nimitz thought to himself, has taken advantage of men before.

Nimitz caught a cab to a hotel near the airport.

The storm was at its height. The streets were empty. It was suppertime, but dark as a wild eerie midnight. Nimitz sat in the back of the cab, clutching a huge stack of paraphernalia on his lap — mylar fins, ribbed with old car aerials, a scaly skin fashioned from a body stocking and large sequins, spiny dorsals, sheet metal gills. The cab wallowed and skidded through the snow clogged streets. Occasionally snow plows would lunge across the street in front of them, their disaster lights spinning crazily.

"You're going to a masquerade party on a night like this?" the cab driver remarked.

"No . . . " said Nimitz quietly, the lights of the city playing over his face one last time. "I'm going to the ocean. To become a fish."

The cabbie nodded. "Sorry I asked."

At the hotel door the cabbie sulked, refusing to help Nimitz unload his gear. Nimitz paid him with a five dollar tip, his bare hands freezing in the bitter January wind, and then carted his equipment to the brightly lit aquarium of the hotel entrance.

He stood in front of the desk, his fins piled beside him, and rubbed his hands together for warmth. Bits of snow melted in his tousled hair.

"Mr. uh . . . don't I know you?" the desk clerk asked.

"I doubt it," retorted Nimitz. "I'm on my way to the ocean. I'd like to rent a room for a few hours, until the airplanes start moving again."

"Of course, sir."

"And I'm expecting a call from the airlines regarding my reservation. Other than that I want privacy, all right? No visitors —I want to get some rest."

"Yes sir, of course." The desk clerk tossed a finger. A bellhop materialized at Nimitz's side.

"You take the suitcase. I'll take the fish outfit," said Nimitz.

The bellhop led him down the hall.

He wasn't in his room more than ten minutes, testing the shower, testing the color television, ripping the sanitary band off the toilet seat, when a key sounded in the door and the lady reporter came into the room. "I'd like to introduce myself," she said.

Nimitz relented.

The girl said her name was Kate Mathews, freelance journalist, down on her luck. "At at hundred bucks a story do you think I'm getting rich?" she said. She was already sitting on the edge of the bed, but there was a resigned look on her face as if she expected to be expelled from the room as quickly as she came in. Her leather coat was unbuttoned, and she didn't have a light for her cigarette. Nimitz didn't smoke.

"I'll talk to you for five minutes. These rules please . . . no tape recorder, and no story until I leave town."

"Okay," she said. "No sweat." She was still looking for a match for her cigarette. She found one, lit her cigarette, and slipped out of her leather coat. She was wearing black slacks, fawn sweater and a crimson silk scarf knotted around her throat. Nimitz appraised her bosom. This is one thing I'll miss, he thought to himself. A female trout or salmon is gorgeous, admittedly, but the human female isn't that bad either.

Settled, with her knees crossed, her Benson & Hedges aloft, her hair loosed and shaken down, she glanced at Nimitz and smiled. "Now . . . what's this about becoming a fish. Is this another one of those Fly-to-the-Sun promotions?"

Nimitz explained that he was serious. He showed her his fins, his weight belt, his underwater topographical maps of various ocean regions — all tucked away in water proof pouches — his scaly outfit, designed so that other fishes would accept him, and most important of all, his solid state rebreather. He laid all the gear out on the bed, explaining the function of each, and told her that he'd test the outfit one more time, to make sure he hadn't forgotten anything.

Kate Mathews watched with a look of disbelief as he stripped down to his jockey shorts and climbed into the fish outfit. In a matter of minutes he was fully dressed — in silver scales, rattling gills, and a great quivering array of gaudy fins. From around his neck, in the manner of a French cavalier, hung a lacy ruffle of quills. He waddled carefully to the mirror, studying his image with narrowed eye. "I put a lot of thought into this. You know, your average person would think I was crazy. They'd say 'Nimitz, you're crazy. Why not become a dolphin if you're going to all the trouble?' But that's just their own prejudice coming through. Dolphins share a lot of similarities with human beings, so naturally we think that dolphins are wonderful. And nobody mentions that the Japanese slaughter them by the thousands, so there's a real risk involved. And not only that . . . dolphins breathe air and I don't want to have to go up to the surface all the time. I've had enough of that."

He stood sideways, glancing at himself in the mirror, and awkwardly rearranged one his ventral fins. "I finally settled on the rooster fish. I'm one of the most grotesque creatures in the ocean, in a sort of flamboyant way, and also . . . " he added with a modest smile, "I'm deadly poisonous."

Kate Mathews stared at him for a long moment. "This is a joke," she said flatly.

Nimitz shook his head. His gills rustled. "But you don't have to stay here, if you don't believe me. I mean you asked, and I'm telling you."

"Well you can't just become a fish!"

He sat on the edge of the bed, crossed his fins patiently in his lap. "Well yes, actually . . . I can."

She stared at him, as if making some quick appraisal of his sanity, and he stared back. There was the faint sound of winter buffeting the outside walls. "You see," he began "it's a well accepted fact, these days, that the physical world is really just an idea. It's not real, but just a sort of stage setting that we've all decided to work on. Any physicist will tell you that. Any physicist will tell you that once you divide an atom a certain number of times there's nothing left. Nothing! At some level, then, there's no such thing as matter!"

She nodded sourly. "Heavy."

"So if being here, in this room, in this city, in this world, is just an idea, then I'm changing my mind, that's all. I'm just changing my mind."

"Well . . . I don't have the mental power of say, a yogi or somebody like that so I have to cheat a bit. I don't expect to turn right into a fish just by snapping my fingers. I'm more reasonable than that. I figure I'll have to be down there, concentrating real hard for a couple of weeks before I get any results."

She nodded, then shook her head. "You can't do this. You can't take these philosophies and apply them to real life, they're not meant for that. Where will you live when you're down there? How will you swim with all that crap on? What will you eat? How will you breathe?"

Nimitz smiled benignly and displayed his solid state rebreather, which was a black steel and rubber device resembling a harmonica. "With this . . . I can breathe underwater just like a fish. It's good for up to two years . . . Cousteau designed it years ago but suppressed it because it would kill off his SCUBA royalties. Not many people know about it. I had to buy the plans off this Florida dope dealer I know, and it cost me plenty."

She examined it dubiously. "This little thing?"

"Sure. It works just great. You just pop it in your mouth and breathe through it. It separates the H_2 from the 0. Hydrogen bubbles shoot out those little vents on the side and oxygen flows in through the mouthpiece. It'll have to do until I get my gills operating."

She peered at his gills, several layers of clinking sheet metal with meticulously handpainted scales. "But . . . where will you live? You can't just swim around like a fish with that monkey suit on."

He unbuttoned his gills at the throat and smiled. "Of course not. I'll tend to settle down off reefs in about forty feet of water. I prey on crustaceans so you'll tend to find me where there's a steady run of shrimp or squid or lobster. Give me some clear, clean water, a sand bottom, and maybe a bit of riprap or coral nearby and I imagine I'll do very well."

"Really," she said. She was regarding him with unwavering fascination. "And you seriously think you can get away with this? You don't work for some goofy ad agency?"

He stared back at her, his eyes equally intent. "No I do not."

"And you think that . . . mouth organ thing will let you cruise around under water indefinitely?"

"Oh yeah. I just got to keep it filled with baking soda."

"You've got to keep it filled with . . . baking soda?"

"Yeah . . . the baking soda makes the bubbles. Along with the H_2. Here, let me show you. I should test it anyway."

Nimitz stood up, clumsy because of the way the fish skin bound his legs together, and wiggled into the bathroom. He heard her coming behind him, but couldn't see with the ruff of fins around his neck. He bent over stiffly and turned on the bathroom tap, and spoke loudly the water's roar. "My name is Nimitz, by the way," he said.

"I know . . . your name is on the billboard remember?"

"Yes. But I'd like to forget. I hadn't intended to become a notorious figure so early, but my plans fouled up."

She was turning over the breathing device in her hand, looking up at him expectantly. He was taller than her but not by much.

"Allow me," Nimitz said. He shut the tap off and took the rebreather from her hand, paused for a moment and gazed down into the half-tubful of swinging water. He clamped the rebreather in his mouth, looked at her, waved goodbye, and then plunged his head into the water.

Seconds passed, and more seconds, and then she thought she detected a queer tremor in his shoulders. She seized him by the gills and dorsal fins and wrestled him bodily from the bathtub. He fell backwards onto the floor. She fell in a tangle beneath him, and as he gasped and coughed violently she scrambled to one knee, forced him to lie flat on the wet floor, and prepared to administer mouth-to-mouth rescusitation.

"Easy, easy . . . " she soothed. "You're not going to drown."

"I know I'm not going to drown!" he protested, his voice nasal from the thumb and forefinger clamped on his nose. "I was going to be fine! There was no problem! Didn't you see the H2?"

"No I didn't see the H2," she retorted, mimicking the quack in his voice. "If it was working so well why is your face purple?"

"Eh!?"

"Why is your face purple?"

He sat up, straightened his fins. "Excitement I guess . . . I don't know! You try it. If you don't think it's exciting to be breathing air under water, man's oldest dream . . . "

She made a cynical snort.

"Looks like I spilled a little water on you," Nimitz said.

She nodded, looking down at the water splotches in her slacks, the thin sweater drenched and clinging to her bust. "I guess I got excited," she said. She gave him a crooked smile.

At that moment the telephone rang. Nimitz wriggled and flopped on the floor struggling to get up.

"Here, let me help," she said.

"Get the phone."

Nimitz lay on the floor and listened as she answered the phone. Water, his element, soaked in through the fish skin and established a chilly presence in his undershorts. "It's the airline," she called out. "There's some flights starting to operate again. You've got a reservation on Flight 203 to Cozumel, but that's postponed until sometime tomorrow morning. And you've got a reservation on Flight 109 to Miami, but the flight is held over in Toronto . . . And you've got — "

"All I want is to get to the sea!" he blurted. "Anywhere on the sea! Doesn't she have anything tonight, going to the sea?"

There was a long interval, and Nimitz listened intently to the voice in the other room. Her voice was calm and pleasant, and Nimitz was beginning to think that she was a little unbalanced.

"There's Skybus to Vancouver at midnight. It's leaving on time, and there's till two seats left."

Nimitz struggled to his feet. "Yes! I'll take it."

Kate Mathews cooed into the telephone. "Wonderful. We'll take both of them," she said.

In front of the airport there were taxi cabs clustered like predators, their lights flashing in ominous synchronization. The cab containing Nimitz and Kate Mathews slid to an icy halt in the loading zone. Nimitz paid the cabbie and exited clumsily. Still in his fish costume, having committed himself to never again remove that freely chosen badge of identity, he slipped on the packed snow and bent one fin against the taxi door, Kate Mathews exited from the cab behind him, carrying a luggage bag and taking his arm as they slipped and skidded across the road. "It's only a caudal fin," said Nimitz. "I'll hardly ever need it. Anyway . . . maybe it'll heal."

"I'll get some tape somewhere," Kate Mathews said.

Overhead, above the streetlights, the cloud cover had torn off and the sky was clearing. There was several stars, tiny chinks of light, visible in the huge dark emptiness but the wind blew chips of ice into their faces, and they both exclaimed aloud as they rushed towards the door. Kate Mathews, her own clothes thoroughly soaked from the debacle in the hotel bathroom, had changed into an outfit assembled from Nimitz's suitcase. As she expected, his clothes were somewhat too large and consistently fish-oriented, with "Save the Whales" and "I'm a Bass Buster" tee shirts predominant, along with sweaters plastered with fishing club crests, "Tackle Tester" and "Go Barbless" baseball hats etc., but she managed to put together an outfit she thought reasonably anonymous. Wearing wool breeches, an old British army khaki shirt, canvas vest, straw creel hung over her shoulder as a purse, and a crush hat, festooned with numerous tiny trout flies, she thought she might pass for somebody marginally normal, perhaps even chic. However, as they entered the cavernous light of the airport terminal, aswarm with strangers, she drew near to Nimitz's fin. "I feel a bit conspicuous," she whispered, as they walked to the ticket desk.

"How do you think I feel?" he retorted.

Nimitz paid for their tickets. "I won't need money where I'm going," he sighed. There was a two dollar bill in his hand. "This is it. The last money I have as a human. Should we blow it foolishly?"

They secured their tickets, checked their luggage and walked to the boarding gate. Nimitz went through the metal detector first. A female security officer, smiling as if she were overjoyed to see them, ran a hand detector up and down their bodies. Nimitz, at first concerned that his fish costume would cause consternation at the security gate, saw that amongst the other passengers lined up for the Vancouver flight — aging hippies, loggers, painted ladies, seven foot tall Rastafarians, radical nuns, skeletal drug addicts — he was barely noticed. They walked down the hall and down the long umbilical tunnel into the A-320. They sat, waited, there was a whine, the engines staggered thunderingly alive and they began to roll, squeaky as a carriage, across the concrete ramp towards the runway. Nimitz pressed his forehead against the window and mentally photographed all that he would never see again —lights of the city, crawling headlights, cold pavement swept by even colder snow. A moment later the landscape swung through an abrupt ninety degree arc and the jet braked to a stop. There was a long moment, a total silence inside the gloom of the aircraft.

Nimitz looked at Kate Mathews. She was pretending to look straight ahead, but he had the sense that she was studying him. She seemed sneaky, but in a constant and predictable and quite playful way. The trout fisherman's hat was perched on her abundant hair in a roguish tilt and she was twiddling her thumbs. As if reading his mind she whispered to him from the corner of her mouth. "I saw your picture on the billboard and that's why I'm here. I'm not really after a story. I'm after you. I know what kind of man I like and the face on the billboard sparked my interest. And then I found out that you're going away and never coming back, so that was three strikes and I'm out."

She proffered her hand, palm up, as if they were making a deal.

Nimitz took her hand, profoundly moved. He hesitated, as if searching for the proper words. "If you were a rooster fish," he finally whispered, "I would like to spawn with you."

"Oh thank you, Nimitz," she replied, squeezing his hand.

The jet began its takeoff roll. With the thunder of engines they were pressed deep into their seats. Nimitz was imagining what it would be like to spawn with Kate Mathews. "Do you know how to swim?" he asked, as the plane lifted off.

It was like the hell-bound plane, Nimitz thought to himself. A full moon slanted in through the heavy plastic portholes and the plane bucked and swooped its way westward. At one point the pilot announced that were flying into a one hundred and twenty mile-an-hour headwind, thus the buffeting, but though he changed altitudes the bouncing continued. Their departure time from Winnipeg was midnight and their estimated time of arrival in Vancouver was midnight, and as they rocketed westward, locked in time, the strange-looking passengers who hulked up and down the gloomy aisles, or brayed drunkenly throughout the airplane, seemed like flies caught in amber, living exhibits in some future museum. Nimitz, with a leaden despair for his own species, studied the plastic moldings, vinyl seat backs and mysteriously patterned rivets around him and tried to divine the process by which human civilization had come to this noxious climax. Personally, he suspected that evolution made its first mistake when the first amphibians crawled up out of the sensible sea.

Finally the plane began to descend. Kate Mathews, who had been sleeping with her head upon his shoulder, stirred drowsily and he patted her knee. He felt like they were married. "We're going down."

She leaned across him, her elbows heavy in his lap, and peered out the porthole. A moment later she said, "Look. There's the lights of the city."

They landed at Vancouver International and picked up their bags. Even inside the terminal teeming with crowds, they could smell the damp west coast air. They went outside and it was lightly raining. The everpresent cabs idled at the curb and a tangle of roads, black and shiny as oil under the streetlamps, all led towards the lights of the city. "What now?" Kate Mathews asked.

"This way," Nimitz said. "I used to know a guy . . . "

They walked down the road for half a mile. When they were out of sight of the main door of the airport Nimitz went down into the ditch and spread the barbed wire fence. "Hop through," he said. He was shivering. Already the rain had leaked through the hand sewn scales of his fish skin.

"What gives?" she said, as they began to slog across the muddy field.

"This is actually an island, Sea Island. When they built the airport there were some people living on this island, but they kicked them all off. I know a guy who's sort of a hobo who lives in one of the old houses up here. He's a good guy, we used to work together. Anyway, maybe he'll put us up for the night. He's thinking of becoming a fish too."

Soon a dark row of houses, with not a light on, loomed ahead. The wind seemed to be picking up and Nimitz moved boldly through the yards, hurrying against the quickening rain. "It's this one," he whispered loudly. "But it doesn't look like he's home."

Around the back door, which was piled with fresh-cut firewood, there were many signs of occupancy —dog dish, rubber boots, swede saw. Kate Mathews spied a note on the door. "Look."

"DEAR STRANGER," the note read, "COME ON IN AND HELP YOURSELF. BUT PLEASE REPLACE WHAT YOU USE. SPLIT WOOD IF YOU GOT NO MONEY. PERSONAL FRIENDS PLEASE IGNORE THIS SIGN. I'M SHANGHAIED TO BELLA COOLA. CY."

They went in the door and Nimitz groped through the kitchen, locating a lantern and a wooden match. The room flared alight — kitchen at one end, fireplace halfway through the room and old double bed at the far end. "I want a coffee," Kate Mathews said.

"Me too . . . I'm cold."

"Take off that fish outfit. You must be soaked."

"I'll take it off and light a fire. I don't mind, since it's my last night as a hairless primate."

Nimitz lit the fire and took off his fish skin. His shorts were also wet and he removed them, hanging everything by the heat of the fire. His torso, hardened by years of travelling and outdoor labor, was sculpted in shadow by the firelight. He was not ashamed to be naked in front of a woman he barely knew. It was his preference for basics that convinced him to become a fish in the first place. He got into bed and pulled the blankets to his chin, shivered.

"Hurry up," he said. "I'm warming it up."

"Warming what up?"

She came to the bedside with two steaming mugs of coffee. Nimitz watched her undress. He decided that she was undoubtedly the most straightforward, witty and nubile woman he'd ever had the pleasure to watch disrobe. She climbed under the heavy quilts, shivered wildly from the cold and wrapped herself around him. "Oh my," she said. "Oh my . . . "

Afterward, in the total dark, with the fire down to only crawling embers, she stirred her sleepy warmth against him and kissed the side of his neck. "Nimitz . . . are you still awake?"

"Well . . . what's that strange noise outside? That . . . thumping, swishing noise. It can't be that windy, can it?"

Nimitz smiled. "What, didn't you realize? No . . . I guess in the dark you couldn't see and I forgot to tell you. That sound is the surf hitting as the tide comes in. We're only about fifty yards from the sea."

Dawn broke stormy and dismal. For hours, as wind and rain slapped the windows, Nimitz and Kate Mathews dozed under the covers. Occasionally they would waken, nuzzle like cats, and ease their limbs into some new model of entwinement. Outside, the sea growled patiently.

Finally, after sleeping all of the morning and much of the afternoon, Kate Mathews opened her eyes to sunlight in the window. She rolled over to tell Nimitz but he was already awake, staring up at the ceiling. "When are you going?" she asked.

He looked at her. "Soon, I guess. I was going to go early in the morning but I hate to go swimming when it's overcast."

They rose from the bed and dressed. Kate Mathews wriggled into Nimitz's old fisherman's sweater and moved about the kitchen making coffee, her hair a luxuriant mane. Nimitz, strapping on his gills, gazed at her fixedly. His eyes were soft but the muscles of his jaw twitched with determination. Finally he moved up behind her and placed a fin on her should. "Kate," he said.

She sobbed and threw her arms around him. "I don't want you to become a fish!" Her tears ran onto his scaly chest.

"Kate, Kate . . . " he whispered. "It's not what you want, or what I want, or what anybody wants that's important. It's bigger than that. It's survival of a species. At one time we crawled out of the sea, and now it's time for us to go back, don't you see?"

She nodded.

They drank their coffee and went outside.

It was a brilliant day, the sky blue as a flag. The sea was a darker purple, redolent with salty breezes, and across a line of dunes, drift logs and cane grass the surf was dumping lazily on the beach. Nimitz walked boldly through the sand, his ostentatious rooster quills shivering colourfully in the wind, and seagulls swerved drastically overhead, screaming.

There was a rowboat on the beach and together they pushed it into the water. "Do you know how to row?" he asked.

"Shut up," she replied.

She rowed and he sat in the rear of the boat, going over his maps.

"I'm going to swim out to the end of the Strait of Juan de Fuca," he told her. "And then hang a left and head south down the edge of the continental shelf. If I keep travelling I should make the Coronado Islands in four or five weeks. There's lots happening down there, the waters are teeming with life . . . I'll take it easy there for a while, rest up, prey on the plentiful crustaceans, then it's make westering . . . head out. I got seven thousand miles of Pacific Ocean to explore, not to mention what lies beyond, like the Great Barrier Reef, Sunda Straits, South China Sea . . . "

She stopped rowing. They were fifty yards from shore, bobbing gently. Her chin was propped on her hand and she wasn't looking at him. And then she looked up at him and she was focused, bright. "Good luck Nimitz," she said.

He shrugged. "As long as I don't get speargunned by some tourist or netted by some Russian trawler I should be all right."

He pulled the fringed collar and fish hood up over his head. The glassy eyes, large as saucers, stared at her unseeing. "Next time you're at a fancy cocktail party," he said, the large fat lips flapping, "take a good look at the seafood hors d'oeuvres. It might be me."

She pried open the huge lips and took one last look at the human face inside. She kissed him, he kissed her. "Good bye," he said.

"If you change your mind you'll find me back in Winterpeg, working for a living."

"Evolution can't reverse itself," he said.

He stood up, put the rebreather in his mouth and leapt into the sea. Water exploded around him, flashes of colored light. Jeeze it's cold! He was going to shout, but realized with his weight belt he was already sinking. He breathed deeply, once, twice, and a rapture began to flood

Jake MacDonald

into his brain. Below him he saw the spiralling depths coming up to meet him, the sun winding down like a staircase of gold.

The Wild Plum Tree

Sandra Birdsell

ESSAY
The Wild Plum Tree

It is more than a shrub but not a tree, bark is smooth when young.
Inside, white sapwood, porous bark splits with age and leaves
narrow tipped, fruit slightly reddish with blood
flowers showy white gracing
southern end of Manitoba and other provinces,
of no commercial value.

Mr. Malcolm is English 100. He is also Betty's Mathematics teacher, History teacher and Language Arts teacher. He is straight from Jamaica and looks to pregnant wayward girls and delinquents to teach him all they know about Manitoba.

"Now surely," he says, "you must know more about this subject. It was your free choice."

Betty shrugs, feigns indifference. The essay is the best she can do under the circumstances. The reference books in the classroom are *The Books of Knowledge* and *Weeds, Trees and Wildflowers in Canada*. Some of the girls have taken a bus down to the public library on William. But not her. What she doesn't know, she will make up. That's life, she tells herself.

Sandra Birdsell

"But you see, I asked for six pages, at least," he says. He wears pastel colours. Pale green polyester pants, a pinkish tie against a coral coloured shirt. She ignores him, looks out the dusty window down into the city. The rapid darting of traffic intrigues her. Where are all these people going to, coming from? And why? It seems pointless. She saw shadows in the graveyard last night. She'd sat on the radiator in her room looking out and thought how appropriate: a graveyard in the back yard of the home for wayward girls. They were all burying things, their past, their present, the things that came out of them. And she saw down there, lithe phantoms sprinting from tree to tree, leaping up from the hard granite stones. Today, several of the tombstones are toppled into the grass. The praying virgin with her blind eyes and reverent posture, hands held up in frozen supplication, lies on one side.

"Did you not understand my instructions then?" the teacher asks.

"Yes, Mr. Malcolm, I understood your instructions." She wants only to be left alone.

"Mr. Jackson."

"Yes, Mr. Jackson." His name is Malcolm P. Jackson. You have never heard the sound of a mob, he has told them. He'd sat on the desk in front of them, swinging his knees in and out, like a young child needing to urinate. I was a boy when I once heard such a mob. It was like the sound of a swarm of angry bees growing louder and louder. Let me tell you, it was not a pleasant sound. Angry people. A mob rushing along the street. I was very young but I learned quickly to be afraid of the mob.

"Well then, if you knew the instruction, then why have you handed me this?" He holds up the single sheet of paper. The classroom has grown quiet. The girls stop talking to listen.

"Because I felt like it."

Several of the girls titter. Betty has not said this for their benefit. She only needs, wants to be left on her own. A detention is a way to accomplish this end. Mr. Jackson sets the paper down, takes a piece of yellow chalk from his shirt pocket and rolls it from hand to hand.

"My dear girl. Listen. In my country, education is a privilege. Only the cleverest people go beyond grade school. Our parents made great sacrifices for us. We're grateful. With us, it is never a question, whether we feel like it or not, we do it."

"If you're so smart," someone says, "then why are you here with us?"

He pretends he hasn't heard, but the muscles in his jaw contract suddenly as though he just bit into a stone.

Betty wants no part of their taunting. She wants to be away from them all, to be able to sift through all the information she has gathered, to make some order of it.

"Surely you could do better than this," he persists. "There must be more you could write about the wild plum tree."

Even now, she smells the fruit of it. The tart flavour, taut skin splitting in her mouth, the slippery membrane of its meat, a piece of slime at the bottom of a quart sealer jar of homemade wine coming suddenly into her mouth like a great clot of blood. There is too much to say about the wild plum tree. The assignment has paralyzed her.

"Yes, Chocolate Drop. I'm sure there is." She uses the girl's private name for Mr. Jackson.

His nostrils flare. The room grows silent. Then laughter erupts, spills over. "Chocolate Drop," a girl says and then they all say, "Chocolate Drop."

His eyes dart about the room. Betty continues to stand before the window toying with the frayed cord on the venetian blind. Thousands of girls have stood at this very same window and played with this cord. It's marked with their anguish, their boredom and frustrations.

"Well um," Mr. Jackson says, bouncing the chalk from palm to palm. "Well um." The palms of his hands are tinged pink. The skin has been worn away. It's from masturbating, flogging his meat, the girls say. He clutched at his crotch frequently in the classroom. Adjusts his testicles before he sits down on the edge of the desk to confront him.

"Who needs you, Chocolate Drop," a girl asks.

"Well, Miss," Mr. Jackson says to Betty, "You see what you have instigated? You may call me what you like. What can one expect from Satan's daughter."

Betty yanks the frayed cord. It snaps free and falls to the floor. Several girls leave their desks. Mr. Jackson turns and faces them quickly. "Well um," he says. "That will be ten pages now. You seem to think she is a humorous person. Do you think ten pages is also funny?"

They groan. "You can't make us do ten pages," a tall girl with angry grey eyes says.

He strides to his desk, pulls open a drawer and takes out a wooden ruler. "Ten pages, I said." He bangs the ruler against his desk.

"Fuck off," the tall girls says.

He walks swiftly to her and whacks her across the face with the ruler. Smiles fade, all movement suspended. A red welt rises on the girl's cheek. "And who else wishes to express themselves in such a manner?" he asks. The girls, one by one return to their desks.

"You heard her," Betty says. "Go fuck yourself in Jamaica and leave us alone." A flood of tension is released suddenly. She feels the teacher's wooden ruler bounce off her shoulder blade. The girls laugh and call out their individual hate names for Mr. Jackson. An eraser bounces off the wall beside his head. He backs slowly over to the classroom door and stands with one hand on the knob. His lips are flecked with spittle. "Ten pages, you naughty spoiled children. When you can control yourselves, we will continue this class," he says and flees.

Control themselves. Is it lack of control then, that has brought them all to this place? The windowpane is cool against Betty's forehead as she looks down into the street. A young man cuts through the cemetery, hands plunged deep into his pockets, he walks with his shoulders hunched up, a cigarette hangs from his mouth. He glances up at the window where she stands and is gone.

Notes for essay on wild plum tree
Mr. Malcolm, English 100

the beginning

Suddenly you face across the street where once there was only a coulee with bullrushes, twitch grass four feet high, God and Indian arrow-heads; a brand new house.

But first, machines squashed frogs and garter snakes and a pen once lost and never found and then plowed them beneath tons of landfill from a field where they also discovered the skeletons part of which Laurence brought to school. (the skull)

Then, when the four and a half member family move into that new house; the dark haired woman has a bump in front so she is probably pregnant, being the oldest of six teaches you to watch for those things; the beginning ends.
through yellowing lace curtains
I have always watched
the games of others
hiding and seeking the waning sun
shadows the mourning dove's
spotted grey
bird sounds temper the shrill play
sounds
that strike my note
of sorrow
I have not found anything good
in tomorrow

Sandra Birdsell

Notes before the beginning (big inning)

Leaves (somewhat hairy) of the dog mustard plant, which, like the mother of seven, originated in Europe and were first found in Canada at Emerson in 1922, tickle bare legs when walking in the coulee. And their flower, clusters of pale yellow stain white organdy, which also scratches bare legs when walking, sitting, standing period. When you wander with Laurence in the coulee, he carries your shoes and you can feel the spongy ground and make it squeeze up between your toes and then he shows you his hidden pool
and in the deep pool
melted snow yellows
bright all the dead grasses
pink granite stones and your face
rising and falling as feet dipped clean
drip the surface and make you wrinkle

Russian pigweed stands as high as you because you are eight, but Laurence's head is a little above it. The plant is like the two of you, one plant and two different kinds of flowers, male and female.

And God is also in the coulee, moving before you. You can feel his breath on your body, coming through the organdy you have worn especially for Him because it is Sunday.

And Laurence, even though he does not go to any church is of the same plant that nods in the same breath. But for some reason, the mother of seven doesn't think so which is why you walk among the Russian pigweed, so she can't see you and get angry and send you down the road to your grandfather's house to get a lesson in the Bible.

God you were
there inside
my knees and elbows
scratched raw

crawling from imaginary
Indians
would take my yellow hair
make a belt or something, God
your voice
fades faster than games
of Indians don't last
forever

"Betty uses foul language and shows disrespect for the property of the institution," the social worker says. She reads from the teacher's report. She wears black cats' eyes shaped glasses and adjusts them before she speaks again. Betty can feel her father's shyness of this woman, his eagerness to appease and have everyone agree quickly that everything will be fine so that he can go home and report to Mika with a clear conscience that he's done his best. He sits on a chair beside Betty. They face the social worker's desk beneath the window. The room is a basement room. The window is at street level and Betty watches and counts the feet of people who pass by on the sidewalk.

"If you won't adhere to the rules of this institution, what choice will we have, but to ask you to leave it?"

"Certainly, she's going to follow the rules and regulations," Maurice says. "There's no maybe about it."

He plays with the brim of his hat and looks down at the floor. He's put on his suit and tie and taken the bus in from the country especially for this meeting. He's deeply embarrassed. He cannot bring himself to say the words, "pregnant" and "social worker."

The woman writes something on her pad. Betty wonders if she is writing, "father is co-operative," or "supportive father." Of whom and for whom?

"What about rules regarding hitting students with rulers?" Betty asks.

Sandra Birdsell

"Listen here," Maurice says, suddenly irritated. "What makes you think you can ask that, eh? You're not in any position here to ask questions."

"And what position am I in?"

Maurice is flustered. He twirls the hat between this thick brown fingers, clears his throat several times.

The social worker gets up quickly. "I think the two of you need to talk alone. It's important that we reach an understanding today." The door closes behind her. Maurice relaxes. He wipes his brow, sits up straighter and looks about the room for the first time. The walls are cement block, unpainted. There are no pictures on the walls. "This here place is not so bad," he says. "I don't know what you're griping about."

A black mongrel zig-zags across the boulevard and sidewalk. It stops and looks down into the room, sniffs and then continues on its way.

"You don't have to live here. I hate it."

"Well now, that wasn't our doing, was it?" Maurice says. It's the closest he's come to mentioning her pregnancy. "Anyway, it's a darn sight better than being out on the street because, believe you me, that's where you're headed if you don't shape up."

Betty stifles the urge to laugh. Shape up. She is rapidly shaping up. She knows that her parents' number one concern is her shape. They're afraid that she might be expelled from the home and shame them with her bulging presence in the community. It's the only reason for his trip into the city. She knows she's been cut off, that she can't look to either of her parents for anything.

"It's okay," she says, "I'll be okay now. It's just been hard to adjust."

Maurice brightens. He looks at her with a wide smile, his eyes uneasy though, carefully avoiding looking at her stomach. "Adjust, absolutely. I can understand that. Certainly it takes time to get used to new situations."

"Losing your home is a new situation all right."

"Eh?" His hands stop in mid-air.

"I feel as though I have no home." For one second she wants to fling herself at him, bury her face into this shoulder and hold on.

Maurice works furiously as he flicks non-existent lint from his hat.

"Well, that's not quite so," he says. "You've still got a home. You're only here for a few more months, that's all. Once it's over, it's over." He stands up puts his hat on, adjusts the brim. "You've learned."

I am learning to control myself, no more fucking. "In a few more months, I'll have my baby." She wants him to think about this.

"On that score your mother and I agree. You can't bring the bastard home." He takes his wallet from his pocket. "Just in case you need something," he says and hands her several bills. His hands are shaking. She takes the money from him. Everything is okay, taken care of, he'll tell Mika. You know, it's not easy, it takes time to adjust to these things. All she needed was a little talk and a little time. He's in a hurry, anxious to be away.

"I have to go," she says.

The door closes behind him. She waits. She sees his feet pass on the sidewalk along with the feet of another person, strangers passing by and her father is one of them.

Notes for the essay: Bible lessons at Opah's

Opah means Grandfather. Omah means Grandmother. (This is for the benefit of Mr. Malcolm, English 100, the Chocolate Drop who came directly from Jamaica and wants to know everything he can about Canada) The lesson for today, Opah says is: HOW GOD LED HIS PEOPLE OUT OF THE LAND OF EGYPT. But then he forgets and his sky blue eyes melt into the horizon and he speaks of hundreds of people gathering around twenty-eight train cars in Russia. They are coming, these people, like the dog mustard, only a year later, to spread out across the fields of southern Manitoba. Faith is the Victory, Faith is the Victory, Opah hums, wiping tears from his face and Omah comes out from the pantry wiping hands of flour onto her apron. There is a boy in the garden, she says. They still dream of thieves and Bolshevik murderers. Laurence is waiting for the lesson to be finished so that there will be someone to go fishing with. He has only one friend because he is on welfare.

First you learn, Opah says, no longer can you get into heaven free because of your parents or grandparents. When you're twelve, you're on your own with God.

He makes you learn the ten commandments even though you know Emily, who lives across the road, whose father is a doctor and drives a Lincoln and with his money has built the gingerbread house that now has a patio and one more child added, which looks out over another row of houses where the coulee once was, this girl, whose father's building also destroyed an Indian burial ground, will not hesitate to walk across the friendship and go fishing with Laurence.

—round-leaved mallow is different from common mallow and is a nuisance only in the prairie provinces where it nudges aside Kentucky Blue and Shady Nook grass but that doesn't matter because you can't really eat cultured lawn the way you can the nutlets of round mallow an after school treat not double bubble gum or fudgsicles but a prairie weed that stayed behind to live in town to colour green your teeth you forgot to brush today but ants don't brush do they or for that matter neither do grasshoppers they squirt tobacco —

too bad   Emily can't eat round-leaved mallow

too bad   she has to eat juicy fruit cracker jack and all that crap

too bad   she isn't a grasshopper or an ant

I would press her lightly with my toe and scare the shit out of her Emily is a stinking willie.

She is poisonous inside.

To her, fishing with Laurence is an opportunity to practise lying.
She is like a plum rotting in the grass.
I lost Laurence one summer
didn't last and he was gone
I looked: in the garden
*   in the poolroom*
*   bowling alley*
*   cafe*
*   fair grounds*
no Laurence

Look — he has waited long enough for you to go fishing.
It's your fault you learned the ten commandments.

And now Emily wears his arrowhead around her neck. Your arrow-
heads gather dust in a cigarette box in the rafters of the icehouse while
she, whose backyard has a patio surrounded by stinking willie, wears
his arrowhead because plum wine is strong enough inside Laurence
that no longer does he care that occasionally he is on welfare or that
at ten he had lice.

The small lamp in the corner on the table spreads a pink glow in the room. There are six girls in various stages of pregnancy dressed in bathrobes, feet tucked up beneath them, one lies flat on her back, she is only in her third month. "When I get out of this place I'm going to slash the bugger's tires, all four of them," the girl with the angry grey eyes says. They have been telling "how I lost my virginity" stories. Betty listens, she has not contributed and she knows they expect her to soon. She thinks that only this tall girl has been honest.

"I used to tell my parents I was staying at a friend's house," one of the girls says. "They never checked, usually they never checked, that is. The one time, wouldn't you know it, my girlfriend's father answered the phone before she could get to it? And made her tell my Dad where I was? God, I almost died. There I was, Rick doing it to me, you get what I mean? He didn't even knock —"

"Doing what?"

"Aw, come on, you know —"

"Was it big, small, did it hurt? You've got to tell a better story than that."

"I opened my eyes and saw my father. He just stood there staring and didn't say anything. It gave me the creeps. Like, for a minute, I didn't know what he was going to do. Then he went and waited for me in the car. When I came out he was sitting there crying. I felt like a piece of shit."

The girls moan sympathetically. They stare at their feet, at the space in front of them. They are all getting into shape, out of control, Betty thinks. Sometimes one of their boyfriends visits them and then the rest of them slouch in corners, snapping gum, dissatisfied until he leaves. Where's your boyfriend, they've asked Betty, sixty-five girls who have eaten too many sweets, superior because they have visitors, more righteous for a time, than her.

They turn to her. They wait now for her story to begin. I was twelve. He was an old man. At first he just used his finger. I screwed sixteen men this year and have written their names down in a scribbler.

"His name is Hank," she says. "We're in love. He wants to marry me."

The tall grey-eyed girl rises first and the others follow her one by one and file out of the lounge. Woolworth diamonds sparkle on their fingers. Now, at last, she can be alone.

Notes for the essay: hide and seeking

Laurence's anger moves in circles, his teeth on edge against an unnamed foe burned off in the sound of his motor cycle held into place by centrifugal force around and around. His anger spent, the dust settling, he stops moving, stands beside you and finally you are once again behind him, your arms about his narrow leather waist climbing the yellow fields, cutting a swathe through black-headed cattails

(fire torches, good for, eating) in the ditches beside the highway, up and down Main Street. He doesn't speak, but only with others does he need to, you never cared his silence was like a lady slipper growing beside a swampy marsh. He takes the old skull from his saddle bag, lines it up on Main Street, takes a run at it and shatters the old bone like pieces of coconut shell skittering curses across a table top. Don't do it, you think, but it's his skull, he can do what he wants. You ride and drink until the sun is down behind old weathered caved in barns and he pukes plum wine, purple and violent into the grass at your feet. He lies you down and you are surprised at his fumbling,
thought he would know
how to do it better
and so you help him with his clothing and guide him. (Was it big, was it fat or small, did it hurt? Come on, you've got to tell a better story than that.)

His nostril in your eye and when he turns his head you notice: hair in his ear, dirty. Emily, Emily, he says, not your name, but hers and his nostrils puff out warm plum air and his mouth, not gentle, smells of sour jam as he pins you to the earth but the worst is that after, he pulls grass from your hair, says he's sorry and treats you like a friend you are —

Listening until the sound of the engine is a distant whine on the highway an angry wasp, a wavering line of sound straightening, becoming threadlike, thin, and then it snaps and —

Betty switches off the lamp. The traffic below in the city street is a ribbon connecting people together. The gravestones sheltered beneath the trees seem to move into the light filtering down between the tree branches. She hears a sharp whistle, like a signal and the figures rise up from among the stones, gather beneath the street light and plan their night errands. She watches and waits for tomorrow.

The Sign

Per K. Brask

N ow he was lying under a sign, hanging from the post next to him, observing it swing back and forth in the warm breeze as the friction of metal against metal where sign and hook met produced a squeaking noise. He had read somewhere that the first step in any quest for knowledge was for the observer to estrange him/herself (no, where he had read it the author had only mentioned "himself") from the observed object in order that it should not appear "natural", "familiar" or "expected" to the observer. He couldn't for the life of him remember exactly where he had read it but he placed the author of the notion somewhere in the late eighteenth/early nineteenth century, probably a German thinker. He, however, was simply lying there watching the swinging of the sign, contemplating its sheer irrelevance; yet he felt some small absurd pleasure in being there to observe it.

He had noticed while crawling towards it that the sign had no writing on it. He thought that it had probably burnt away. Although that could be a wrong assumption, too. It was clear, though, that its former purpose would never be revealed to him no matter how strenuously he might apply himself. He felt that he should never know the world again by means of estrangement or any other means, for that matter. He wasn't sure why he felt this so certainly. It just seemed to be so.

He couldn't remember who he was or where he was. All he knew for certain was that when he woke up he had found himself lying on the warm, singed ground. It had been and still was dark. Something had certainly happened to him and to his environment, for despite the lovely quiet breeze everything smelt burnt and he had lost a foot. In fact, the only thing he could remember from before he woke up was an excruciating pain penetrating deeply through every single bone from the ankle to the back of his head. He couldn't remember why or how it had happened but he felt thankful that he couldn't feel any pain now. All he had to go on was the memory of that pain.

Though his eyes had adjusted to the dark he had no real sense of familiarity with this place. From the small hill where he was lying all he could make out was the uneven ground surface apparently extending forever. Nothing seemed to create a barrier for his sight. Occasionally when he looked up he would catch a glimpse of a star before it was again hidden by a cloud. In the very far distance he could see lightning, though it appeared to be stationary, ramming down on the same spot at exact intervals. He couldn't hear the thunder if there was any. But for the darkness he might have been able to identify the place better.

"It all started with the death of Danton," he though to himself. He didn't know what the meaning of or reason for that thought was. He knew that Georges Danton had been an extremely intelligent revolutionary during the French Revolution who had headed the Executive Council as minister of justice. Danton's death was ironic to him because this progressive hero, setting his love of life aside, had approved of the massacre of September of 1792, in order to avert further chaos by satisfying the plebians' craving for revenge and blood. However, when Danton later recognized the terror he had unleashed, he called for mercy, only to find himself labelled a traitor and sentenced to death.

He smiled, though he didn't know exactly why he had thought of Danton. He took it as a sign that he possessed the will to overcome his present situation. What he had meant by "it all started" he wasn't sure. What had "all started" beyond the fact that the French Revolution as well as the earlier ones in America and Britain had ushered in a new era now coming to an end? Questions, Questions. He too was using estrangement while seeking familiarity. He had now successfully located himself as a member of the human race sometime after the French Revolution. In fact, he even knew, despite his lack of personal memory that he was in Canada in the first year of the twenty-first century. He knew this the same way he knew that his left foot was missing — without pain but with certainty and a slight fear of taking a closer look. He leaned back, resting on his elbows. The monotony of the swinging sign eased his mind for a moment and he felt comfortable again. He felt that he could lie here forever. He hoped his ankle wouldn't start to hurt.

By looking at his hands, though they were covered in soot, he estimated his age to be about fifty. He then felt that he was a father and that his first grandchild was on the way. A new role in life. He felt himself getting excited. Again, he took refuge in the sign. He was now feeling a pain in his mind not dissimilar to what he had felt earlier when he lost his foot during . . . He pressed hard to conclude this thought. He knew that his brain had stored the information somewhere and if he could only find the correct trigger he would instantaneously know who he was, where he was and how and why he lost his left foot and why it didn't hurt. The lack of pain scared him.

He felt that he didn't want to know any more for a little while. Maybe he should start to consider how to get away from this strange place, find something to eat and drink, call the police and let them discover his identity. Somehow he was too tired even to entertain thoughts of such plans. It seemed peculiarly futile, even somewhat arrogant. He decided that he should probably stay here and rest till the morning when he would likely be found and events would evolve quietly, logically, necessarily. He didn't believe that that would happen but he decided to stay, nonetheless. He didn't know which way to crawl, anyway. Not knowing where he was made it difficult to determine where to go, even if he had had the desire to go anywhere.

When he had woken up earlier he had felt his name started with the letter P but he was unable to determine the rest of the letters making up his name. Apart from his life, his name was the first thing he had been given. Now he would take on life with a letter. A beginning, perhaps. He was used to beginnings. The process of becoming. He would need to remember to be able to start again. He started to cry. Through the tears the sign appeared to be changing shape and to produce very subtle shades of dark purple to black. He knew that he cried rarely. Not because he lacked emotion but because self-pity seemed unacceptable to him. These tears, responsible for such visual delight, were a communication from his past and they were connected with his feeling that he had (willingly or unwillingly, he didn't know) been part of certain events that had led him here. On the other hand the tears could have resulted from a subconscious reflection on the pain he had experienced when his foot tore off. Both hypotheses seemed satisfactory and he decided for the time being to assume that the reason for his tears was a combination of the two propositions. He could still feel in his mind a great deal of resistance when trying to break through to knowledge of earlier events. He would have to try to take his subconscious by surprise to get it to release the information he wanted. The only way to get out, to move ahead, would be to go back in time. He had to find a trigger.

Turning to lie on his side he noticed that the lightning in the distance had stopped. In fact, the variations in purple and black which he had seen in the sign through his tears had been produced by the fractional clarity resulting from the clouds slowly separating to let a little more starshine through their cover. P sat up to see if the trail of blood which his leg had left behind could tell him where he'd come from. Though patches of blood could be observed as a dull glisten on the ground, when he strained his eyes it was still too dark to give him any better sense of his path up the small hill to the sign. In his field of vision appeared mainly more of the same singed ground. However, a hidden suspicion that he had been a fire victim seemed to be substantiated by five burnt bricks he could just barely see and identify at the extremity of his vision immediately beyond a turn in his trail. He had evidently turned to avoid them earlier on. But where were the firefighters? Or hadn't they noticed him and left, assuming they had rescued who and what they could?

Per K. Brask

There was an undefinable lack of reality in both questions. These were questions belonging to a context different from his.

He looked to the sign again. It had stopped swinging. He had not noticed this earlier, he had not even noticed that the sound had stopped. This unsettled him. He depended on his capacity for identifying clues. He felt fortunate that at least the sign itself was still there. Slowly, he regained his sense of ease, working himself back to calm by forcing his mind to dispel fear.

He decided that he would try to affect a new, although random, perspective by standing up. He grabbed on to the signpost and slowly hoisted himself up to a vertical position by the sheer force of his arms. He lifted his left leg slightly so as not to cause any jolts in it by touching the ground or the post. It was a cumbersome manoeuvre which convinced him beyond doubt that his body and its functions were in a state of deterioration. Slowly but surely his power was disappearing. As he climbed up the post he could smell the burnt metal and as disintegrating particles from this found their way up his nose he was compelled to sneeze. His body jolted and hurt. When he looked up again the lightning in the distance had resumed its ramming action; yet all was quiet. An uncomfortable silence surrounded him. He had never witnessed such strange meteorological phenomena. He consciously avoided speculating on the meaning of this environment, at least momentarily, by looking towards the sky. The clouds were continuing their slow, almost imperceptible separation. He could make out a star behind a thin stretch of cloud. He knew he had often looked up into the cosmos in his life. Not seeking answers, but perspective. To P the infinitude of the cosmos seemed to make meaning possible. The infinitude of possibilities set the "frame" for the specificity of life on earth . . .

His leg started to hurt with an incredible piercing pain which throbbed from his wound up through his left hip joint and further into his spine. He screamed.

Lying back on the ground again he tried to forget the pain by focusing intensely. Every black pebble and stone, every speck of dust within his immediate range would be accounted for. It was only after he had been aware of it for a brief while that he noticed that the earth at a particular, small area was caving in ever so slightly. Then two vibrating headlike antennae became visible and shortly thereafter the full body of a small beetle approximately one cm. long appeared before him. From its shiny green oblong shape, its brassy, bluish elytra, the tiny punctures on its head and pronotum and the round vertex, he deduced that his visitor was quite likely a *Chrysochus auratus*, a Goldsmith Beetle.

He leaned closer towards this intruder while its antennae vibrated in search of information. He felt tears in his eyes again because he now knew where he was and why he was there. The trigger had been found. Or rather he could no longer prevent himself from knowing. The terror had become real. The possible had become actuality. Not, he knew for certain, as an act of insanity. It had simply required a particular form of sanity, an unacceptable form of logic.

P still didn't know who he was but never had such an otherwise essential issue appeared so utterly irrelevant. In fact, he now wished to die before he would accidentally find out. He had discovered his will to die.

He heard the underground elevator's high, soft hum. Then he saw the search lights from the rescue vehicle circle around itself. It was moving towards him from a distance of about a km. He pretended to be dead. He stopped breathing as the vehicle emitting no pollution of any kind moved toward him. Whoever or whatever was inside the vehicle obviously assumed he was dead for it didn't slow down or take any particular note of him as it passed by.

After a safe while P bent down and tore open his wound, ripping loose his flesh so that he could bleed to death. Behind the pain his last conscious thought was: "Now Dionysus lives only among beetles". He never had time to discover why he had this thought for he had barely finished it before he died.

Belle in Winter

Sharon Butala

W here the hell's Lace?" Sig snarled. Annabelle was dishing up food at the stove with her back to him, but in her mind's eye she could see the furious jerk of his shoulder as he stabbed at the platter of meat, or tore apart a slice of bread.

"On her way, I expect," she said. Behind her there was a scuffling noise and then the crack of a slap. The sound broke the rhythm of her ladling of potatoes from pot to bowl, a slight break, and then the motion of her arm resumed. When the pot was empty, she turned to the table. Jack and Eldon, her two eldest, were methodically shovelling in their food, paying no attention. Both were bigger than their father, and having passed twenty, were no longer victims of his impatience and anger.

Sig's glare was fastened on Melody, who sat motionless, staring at her plate. Annabelle carried the steaming bowl of potatoes to the table and set it down in front of Sig Jr., placing her body between her husband's reach and Melody.

"Here Sig Jr.," she said. "Eat up." She wanted to place her hand on the red patch on his cheek, to absorb the sting in her own palm. Sig was a mistake, coming five years after her sixth child, Melody. Sometimes when she saw his pale head pass the window where she was sewing, or heard his voice calling down from upstairs in the early morning, her feeling of special tenderness toward him would be replaced by an unexpected flash of rage, which came and went so quickly that were it not for her trembling knees and unsettled stomach, she would not have believed it had happened. She knew Sig had shifted his murderous stare to her. Her face tensed into an expression of silent hatred. She sat down in her place and began to fill her plate.

Annabelle could hear the subdued roar of a car with a cracked muffler approaching from the west. As it grew louder, the tension in the room eased slightly. The car pulled into the yard, rumbled unevenly for a moment, and was cut off in the mid-rattle. A car door slammed, followed by the sound of running feet crunching on the snow-covered ground. Jack laughed, "Here comes old Lace," just as she rushed into the room in a cloud of steaming vapour and slammed the door behind her.

"The old bastard kept me late again," Lacie said as she pulled off her coat and tossed it over the broken-backed chair by the door. She dropped into her place and reached with a fork toward the meat platter. "I'd swear the old bugger's after my body." Jack grinned at her, not forgetting to chew. Eldon glanced at their father.

"Don't come to the table talking like that," Sig said. "He give you a good job. Work don't hurt you none." He don't care if old Malcolm's pawing at her, Annabelle thought, as long as she brings home her paycheque. Beside her, her husband was ripping at his food and gulping it down with huge drafts of water. He eats like a coyote, she thought. Like he's afraid somebody'll steal it off his fork. It always seemed to her that he might start on one of the kids next. She held her fork poised in front of her mouth.

"If the old bugger lays one finger on you, he'll have to answer to me," she said slowly.

"I can handle him, Ma," Lacie said. She piled potatoes onto her plate. "He don't scare me none." Annabelle couldn't suppress a laugh.

"I'll bet he don't," she said. Even her father, in whom rage seemed to perpetually simmer, didn't scare Lacie. Annabelle knew it wasn't fear that had so far kept Lacie from moving out now that she had finished high school, the way that Skye had and Allan too. She supposed Lacie just hadn't seen the advantages of her own place yet.

Outside there was the sound of tires crackling on ice and snow, and then the soft purr of a motor that faded into silence. Sig got up from the table to peer out the window, polishing the steam off with his sleeve and cupping the other hand to screen out the reflections.

"It's Roy McKenzie," Eldon said, stooping to look over his father's shoulder. Sig ran both hands over his thin hair, and then opened the door just as the visitor knocked.

"Roy," he said. "Come on in." At the table everyone continued to eat except Annabelle who had placed both hands on her lap and lifted her face toward the visitor.

"I won't come in, Sig," Roy said stepping just inside the door so that Sig could close out the frigid air. He made the kitchen seem smaller and warmer, as though his size and the rich glow of his dark skin gave off a heat that the pale-skinned, silver-haired Svennes family lacked. "Caught you at suppertime, sorry about that." He grinned at each of them. "Hello, Annabelle," he said. Sig's sinewy body looked small beside Roy.

"There's lots," she said shyly. "Sure you won't sit down?" He needs a haircut, she thought, and imagined her hand cupping his skull, the thick black locks curling around her fingers. Lacie had been staring at her mother. Suddenly she breathed in sharply and set her fork down. Annabelle heard the intake of breath and caught the movement from the corner of her eye.

"What's the matter, Lace?" she asked in an undertone, trying to keep her voice matter-of-fact. Lacie looked flustered, reached for the bowl of carrots.

"Not a thing, Ma," she said. Annabelle darted a look at the men. Sig was saying, "Be glad to sell you a butcher hog. You want to take it now?"

"Oh, no," Roy said. "I just thought I'd stop by when I thought of it. Lisa's been after me for weeks. She likes pork roast now and then."

"Ja," Sig said. "Pork is good now and then."

"Well," Roy said. "I'll be going then. Lisa says drop over for coffee, Annabelle." Annabelle did not dare to look up.

"Yeah, tell her thanks. I will one of these days," she said.

"Gotta go. Thanks a lot, Sig. I'll pick it up next week. Good night." While he spoke, Sig opened the door for him and Roy stepped outside. His last words floated into the kitchen from the darkness outside. Sig shut the door and sat down. There was the faint murmur of the motor again.

"Must be driving his Caddie," Jack said.

"Bet it set him back forty thousand," Eldon said.

"He can afford it," Sig said. "All that land. He don't have to keep no pigs."

"He works hard," Lacie said.

"Like hell," Sig snorted. "His wife's old man left her plenty. Set them up good." He shoved vegetables onto his fork with his knife. Lacie looked over at her mother again. Annabelle looked steadily back.

Annabelle was carrying water to the pigs. Usually Eldon and Jack looked after this chore, but on this raw winter day they had gone to a cattle sale in Maple Creek. The water should have been piped into the corral, but Sig either had never had the money to do it, or as Annabelle thought, let his family carry the water across the yard out of pure meanness. She brought the water in two pails up the slope from the yard hydrant, across the yard to the corral where she set them down and opened the gate. Then she laboured across the corral to the pigpen and dumped it over the fence into the trough. The sows crowded around drinking noisily.

After her third trip she stopped to rest, leaning against the corral panting, her breath making white puffs in the still, sharp air. A half-ton bumped into the yard, the stockracks on the back rattling. It was Roy McKenzie. Annabelle straightened and her hand flew to her hair to touch the scarf that covered it. She waited by the corral gate as the truck bumped slowly toward her and came to a stop.

"Morning," Roy said, smiling at her. He put his hand through the open window to the outside door handle, opened the door and climbed out. He was very close to her. She could see a fringe of black chest hair curling around the neck of his red shirt where the top button was undone. She wanted to bury her face there, to warm it in the heat that radiated from him, to taste the salt of his skin on her tongue. "Sig here?" he asked, looking around the yard. She lifted her eyes to his face.

"He's over at Maple Creek at the sale." Roy hesitated.

"I came for that pig," he said, shoving both hands into his windbreaker pockets. "Oh well. I'll come back tomorrow." He turned to get back in his truck. Annabelle took a step forward. She almost reached out to touch his shoulder.

"You and me can get him," she said. "He isn't wild." She started walking toward the barn. "Bring the truck," she called to him over her shoulder. Roy started the truck and drove over to the barn where he turned it and backed it against the open door. Chickens scattered at his approach.

They squeezed past the truck box and stood side by side in the darkness waiting for their eyes to adjust to the light. The air was warm and pungent with fresh straw and manure. In the stillness she could hear him breathing. She lifted one hand slowly. It brushed the rough texture of Sig's old coveralls that she was wearing under her parka. The feel of it brought her back to the reality of her body, its corruption from the births of seven children, the flaccid stomach, the ruined legs. She wanted to throw herself onto the straw-covered floor and give herself up to despair.

"I'll make a ramp," Roy said. He went over to some straw bales that were piled against the wall and dragged them, one by one, to the foot of the truck. He began to stack them into a rough ramp. Annabelle watched him, her muscles slack with misery. There was a grunting and rustling of straw in the back of the barn. She turned her head toward the noise and began walking toward it. In one stall she disturbed a sow with a brood of piglets. Farther down she found the animal she was looking for.

"Here Roy," she called. Her voice sounded strange in her ears. Roy came down one side of the aisle behind her and together they chased the pig out of its comfortable nest, down the aisle toward the truck.

"Nice looking one," Roy said. The pig stopped at the foot of the bale stairs and balked. It turned first one way and then the other, trying to go back down the aisle between them. "Hah, hah!" Roy said, lunging at it. The pig turned again and with the two of them close behind, ran slipping and squealing up the ramp into the truck box. Roy hurried behind it, shut the endgate with a bang, and jerked down the stockrack door. He turned to Annabelle.

"Well, Belle, that's a good job well done!" He was laughing. She had not been called Belle by anybody since her mother's death. She had forgotten how the kids at school had called her that, and how she had hated it, because Belle was the name of a workhorse, and she would not be a workhorse, a beast of burden, like her mother. She would be a secretary in some clean, well-lit office in town. The name from him was like the precise cut of a fine-bladed knife, half-painful, half-welcome. She wanted to say something to him so that he would know she was there, so that he would know she was Annabelle, a person, a woman. She cleared her throat.

"Long time since anybody called me that," she said. He was already turning to the truck.

"Is it?" he said. "It's a good, old-fashioned name. Always liked it."

"Want coffee?" she called to him, but he was already climbing into the cab and starting the motor.

"Better not stop," he said. "Lisa wants me to take her to town this morning. Thanks anyway." He roared the motor. The truck started to move away. "I'll settle up with Sig," he called out the open window. Annabelle watched the truck leave the yard, make the turn at the far gate and then disappear down the grid and over the hill.

It would soon be dark. Up and down the main street half-tons were parked with their motors running, sending up indigo and mauve clouds of condensed vapour. The lights in the store windows made yellow rectangles on the icy sidewalks. Annabelle, in town to give Lacie a ride home, hurried down the street with her face hidden in her coat front, the collar turned up. When she came to the sign tacked to the wall that said, "W.R. Malcolm, Solicitor," she pulled open the door beside it, stamped the snow off her feet and started up the red-carpeted stairs.

At the top she pushed open the glass door and went inside. Nobody was there, but Lacie's coat hung on the coatrack and her boots sat neatly side by side beneath it. Annabelle, noticing that the inner door into Malcolm's office was ajar, walked closer to it and tried to peer into the gap.

She saw a man and a woman standing with their arms around each other, their bodies pressed together. The man had his right arm around the woman, the hand spread out clasping the woman's left hip. His left hand, the one nearest Annabelle, was reaching for the woman's breast. The woman had her arm up as if to touch his face. Her face was hidden by his head. It looked as he might devour her.

When Annabelle gasped, they dropped their arms and snapped apart. Roy lifted his head and Lacie swivelled around. When Roy's eyes met Annabelle's his already ruddy face flushed a deeper colour and his jaw dropped open and then clicked shut.

"Mom," Lacie said weakly, her voice trailing off. Nobody moved. The room had grown intensely hot, like the summer heat that radiated off the prairie, distorting things. Lacie's red dress rippled like flames before Annabelle's eyes. Her pale gold hair shimmered. Roy grew larger, his dark pants and sheepskin coat swelling, his head growing massive, like a bull's. He came toward her and she turned sideways and took a step back to let him pass. The door swung shut behind him with a hiss.

Lacie came past her mother into the outer office and opened her desk drawer. She took out a comb, ran it through her hair, put it back, closed the drawer and went over to the coat rack, passing Annabelle again. She sat down on one of the vinyl-covered chairs which squeaked and let out a sigh. She slipped off her shoes and pulled on her boots taking a long time with the zippers. Annabelle watched as though she had never seen boots before. When Lacie was ready she stood up and the two of them walked out of the office and down the stairs, Lacie ahead and Annabelle following behind.

When they were out of town, humming along in the darkness, Lacie spoke. "It's nothing, Ma. Nothing. I don't know why you're making such a big deal of it." Annabelle could feel her give an angry shrug. "Honest to god," she said. "It doesn't mean a damn thing." She was quiet for another mile. "Lots of men like to kiss me. That's all there is to it. I'm pretty, you know," she said accusingly to her mother. They turned into the yard. "I'm sorry it was him," she added softly. Annabelle stopped the truck and opened her door. Her hands had begun to tremble. She wanted to ask what Lacie meant by that, but she was afraid to. She climbed out of the truck and went into the house without speaking.

When morning came, Annabelle rose, every muscle aching as though she had spent the night in the hands of torturers. She stumbled in the darkness on the chilly linoleum to the kitchen where she began to make breakfast. Jack and Eldon left for Medicine Hat without waiting for the coffee to perk. Sig sat at the table as he did every morning and fixed his eyes on a spot on the kitchen wall. He didn't speak to her. Sig Jr. and Melody hurried into the kitchen grabbing toast and milk and accusing her, "We're late, Mom. Why didn't you wake us up?" They snatched their lunches, held their toast in their mouths, juggled their books in their arms and ran for the school bus with their coats flapping open. Lacie came down, sleepy-eyed, wearing a red plaid skirt and a yellow sweater a shade darker than her hair. Annabelle poured her a cup of coffee and set it in front of her.

"I'm thinking of getting a room in town," Lacie said. Annabelle didn't speak. Sig shifted his gaze to Lacie and then went back to staring at the spot on the wall.

"It's about time," he said. Lacie ignored him.

"Too much driving and my car not working half the time. You gonna take me this morning?" she asked Sig. He nodded. Annabelle sat down. Sig dropped his stare from the spot on the wall to Annabelle's chest where her dressing gown had fallen open and the torn frill of her pink nightgown hung out. His jaw worked as if he could not find words to express his fury. Abruptly he scraped his chair back and said to Lacie, "Well, come then if you're coming, or I'll leave without you."

"Jeeze," Lacie complained. "What's eating you this morning?" But she rose quickly and put her coat on. Sig had already gone out to start the truck. "Mom, I'm gonna stay at Ruthie's tonight." She hesitated when Annabelle didn't answer, but then she went out calling a muffled "'bye" over her shoulder.

Annabelle didn't move as the door shut behind Lacie and the truck pulled out of the yard. Some time later she rose and, like a sleepwalker, drifted into the living room where she stared out the window at the grey winter sky and the plain that tilted upward into low hills.

As she watched unblinking, the sky deepened to the blue of late fall, and fluffy white clouds began to skid by as though a film had been speeded up. All along the curve of the sky, tall bleached grass pressed eastward, lying like a woman's hair along the earth. She imagined reaching out and running her fingers through the grass as though it were human hair, Lacie's hair, and it would slide through them and float to the ground like so many fine-spun glimmering threads. As she watched a great wind came up and tore the grass away, leaving behind only bare brown earth that shrivelled, dried, and then opened in ugly cracks that crept toward her like thick black snakes. She blinked several times. Someone was knocking on the door.

She walked into the kitchen. The door opened slowly and Roy McKenzie stepped inside, closing the door behind him. He cleared his throat.

"Annabelle," he said. Some of the colour had faded from his face; he seemed diminished, less brutally masculine. "I came to talk about yesterday," he said. "Sig gone?"

"Yes," Annabelle said. Without taking her eyes off him, she sat down. Roy sat in Sig's empty chair. The fridge hummed softly. Roy cleared his throat again.

"Look," he said. "I'm sorry about that. It wasn't anything." He shifted in his chair. "Lacie's a good girl," he said. Seconds passed. "No, she isn't," Annabelle said. It was the first sentence she had spoken since she had seen them together. Roy dropped his eyes. His lips began to work as though he were trying out different ways to say something.

"Look," he said again. "It's Lisa. I come to ask you not to tell Lisa." His eyes flew to hers and fastened there. He grasped his thighs with his hands and cleared his throat again.

Annabelle said, "I love you," and then gasped.

"What?" he said, moving back in his chair. Annabelle lifted her hands. She stood, surprised to find herself on her feet, and with one pull tore open her dressing gown and nightdress.

"Roy," she said advancing to him. He had risen too, almost falling over the chair as he tried to back away. He stared at the breasts that sagged blue-veined and flat against her ribs. "I love you," she said again. She reached out for him and clutched his jacket with both hands. He loosened one of her hands with his, banging his back against the kitchen door as he retreated. He pulled the other hand loose and, fending Annabelle off with his forearm, grasped the doorknob, pulling open the door, and pushing her back. When he finally escaped through the door, slamming it behind him, Annabelle wailed and pounded on it with her fists. She would kill him. She had seen his face. She would kill him. She opened the closet door and fell to her knees, scrabbling through the castoff rubber boots and jackets, searching for Sig's gun, when suddenly she wanted a knife. A knife was what she wanted.

She ran to the cupboard and jerked open the drawer where the knives were kept. It came out all the way and the contents flew all over the floor, skidding under the table and clattering against the stove. She spun around as if to go back to the closet for the gun when she thought, I have to stop Lacie. I have to save Lacie. She stopped, frozen to the spot. She could not hurt Lacie. She fell to her knees and pounded her head on the floor and beat her thighs with her fists until, exhausted, she began to weep as if she were a child again. She got up from the floor and stumbled upstairs to the bedroom.

She intended to pack and leave at once, but first she thought she would lie down for a minute. She was very tired and it seemed to her that all the light in the room was grey, that the colour had bleached out the objects she looked at. Her head was aching with heavy, palpable thuds. She lay down on the bed and covered her face with her hands. Immediately she could feel Roy beside her. She could feel his body heat warming her arm and thigh, his breath on her face, hot and moist, smelling of tobacco and faintly of whiskey. She lay without moving. Presently the sensations grew heavier, more oppressive, till it seemed to her that she felt his weight full-length on her, growing heavier and heavier until she felt herself melting into him. Her eyebrows felt denser; she lifted one wrist and looked at it. In the light it seemed thicker, and she thought she could see faint black hairs growing on it. She moaned and it seemed that the sound echoed in the bass of Roy's voice.

She pulled herself upright and went into the bathroom where she stared at herself in the mirror above the sink. She reached up and touched an eyebrow. It felt cool, thin and smooth under her finger and with her touch the illusion vanished. It was only she, Annabelle, looking wild and old and immensely ugly. She forced herself to look. Then she went downstairs to the kitchen where she bent and picked up the scattered utensils. She set them back in the drawer and put the drawer back in the cabinet. Then she sat down at the table again.

The linoleum was so thin that the pattern had worn away in places leaving black patches. The table was scarred and nicked, the room dingy from faded paint. It had been a poor farm when she had come here thirty years before, she thought, and it was still poor. She and Sig and the boys would always have to work like dogs to stay alive. Sig was a mean-tempered, violent man who did not love her, never had, she supposed. She could not bear to think about Lacie.

I'll leave, she thought again, and walked to the window thinking what she would take. Her eyes wandered to the frozen ground beside the house. I will take a shovelful of earth from my garden, she thought. I will take the kitchen table where I diapered my babies. I will take the rag rug my mother made me from Melody's room. I will take Sig Jr. She turned away from the window and sat down again.

Annabelle was carrying water to the pigs. She struggled up the slope from the hydrant, crossed the snow-covered ground to the corral where she set her two pails down and opened the gate. Then she laboured across the corral to the pigpen and dumped the water over the fence into the trough. The sows crowded around. She picked up the empty pails and started back for another load. She crossed the corral, opening the gate and shutting it behind her, her breath making white clouds in the sub-zero air. She started down the slope to the hydrant where she filled both pails, lifted them, and started up the slope again. At the top she stopped to rest. In the still, wintry air she could hear the hum of a vehicle coming down the grid from the west. She rested till it came into view. It was travelling fast, heading east past the Svennes farm. It was Roy McKenzie making another of his innumerable trips from town to farm.

Annabelle stooped again and lifted each pail carefully, one at a time, keeping her eyes on the water as it tilted and then washed back and forth in its container. She took a jerky step forward, balancing her burden, and her eyes lifted themselves to the truck, following it as it passed on by till it disappeared out of sight over the hill.

Mick and I and Hong Kong Heaven

Lois Simmie

Mick has been dry for two months, not so much as a sip, and if I believed in miracles the way these A.A. people claim they do, I'd have to say this was one. I can't say I care for it.

It all started with a twelve-step call, and if you don't know what that is I'll tell you, in case anybody ever wants to make one on you. A twelve-step call is where a couple of alcoholics in A.A. go and see someone and try to get him to stop drinking. Well, they only go if they're asked, and I phoned them so I feel responsible, but I never meant them to take over his life like this — I never thought he'd stop completely, like some temperance nut. I only wanted him to slow down and stop trying to kill himself.

Mick is a lovely person most of the time, which is why I have lived with him for a year and a half, I figure most of the time is as good as anybody's going to get. But now everything's changed, and I just want things the way they used to be. I can't stand the way he looks at me now when I have a drink, like a missionary who's caught a cannibal boiling somebody's head in a pot. A missionary who's going to teach you to eat berries instead. But even though Mick on the wagon is not one of my favorite sights, I have to admit he seems happy, I suppose because he's found all those other people in the same boat, or on the same wagon, I guess you'd say. Anyways, the day I met him, A.A. was the farthest thing from his mind.

I was laying in the back yard on my day off, sunning myself in my purple bikini and sipping a cold beer, which is the only way to spend a hot July day if you don't have a pool or a summer cottage. I was reading this Harlequin romance about a girl who is hired by a real bastard to pretend she is his fiancée in Hong Kong, a job she takes to keep her brother out of jail because he stole money from this guy whose fiancée she's pretending to be. Of course the real bastard is tall, dark and handsome and hard as a stick. All of the men in those books are hard — hard lips, hard stomachs, hard jaws, not an ounce of fat on any of them, even though they're always swilling down champagne and eating all kinds of fattening stuff in fancy restaurants where the headwaiter knows them. Another thing they always are is rich.

Anyways, this guy treats her like dirt because she's just a mousy parson's daughter, until she gets into all the fancy clothes he bought her so she'd look like a rich man's fiancée and then she's a knockout. Of course she hates him and has the hots for him at the same time.

Well, like I said, I'm just laying there minding my own business when Henry starts barking like crazy. I shared the house with two other nurse's aides, and when we rented it this evil little chihuahua called Henry came with the deal. I don't blame them for leaving Henry — he was fat and had no hair and just sat around on his bare behind growling to himself with a crazy look in his little bug eyes.

So Henry is going bananas having something to actually bark at, and I'm yelling at him to stick it in his ear, when this long, hard man in a green meter-reading uniform ambles around the corner of the house. He looks me over real good and his eyes light up like maybe Sask Power wires them for electricity.

"Hi, mate," he says to Henry, who is trying to tear his pantleg off.

"Grrrrr OWOWOWOWOW! Grrr OWOW!" Henry replies, around a mouthful of green material. His little bow legs are braced on the sidewalk and his nose is wrinkled all the way up to his forehead.

"Aow, come on mate, you'll give yourself an ulcer," says this movie actor pretending to be a meter reader, and he pats old Henry on the head.

"Growl, growl," says Henry, but you can tell his heart's not in it any more, and before you know it this guy is down on his haunches scratching Henry on the bare belly, which is wriggling at the sky.

Then this beautiful man is looking over at me like maybe I might need my belly scratched. "Helloaw there, luv," he says. And then he smiles.

It was the smile that did it. That and the bluest eyes this side of Paul Newman. Anyways, before you can say kilowatt hour he's sitting beside me on the blanket, pouring a bottle of my beer down his throat.

"Ahhh. That hits the old proverbial dry spot," he says. I *think* that's what he said, he talks like the Beatles only more so, and half of it goes right past me. He stretches out his long legs and leans back on his elbows like he's planning to stay awhile.

"Where did you get this magnificent beast?" he asks, scratching Henry on the bald head. Henry thinks he's died and gone to Heaven. So I tell Mick about my roommates and my job and pretty soon we're talking up a storm and I go get us another beer.

Now you hear a lot about women's throats being beautiful, but I have never seen a lovelier sight than the muscles sliding under the smooth, tanned throat of this meter reader as he tips back his head and guzzles my beer. I got so fascinated watching it that I just kept offering him one after another and I never in my life saw anybody drink like he could. Not even my old man. It was like he was trying to put out a fire in his stomach.

"Whoever said redheads can't wear purple are loony," he says. He was spending considerable time looking down the top of my bikini, in a nice way.

I was looking him over, too; in fact I couldn't stop looking. He was a real classy guy, even if the green uniform was a little baggy on him.

"What's the book about?" he asks, picking up *Hong Kong Heaven* off the blanket. So I told him about the churchmouse and the bastard who would turn out not to be one, and about the churchmouse's crooked brother and their old sick father, the parson, who she's trying to protect, and this guy is killing himself laughing. Pretty soon we're laughing together about everything under the sun. He was from London, England, and I just loved the way he talked. He nicknamed me Bikky right there, because of the bikini, and he's called me that ever since. My name is Angela.

He took off his jacket right away, it being hotter than Hades in the sun, and after awhile he takes off his shirt, too. He has a lovely chest with WHY ME written on it. I couldn't believe it. Not really written on it, *scarred* on it in thin white capital letters, as plain as anything against his tan: WHY ME.

Looking at a guy with a question on his chest should have freaked me out, I suppose, but it didn't. I didn't even mention it, not wanting to scare him away, and he didn't either. I sort of liked that, too — it takes a lot of cool to sit around with a big question carved on your front and not feel like you have to explain it. I always explain everything. Even when people aren't the least bit interested. Anyhow, I didn't give a rip what it meant as long as it didn't mean he was gay.

"Bikky," he says, "you are such a lovely surprise. You remind me of a girl I went to law school with."

I felt suddenly shy. Law school. I thought he was just an ordinary guy. He acted like an ordinary person, though, and pretty soon I was feeling comfortable again.

"How come you're reading meters when you've been to law school?" I asked.

"Oh, I don't know," he says. "I think I passed the wrong bar exams." And he laughs. God, he was beautiful when he laughed.

Well, he kept on drinking and talking and looking down my bikini top like he had nothing else to do and I started feeling nice and warm, which had nothing whatever to do with the sun which had sunk over the other side of the house by the time we finished the third beer. Besides, if I'd been sunning the parts that felt warm I'd've been arrested.

When the case was empty, we jumped in the City Power truck and went to get some more, and before the girls got home from the evening shift, he had talked me right out of my bikini and read my meter, if you get my meaning. He said it was the highest one he ever read, and he must've read lots of them. And ever since, it's been ticking just for him.

The next day I moved in with Mick who lived in a big old house on the other side of town, with a scruffy little yard and a whole lot of funny people living on the second and third floors. It was Mick's house and he rented out rooms. I gradually got used to them all, even the scaly little man with the skin condition worse than Henry's.

At first life with Mick was fantastic, just one big lovely party, and I'd do it again in a minute. I was crazy about him then and I still am, and nobody likes a party better than me.

Mick got fired for drinking beer in my back yard while he was supposed to be reading those other meters, and for forgetting to take the truck back. He forgot everything once he started to drink, which was something I was to find out. After a while he got a job as a waiter in a classy restaurant, but one night he got into the cooking sherry and told a fat lady she couldn't have any dessert, so they fired him too.

"Well, you should have seen her, Bikky. She must have weighed three hundred pounds," he told me, sitting at our kitchen table in the black waiter's suit and white shirt he looked so lovely in. The kitchen table was where we talked over everything. "I just told her to be a good girl and forget about dessert."

"Oh, no." I could see it all, and nearly died laughing. "Was she mad?"

"Mad? She was ready to kill me. So was her skinny little husband, and I was trying to do him a favour." Mick looked injured.

"Do you suppose he likes her that way?" I asked. There was a story about a couple like that in the National Enquirer. He even bought her all this junk to eat every time she tried to go on a diet. He was afraid if she got thin she'd . . . " But Mick wasn't interested in discussing motivation and he hated the National Enquirer.

"Oh, well," he said, getting up to pour a drink. "She'll roll on him some night and that will be the end of the silly little sod. Serve him right, too."

It didn't matter much if Mick worked or not because his folks were rich and sent him money all the time. He laughed and called himself a remittance man, but I got the feeling he didn't really think it was funny. They'd told him not to come home till he quit drinking, though his mother wrote him every week in her aristocratic handwriting with real ink, not ballpoint. I wondered what she wrote about, but Mick didn't say and I would never read his mail. Their loss was my gain was the way I looked at it. I didn't want him to ever go back.

His folks said he was alcoholic and I thought that was really retarded. I mean I like to drink almost as much as Mick. Well, it was like I loved to drink but Mick really needed to drink sometimes. In the middle of the night, even, if he'd been talking to Ralph on the big white telephone. That was Mick's expression for puking up your guts in the toilet, and the first time I heard him being sick, it did sound like he was calling RAAAALPH! RAAAALPH! Mick says you only have to worry if Ralph starts talking back. But I didn't think much about Mick's drinking one way or the other till I heard the tea party story.

We were sitting around the kitchen table having a beer, Mick and I and Buddy, the scaly little man from upstairs. Well, you never had "a" beer with Mick but you know what I mean.

"Did I ever tell you about the time I livened up my mum's tea party?" Mick asked.

Buddy loved Mick's stories, and was grinning away in anticipation, shedding silvery scales of skin onto his old grey sweater. They gleamed here and there when he moved, like he might be turning into a fish.

"I used to play bridge," he said.

Poor old Buddy was as dumb as a doornail, so that was hard to imagine. Mick said he'd fried his brain with rubbing alcohol and shoe polish. His teeth were a kind of mahogany brown, so that must've been his favorite flavor. Buddy has one thing he says to everything: "Yessir, that's quite a thing," he'll say. It's surprising how often it's appropriate.

"Well," Mick went on, "Mum used to have her church ladies in for tea every Tuesday fortnight. And sometimes, if I was in my cups, she'd lock me in my room upstairs. Poor old duck was afraid I'd embarrass her."

"I couldn't stand to be locked in," I said. Sometimes Mick's stories bothered me, even if they were funny.

"Yessir, that's quite a thing." Buddy shook his crusty little head, which looked something like a baby bird's.

"And if I got crashing around up there, she'd just tell her friends that Mick was fixing something upstairs, and then she'd go ahead and bid a grand slam." That's what made Mick's stories so good — he always imagined the parts he couldn't see, like he couldn't know about the grand slam, really, but it helped the story.

"This one day she locked me in, I was needing a drink like I'd just crawled across the desert." As if that reminded him, he held up his empty bottle and grinned at me. I got up and got three bottles out of the fridge.

"I paced around up there," Mick says, "vibrating like a humming-bird, and when I couldn't stand it any longer, I jumped out."

I stopped in my tracks halfway back to the table. "Jumped out where?" I asked.

"Out the flaming window," Mick says, laughing. "Out the second story window right past the tea party in the drawing room."

"Jesus," I said.

Heavy drinking was nothing new to me. The only reason my father wasn't the town drunk was because we lived in the country, but he wouldn't jump out a two-storey window to get a drink. He might fall out of one if he had enough, but that was different.

Mick was laughing, and Buddy was cackling away, showing all his shiny brown teeth. "Yessir, that's quite a . . . "

"Were you hurt?" I interrupted. Sometimes Buddy got on my nerves.

"Hell no, luv. God looks after fools and drunks. I just took off like a shot for the pub, with all of them staring at me over their teacups like they'd just seen an alien landing."

"Yessir, them aliens is quite the things."

"That's when my folks sent for the boys in white," Mick said. He always laughed about being in the loony bin, saying how good he was at making belts and icing cookies. It mustn't have been very funny, though, because that's where he carved up his chest with the razor blade. It was when he ran away from there that they sent him to Canada. To me. Like a Harlequin romance, in a way, him coming from another country and being so handsome and all, and just walking into my life out of the blue.

Except you never found people like Buddy in Harlequin romances. Or anywhere else, that I know of. Mick had found him down on the river bank, with one skinny arm wrapped around a tree so he wouldn't slide into the river, drinking out of a paper bag. Well, out of a *bottle* that was in a paper bag, not actually out of a . . . see, that's what I mean about over-explaining? Or Frankie, the girl who lived upstairs, who carved up her face with a broken thermometer on one of her drug trips. Frankie was beautiful even with the scars. But they weren't all burnouts. There was a short, dark guy on the third floor who wore bright red pants and glasses with rhinestones on them. I asked Mick what he did and he said he got shot out of a cannon, but he actually worked at Safeway's, I saw him there after.

There was usually a party going on somewhere in that house, two or three times a week, but Mick was drinking more and more just with me. Or alone.

One night he went to meet an old friend at the bar, and I stayed home and went to bed. He got in about four a.m. and when I turned on the bedside light he was standing at the foot of the bed, looking like he'd seen a ghost.

"Bikky. Thank God it's you."

"Well, who else would it be?" I said, reaching for my cigarettes as Mick sat down on the edge of the bed. I could feel the cold air coming off him and he looked half frozen.

"Where's your jacket?" I asked, but he just shrugged. He was always losing things. His jeans were muddy and his good navy sweater

121

was covered with bits of dirt and fuzz. He was shaking like a leaf, and I lit a cigarette and gave it to him.

"Oh, God Bikky, I've had a horrid experience. I was sitting in Fast Freddie's with Michael, just talking over old times, and I must have blacked out, because all at once I'm washing my hands in a strange bathroom, and I don't have a clue where I am. Or how I got there." Everybody has a drinking blackout now and then, like not remembering where they parked the car, that sort of thing, but Mick had bad ones.

"It was a half bath off a bedroom and a man and woman were sleeping in the bed. I'd never seen them before." Mick put his head down on his knees and was quiet for a long time, with his hands crossed on top of this dark hair and the cigarette burning right down to his fingers. I took it and butted it.

"What did you do?" I imagined screams, a fight, police.

"I crawled out of there on my belly, that's what I did. It took me an age to get out, I was so terrified of waking them. And the rug was filthy."

"Well, I guess she wasn't expecting company," I said, starting to pick the red fuzz and junk of his sweater and putting it in the ashtray.

"That's not the worst part," Mick said, his voice sounding kind of strange and empty. "When I first saw my face in that bathroom mirror, I didn't know who I was."

After that Mick got worse. He was drinking more and enjoying it less, as they say in the cigarette ads, and he was starting to look like death warmed over. He didn't care if he ever ate when he was on a binge, and he was talking to Ralph a lot on the big white telephone.

He sat and stared into space a lot, too, like he was looking into a big black tunnel he was going to have to walk through by himself, and I was afraid to go to work sometimes and leave him. He tried to kill himself once, sawing away at his wrists with an old dull disposable razor that was plugged full of leg and armpit hair. He was shaking too hard to do it right, anyway. God, it was awful how he'd shake. Sometimes I'd wake up with the vibrations of the bed, and he would be sitting on the edge with the sweat running into his eyes, trying to hold a glass of scotch steady. If he could get it down and it stayed there, he'd eventually fall asleep.

Mick's last drunk was not that spectacular, really. He just kept it up for days, till he kind of drank himself sober, and one night he asked me to take him for a drive in the country. It was one of those wild, windy nights in early spring, and I didn't have to go to work until eleven.

Mick looked ghastly, so thin and white, and we stopped at the A&W on the way out of town, where he drank a large vanilla shake to settle his stomach. He was talking a lot, not drunk talk, but excitable, like somebody'd wound him up with a key.

"God, I feel good tonight, Bikky. I feel so good. My head is clear as a bell." He tapped himself on the side of the head — "Ding dong, Avon calling" — and he laughed and laughed. "Oh Bikky my darlin', the times they are a changing. I can feel it in the air."

"What times? What's changing?"

I had driven out the Regina highway and it was good, being in the country again. The snow was melting fast in the fields, and in the ditches the first patches of green were showing through. Mick was babbling on about how things were going to change, about people being in control of their own destinies, didn't I agree, about how he'd screwed up, he'd admit that, but it wasn't too late to change things — he'd go back to school, paint the house inside and out, go to New York to see an old schoolmate who had a law firm. I'd never seen him so excited, though he wasn't making much sense. Every once in a while he got on this kick about changing everything.

"Spring is here," I said, trying to change the subject.

Mick rolled down his window and breathed in the spring air like somebody who's been shut away for a long time.

"So it is," he says, sounding surprised. "It really is spring." And he didn't say anything for quite awhile, just looked out the window at the prairie, tinged all rosy from the setting sun. With the warm wind pushing behind us, it felt as if the car might leave the road any moment and soar off over the fields. I reached into my purse for the mickey I'd brought because I knew Mick would need a drink, and had a good swig before passing it over.

"A toast to spring," I said.

"Bikky, do you ever feel that you're wasting your life?" Just like that, out of the blue he asks me if I'm wasting my life.

"No," I said, louder than I meant to. "There's no reason why I should."

"I don't know," says Mick, the way people say when they really do know something. He hadn't had a drink, which was strange, and he was holding the mickey on his knees, like he didn't want to get too close to it. "I've been doing a lot of thinking lately."

I reached for the bottle. Sometimes I like it better when Mick didn't think. I didn't answer, hoping it wasn't one of his morbid spells coming on.

"I think we should quit drinking, Bikky."

"We?" I said. "We? Speak for yourself, mate." I'd picked up some of Mick's expressions. I always do that when I like somebody a lot. "You just need to cut down, that's all. You don't have to get carried away."

The road to Last Mountain Lake was just ahead and I hung a left there, thinking to stop somewhere along it and get a beer out of the trunk. I shouldn't have been drinking so much when I had to go to work, but Mick was making me nervous.

"Just cut down," I said again. "That's all you have to do." I glanced at him. He looked worse than before — whiter, with an expression I couldn't read.

"Ah, maybe you're right, luv," Mick finally said, reaching for the mickey, but he sounded depressed again.

It was getting dark, but you could still see. "Look at the ducks," I said, pointing to a shiny slough in the stubble field beside the road. I wanted to get him cheered up before I had to leave him and go to work. "The ducks are back." There were quite a few of them swimming around, one with its head in the water and just its bum sticking out.

Mick didn't answer, and when I looked over at him, he was crying. He was staring out the window, with the bottle on his lap, and the tears were just running down his face. He didn't even bother to wipe them away, and he looked so . . . so *defeated*, somehow.

The road was terrible, up and down and full of potholes, and I was watching for a side road to turn around. We had just come to the bottom of a long, long hill when Mick yells at me to stop, and he was out behind the car before it stopped rolling.

I looked back and I'll never forget it.

Mick was just standing there in that howling wind, not bent over or anything, with a great white flag of vomit blowing out of his mouth and off to the side. It was so strange. Mick's pale face, and the big white banner of puke blowing in the dark.

It was finally over and he got back in the car, leaning his head against the window.

"That's it, Bikky," he said. After awhile he said it again. "That's it."

We drove all the way home with the windows open, he smelled so bad, and I knew he was horribly ashamed.

Back home he sat at the kitchen table for the longest time, with a face as white as death. He looked like a man with his whole life passing in front of his eyes. Then he asked me to call A.A.

I took off his shirt and washed him up right there at the table, from a basin. I felt so sad, like a foster mother who's waiting for the adoption agency to come and take a child she loves more than anything. It was stupid, really, I don't know why I felt like that, but I did. They rang the doorbell just before I left for work, and it was hard to be civil to them. At the same time I knew he couldn't go on like that. He would kill himself.

Well, like I said, Mick has been two whole months without a drink. I figured once he got out of that treatment centre they hauled him off to, he'd be able to have a few now and then, just enough to have a good time. But he's off to those meetings nearly every night, or those A.A. guys are sitting around the kitchen table, swilling down coffee and laughing like a bunch of idiots. I never heard people laugh like they do. I sneak a beer up to Buddy's room sometimes when they're there, but he's not your ideal drinking companion, and I've even seen them eyeing poor old Buddy like they might be thinking of recruiting him. Well, I guess he could sit around saying Yessir, that's quite a thing, at A.A. meetings as well as anywhere else.

Frankie's in the hospital, she o.d.'d again, and I heard Mick talking to them about going up to see her. He wants to sober up the whole world. Starting with me.

I can't get over the change in Mick. I've even seen him down on his knees, in the bathroom, praying. I bet it surprised the hell out of Ralph.

And he's looking fantastic, even better than the day he ambled around the corner of the house into my life. He's talking about going back to university this fall and get a master's degree in law. He's talked to his folks a couple of times and I think they're starting to want him back. He says he loves me, but I don't know. I guess things are just happening too fast.

The other night Mick and I went to a second-hand bookstore, where Mick spent about a hundred dollars. That's the way we spend our evenings now, going to second-hand bookstores. Or having coffee with people. I wonder that those A.A.s ever get a wink of sleep or that they haven't all died of caffeine poisoning long ago. If you ask me, they'd be better off to have a drink now and then. Anyways, at the bookstore I saw that Harlequin romance I was reading the day I met Mick, and I just stood there and sort of scanned it through to the end.

Tall, Dark and Handsome and the churchmouse sail off in a sampan or something like that at the end, kissing behind the sail, with this Chinese guy filling up their wine glasses every time they turn around. Nobody ends up puking in the wind.

Music Lessons

Bonnie Burnard

Most of us who grew up in that time, in that place, in that little sub-class of well-off girls in well-off towns seem now to me interchangeable, like foundlings. We all grew around the same rules, the same expectations. Among the many things we did in my town, with a strangely limited variation in skill, was play the piano. We were all taught to play by Mrs. Summers, though I finished with her alone.

The osmosis which is at work among very young women, beginning always with the one who will tell, the one who will act out a scene for friends gathered round her in some flouncy bedroom, was at work among us. The substance of our minds, like the contents of our closets, was swapped and shared in a continuous, generous game. Perhaps, if we had lost our virginity at thirteen, I would have many elaborate scenes in my memory rather than one. Perhaps not. The osmosis thickened and slowed just as the loss of virginity accelerated. But we knew for a time, we were happy knowing, what the world held. I remember knowing what Mrs. Summers would do when I showed up for a lesson sporting my first bra. I remember knowing that when it was over I would be able to sit on the flouncy bed and say, guess what. My world and my comfort in it depended on the sharing of events. This is part of the silliness for which young girls are, cruelly, ridiculed.

What Mrs. Summers did was exactly as had been reported. She put her hand firmly on my shoulder and turned me under her gaze like a work of art. "Sweet," she said. "Just sweet." And I felt, as it had been guaranteed I would feel, dumb. The surprise was the kindness in her voice and in her hands. She was encouraging our adolescence when everyone else was extremely busy avoiding it. In her time, she said, girls had been bound tight and flat.

Mrs. Summers had, even into her sixties, elegant sculptured legs and wonderful carriage. She had the good shoulders and the deep full bosom of women who love and manage music. Though she played the organ in the Presbyterian Church, she had no affiliation with any of our mothers or grandmothers. She was not a bridge player or a Daughter of the Empire. She did not quilt or make hats or gossip.

Her dark red brick house had a wide front porch and an oak door with three small, uncurtained windows. Before each lesson I would stretch up to those windows and watch her coming to the door. She walked erect, patting her hair to ensure that no grey blonde stands had escaped the chignon, straightening her gown; it was always a gown, full and rich with colour. And always, just before she put her hand to the door, she prepared a smile. With the swing of the door came a rush of smells: furniture polish and perfume and smoke from the fire in the winter. And her voice, across the threshold, "Elizabeth dear," as if surprised, delighted.

The piano was a brilliant black, dustless always, with one framed picture sitting on top, of the two of them, Mrs. Summers and her husband, standing under a grapefruit tree, in the south. I could always feel Mr. Summers in the house when I took my lesson, though he never coughed or answered the phone. He was not seen in church either; if he liked music his taste did not run to hymns or to the plunkings of adolescent girls. They had no children, only a Scottie dog and a vegetable garden.

Each spring he could be seen painting the red front porch steps, alternately, so his wife's students could still get in to her. He would stand back beside his paint can, the brush in his hand and watch us leap up the steps, giving no instruction, trusting our good sense.

Within hours of his death, the doctor's wife let it be known that Mrs. Summers had found him slumped at the sweet pea fence. He had been tidying them, arranging them through the wire. People said he had only a few yards left to do, as if that signified injustice.

His funeral was a big one. He had been the hardware man and a councillor and years before he had bought the Scouts four big tents which were still in use. It was my first non-family funeral. I was determined to go, as were all my friends, because we wanted to see how Mrs. Summers would grieve.

She grieved at her usual place, at the organ. The front row of the church was filled with his people, brothers and nephews and nieces and a few strange children, but she did not take her place with them. She stayed at the organ throughout the service, playing the music or staring at it. I was smart enough to know that she was expressing something through the music but it was nothing I could recognize, nothing I had been exposed to in her living room. I knew only that the level of difficulty was beyond her audience, had likely been pulled up from her time as a young woman at the Conservatory. Toward the end of the service she switched to the chimes, making herself heard throughout the town and into the countryside. I imagined a farmer, not far away, walking across a yard with a cream can in his hand, pausing, his movement stopped by the chimes. After the service the word "appalled" moved through the circles of people standing on the sidewalk and on the grass. My friends and I were not appalled, we were thrilled.

It was assumed that lessons would stop for at least a while but Mrs. Summers put out a few phone calls and said no, there would be no interruption. As I took the steps up to my lessons a week later I wondered about them, wondered who would paint them. I decided I would. I would get my Dad or my brother to help me or I would do it alone, in the spring, when I could be sure the memory of the painting wouldn't hurt her. I didn't tell my friends about this plan; they would have wanted to join me, to help. I wanted it to be a small thing, a quiet, private thing.

I had checked with my mother about what to say to Mrs. Summers, if I should say anything at all.

"Just keep it simple," she said. "Just say you are sorry."

"How should I say it?" I asked.

"Well are you sorry?" she said. "Did you like him?"

"Yes."

"Then don't worry." As usual her help, her preparation, her warning, was unadorned. It seemed inadequate when compared to the enriched and detailed advice of my friends, who had rehearsed their sympathy.

As Mrs. Summers approached the door I repeated under my breath I'm sorry, I'm sorry. The smile she prepared came from a deeper place. She opened the door and I said it aloud just at the moment she was saying my name. I don't know if she heard me.

There was some concern about the vegetable garden that fall but she managed it. It was almost as well tended as it had been. My friends and I saw her when we were riding past on our way to school, stooped low in the varying greens of the garden, bright and undaunted in her yellow pedal pushers and mauve sweat shirt. She wore gloves to protect her hands.

The first change came a few weeks later, when the garden was finished. On the piano, beside the Florida picture, sat another, younger, picture. She was not a bride, was something between a bride and a Florida woman, perhaps thirty. Mr. Summers was slim and grinning and turned away from her as if talking to someone just outside the camera's range.

The following week the picture I had been hoping for was there. She was a bride, though not in white, like my mother. She wore a tailored suit and a wrist corsage and spectator shoes, black and white or navy and white. Her left hand was held in such a way that her ring picked up the sunlight of the wedding day. He wore a suit with wide lapels and wide stripes and felt hat tipped forward, on an angle across his face.

His arm was wrapped around her waist, his hand flat on her stomach. I liked these pictures, liked their arrangement on the piano, facing me.

When the other pictures appeared on the opposite side of the piano, in grey cardboard frames, five of them, I forgot good manners and stared boldly. There were five men, all young. One leaned against the flank of a Clydesdale, his hands in the pockets of his draped pants. One knelt in a soldier's uniform beside a dog. Two others, though not alike, leaned in a shared pose against the hoods of large dark cars. And one of them, with the unmistakable jaw and the eyes I saw every day in the mirror, was my grandfather.

"Lovers," she said. "They're just my lovers, dear."

She was not with any of them.

Word got out of course. Lovers on the piano. It wasn't good. Soon music students were taking the longer walk across the tracks to the new high school teacher who, it was said, was just as qualified, if not quite so experienced.

I didn't take the longer walk. My mother was puzzled; I saw her on the phone, listening, and I knew she was puzzled but she shook her head. "No," she said. "No. I won't be taking Elizabeth away from her."

I didn't ask my mother why she insisted that I continue with Mrs. Summers and though it's too late now, it would still be good to know how the characters arranged themselves in her head that fall. My friends hounded me for a while about the lovers, about the possibility of deeper, darker things, eager for oddity at least, if not perversity. But something stopped me from acting out the small things I saw. I was not puffed up with knowledge, did not feel unique and envied; if they had sensed any of that they would have sliced my fingers off at the knuckles, ending my music lessons forever. I felt alone and terrified.

Mrs. Summers struck my hands with her crossword puzzle book just after Christmas. I remember the mantel was still draped in garlands and the reindeer stood precariously on the snow-covered mirror on the buffet. I hadn't practised much during the vacation; my pieces were weak. Perhaps, knowing I was the only student, I wanted to feel a bit of power over her. She was sorry immediately, or seemed to be, but the next week she rapped my back with her knuckles, telling me to sit up straight, sit erect. Her gowns were no longer starched and crisp, the chignon was gone. Her hair hung loose and coarse and long. Eventually she sat in the brocade chair by the window, leafing absently through old photograph albums while I played. This arrangement suited me but I knew I wouldn't pass my examination if she didn't help me. I wanted badly to play the piano well, perhaps thinking this would please her, in spite of everything.

I knew about winter by then, how it works on women. My father joked secretly about my mother's February moods, telling us not to take things to heart, that spring would bring her back to herself. I hoped spring would work for Mrs. Summers too.

But when it came, when the snow moved in dirty chunks down the street, carried by the run-off, things were worse. Mrs. Summers hadn't helped me at all, my mother seemed oblivious to my flounderings on the piano at home and my friends said they were far ahead of me. The day of my last lesson Mrs. Summers didn't prepare a smile at all and she looked back at me through those three little windows in the oak door. I was bent down unlacing my saddle shoes when I noticed the navy and white spectators from her wedding day. She lifted her dingy gown.

"Remember these?" she asked.

"Yes," I answered.

She wheeled her back to me, going to the piano bench. "Of course you don't," she snapped. "How could you?" She sat down and played for me, pieces I had not even imagined. She began to hiss at her blue-veined fingers as they missed their place, their time. When the half-hour was up she named a date for my examination. We both knew there was little chance I'd pass.

I could have told. I could have given the details to my mother and to my friends, who would have confided in their mothers. I could have lied myself into the glory of victimization. I'd done it before. But I was drawn to the hurt, to the chaos. There was an odd comfort in me. I wondered if I was making what my mother had once called a moral choice, a choice that would make my life easier, or harder.

The steps had always been blood red. I charged the paint and the brush to my father's account at the hardware store and I took our broom over with me and a rag I had soaked with the garden hose. I cleaned the steps and painted every other one, just as Mr. Summers had. She didn't come out that first day, but on the second day I had just dropped everything and begun to wipe the steps again with my rag when the oak door swung open.

"Will you just go away?" she said. "Just disappear."

I held my ground, stood erect with the rag dripping at my side. She watched the tears, unstoppable, sliding down my cheeks. I didn't wipe them away or take the deep breath that brings pride back.

She came at me with her arms out and though there was no way to know whether she was going to pound me or lean on me or hug me, I could not have run. Her hands were firm on my shoulders; the sound she made was loud and brutal and almost young.

Stains

Sharon MacFarlane

H er wrists burn in the icy water. But the water must be cold if she is to get all the stains out. She folds the leg of the jeans, rubs the layers of heavy denim together. With the bar of harsh laundry soap she scrubs the spots over and over. The water darkens with blood. She twists the jeans, wringing out as much water as she can, sets them carefully beside the sink.

When she lifts the tee-shirt a small piece of curled, white skin floats free of the jagged tear, rises to the surface. She swallows, takes a deep breath.

When the clothes — a pair of shorts, a pair of socks, the tee-shirt and the jeans — are all in the washer she sits down at the kitchen table. She's never been good at waiting. "Go home," they told her, "there's nothing you can do here. We'll call you." She stares at the clock, not sure if she wants the hands to move faster or slower. Should she call one of her friends to wait with her? She couldn't bear to make small talk, couldn't concentrate on anything but the pictures that fill her mind. The image of him — grey, unconscious, his dark blood seeping through the bandage, seeping into the white sheet of the hospital bed. No, she will wait now as she waited seventeen years ago for his birth. Alone. She sees again the baby with snowy hair, the five year old in an over-sized hockey uniform, the fourth-grade wise man in the school pageant . . . thinks of all the hopes she had for him.

She goes to the washer as soon as it stops. There is a circle of red-tinged suds on the inside of the lid. She puts the clothes into the dryer, then with an old towel scrubs the enamel lid. She rinses the towel again and again; when it is clean, she hangs it over the tap to dry.

In the kitchen, she fills the kettle and sets it on the burner. She spoons tea leaves into a small brown pot and takes a china mug from the cupboard. When the tea is ready she sits for a moment holding the warm mug in both hands. She drinks two cups but in a few minutes she is thirsty again. Worry parches her mouth, it's always been that way.

She learned to keep a pitcher of water and a glass beside her, the nights she sat up with him when he was sick. With every illness he ran a high fever. When he was a baby and she held him in her arms in the rocking chair all night she wished that she could absorb the heat from his body into her own. Wished him cool — well again — sleeping in his crib with the white quilt tucked around him. When he was three or four, the fevers made him delirious, made him babble nonsense, reach to pluck imaginary balloons from the air. She thought then that when he was older, after he'd had all the childhood diseases, everything would be all right. If only this was as simple as a bout of croup or measles.

The fear has been with her for a long time. She realized that when the doorbell rang at 4 a.m. She awoke instantly, went to the door, saw the policeman standing there. " . . . your son — there's been an accident . . . " She knew then that, somehow, she'd been waiting for those words.

Noon. He'd be getting up about now if this was an ordinary Saturday. He'd come into the kitchen, bleary-eyed, his hair rumpled, wearing only his wrinkled jeans. He'd go to the fridge, take a drink of milk straight from the carton. She'd say, "For Pete's sake, can't you get a glass?" He'd shrug, both of them knowing she wasn't upset about the milk but about his hangover, his boozing, his friends . . . A Saturday ritual that had been going on for a year now. Today — there is only the faint hum of the dryer and the ticking of the clock.

Sharon MacFarlane

When she takes the clothes out of the dryer she spreads them on top of the machine, inspects them carefully, satisfies herself that there is no trace of stains. She folds them and puts them in his dresser. Except the shirt. She takes the shirt to the sewing machine. The gash is so long — from the shoulder almost to the hem — that it distorts the MOLSON logo printed on the chest. Of course he has other shirts — a red one, a soft silvery-grey one, a black one that makes him look even blonder than he is — lots of nice shirts; but he prefers this one. A stretched tee-shirt that shows the world he is a beer drinker — a man.

Booze erases his shyness, gives him confidence. She should have praised him more when he was younger, criticized him less, helped him to have a better self-image. She knows that now. Maybe then he'd have excelled at something — school, sports, drama — wouldn't have needed the booze to make him feel important.

In the sewing room she takes a cardboard box from the top shelf. She must find material to match the shirt. She turns the box upside down, spills hundreds of odd-shaped scraps onto the floor. She sifts through them carefully, picks up, then rejects, five or six. Finally she finds a piece of soft cotton that matches exactly the faded blue of the shirt. She pins it carefully in place under the tear and starts sewing. The machine's zigzag stitches pull the edges neatly together. The mend will be almost invisible. But there is still an inch left to sew when the telephone rings.

Well-Meant Advice

Elizabeth Brewster

I t was, Sarah felt, unfair of Leota to ask her advice in the first place. After all, Leota was the elder of the two, and she had much more experience of life generally. But of course she was terribly upset at the time; she needed someone to talk to; it was natural she should turn to her own sister, wasn't it? What worried Sarah later was, how in the world could she know if she had given the right advice? At the time she thought she was right in saying No, definitely, Leota ought not to press charges. It would be too embarrassing. Later, it occurred to her that she might have been mistaken; the man ought to have been punished, and Leota might have felt safer if he had been. But supposing he had been charged and not convicted? And then supposing he had wanted revenge on Leota?

Leota and Sarah were sisters, both past their first youth. Leota was in her middle forties, Sarah ten years younger. Leota, the product of the earlier days of their parents' marriage, had been given what they thought was the more romantic name, had the more exuberant personality. By the time Sarah had been born, the parents had settled down to a dull life, and gave her a dull name, her grandmother's name, from the Bible. Though it meant "Princess," she discovered later.

The only adventurous thing Sarah had ever done was to move out to Saskatoon from the small Ontario town where she and Leota had grown up; and then she had merely followed Leota, who had come here

Elizabeth Brewster

with one of her husbands and had stayed on after the marriage had
failed. In those early days the sisters had seemed closer than they
became later. Sarah had thought once she might move to the Coast,
but had long ago given up that notion and settled down in Saskatoon.
She had gone to a business school after high school, had worked in a
number of offices after coming to Saskatoon, and was now the chief
secretary in the office of the Dean of Arts at the University. She had a
pleasant cubbyhole of an office next to the Dean's, and enjoyed her
work, at which she was efficient. She was moderately friendly with
Rose Dooley, the receptionist in the outer office. Otherwise, her social
life consisted of visits to the library, the monthly meetings of the
Read-a-Book club, the bi-monthly meetings of a group of Church
ladies, and an occasional outing to the movies with someone from one
of these groups. And, of course, visits to or from Leota.

Not that she often dropped in on Leota without previous notice.
Leota's living quarters were tiny: a bed-sitting room with a hot plate, a
folding table, and a kitchen sink, the bathroom shared with a tenant on
the other side of the corridor. If Leota already had company (and Leota
seemed often to have company, chiefly gentlemen friends) there was not
room in the place to breathe. And anyhow, Leota lived on the opposite
side of the river from Sarah's apartment, larger and more comfortable,
which was just across from the university. (People who were only
slightly acquainted with both the sisters sometimes wondered why they
didn't share a place. It was a subject that, after all these years, they found
it convenient not to discuss.)

Sarah saw Leota most often in whichever restaurant Leota happened
to be working. It was usually a rather grubby restaurant. Leota had
dropped out of school in her second year of high school, just before
her first marriage. When she had to support herself, she was not as
well qualified as Sarah, and took what came to hand, working sometimes as a waitress, sometimes as a short-order cook. She preferred
greasy spoons and hamburger joints to places with more pretensions
of elegance. "I don't like those classy places," she told Sarah. "Everything has to be just so, and then the customers act as if they couldn't

see you. I like to serve just plain folks. They treat you like a human being, even if they can't afford to tip."

Sarah first realized something was wrong with Leota one Saturday morning in June when she dropped in at the Pancake House, where Leota had just recently taken a job. It was downtown, in the Mall, and maybe a cut or two above Leota's usual place. Quite clean, really, with shiny formica table tops. The waitresses wore orange uniforms, laced in at the waist, which pretended to be of some vaguely earlier time. Leota, who still had a good figure and took pride in it, liked this uniform, and the last time Sarah had seen her in it she had thought Leota seemed pleased with herself and in good spirits. But today she looked dispirited; her uniform seemed wrinkled, almost dirty; in fact, to Sarah she looked unkempt. Oh, dear, whatever's wrong? Sarah thought. She'll never last here if she doesn't smarten up. But it isn't like her not to care what she looks like.

For Leota had always had good looks and had kept them. As a matter of fact, it sometimes vexed Sarah that people mistook Leota for the younger. There was the man at the Ex, for instance, who guessed ages, and had guessed Leota to be seven years younger than Sarah. ("Don't be mad, Sarah," Leota had said afterwards. "Men always go by hair colour. You've let yours go gray at the front, instead of having a colour, like me. Get your hair coloured red, and he'll think you're twenty-five.") Today he would have known Leota was older, hair colour or not.

"Aren't you well, Leota?" Sarah asked involuntarily when Leota approached her table, where she had settled with her small parcels.

Leota shook her head, as though there was some mystery. "I'll tell you later, Sarah," she said. "What do you want? Just coffee?"

"Coffee and a muffin, I guess. OK?"

Leota went off dispiritedly, and Sarah stared after her in puzzlement. Bad news of the kids? Leota had a grown-up son and a practically grown-up daughter, from her first two marriages. Neither of them lived in Saskatoon. One of them might be into drugs or something. That was the trouble with kids, you never knew. But she wouldn't have thought Leota would've lost too much sleep over something like that. She would have herself, of course. Maybe just as well she hadn't married and had kids.

Leota came back with the muffin and coffee and plunked them on the table before Sarah, spilling the coffee a little. Sarah stared at Leota's hand, which was trembling. What in the world — ?

"Do you want me to come in tonight, Leota?" Sarah asked. "Are you free, or is this your night to work?" (She had thought of going to that good movie tonight with Rose Dooley; but blood's thicker than water. She couldn't have lived with her sister, but if she was really worried about something — !)

"I work tonight, but I'm free all day tomorrow," Leota said. "Could I come to your place, though? People can hear everything that's said through the walls in that place of mine, and I want to tell you something."

"Lunch tomorrow at my place, then," Sarah said, wondering still more. "Say twelve thirty, then I'll be back from church."

"Oh, you and your church. Well, I can't stand here gabbing. See you tomorrow for lunch, then." And she went off to the next customer, leaving Sarah to digest her coffee and muffin. One of the kids must really be in bad trouble, maybe criminal trouble, if Leota didn't want the tenant next door to hear. Danny, probably. He was her favourite. It wasn't like Leota to be so mysterious.

She did not, in fact, go to church the next morning. Instead she stayed home and made Leota's favourite lemon pudding, to be eaten after the baked ham, corn soufflé, baking powder biscuits and tossed salad. She had a feeling that people who ate out most of the time, as Leota did, ate rather badly, and a good meal must surely be a help if Leota was unhappy about something. Besides, she did not mind showing her sister that, though she was an amateur at cooking, she could turn out a good meal if she wanted to, as well as people who worked in restaurants.

Her little dining table was placed in front of the chief window in the apartment, to get as much light as possible. The day was rainy and sullen after a spell of hot, dry weather. There was a wet weeping birch outside her window, its branches drooping disconsolately. The blue spruce beside it stood tall and upright, though it swayed slightly in the breeze. The lawn across the street on the campus was green, for once without need of sprinklers. The rain was good for the Crop, Sarah reminded herself as she laid the table. Nobody who had lived in Saskatchewan for nearly ten years, as Sarah had, could fail to think of the Crop, though she had seen it chiefly from the air, on her occasional flights to Toronto to visit an old aunt. Now she caught herself thinking, half guiltily, that the Crop might have waited until Monday for rain, and not spoiled her week end.

The door bell pinged. Sarah hurried to open it, and saw Leota, still disconsolate, her eyes red-rimmed.

She hunted in the back of the buffet for the bottle of sweet sherry she kept for special occasions, poured out a couple of small glasses, while Leota hunted in her purse for a box of cigarettes, pulled a cigarette out, and lit it.

"You can't do yourself much harm with glasses as small as these," Leota said. "Well, here's mud in your eye."

She seemed to be fortified slightly, though she waited until they were at the table, with their ham and corn souffle in front of them, before saying, "The most awful thing has happened, Sarah. You'll never believe."

"What is it? Danny in trouble again?"

Leota shook her head.

"Marilyn then? At her age she shouldn't be in Vancouver alone."

"Oh, Marilyn's fine, so far as I know. It's me. You'll never believe," she repeated. She picked up her fork, set it down again, then burst out desperately, "Sarah, I've been raped."

"Raped?" Sarah cried, and dropped her fork in astonishment. She checked herself from saying, "Not at your age." (But rape is no compliment, at whatever age, she reminded herself.) Instead she said, "Here in Saskatoon?"

Leota laughed, in spite of the red rim around her eyes. "You don't think bad things can happen in Saskatoon, the same as anywhere? I could tell you some things that happen here, Sarah, that would curl your hair."

Of course Sarah knew things happened in Saskatoon. There were those little girls murdered in the park. And a woman had been killed in a hotel downtown just the very week she had moved here. But things like that didn't happen to people she knew.

"How did it happen, then?" she asked. "When? Why didn't you tell me right away?"

"It was just a week ago," Leota said. "Went to a party last Saturday night at Lily Boyd's. You remember Lily Boyd?"

"Yes. I met her once at your place."

"You didn't like her. She was tight, I remember. Well, she can be mouthy when she's tight, but she's a good sort, really."

"So there was a party at Lily Boyd's. Go on."

"Yes. Well, it was a pretty lively party, and I'm not as good at staying up all night as I used to be, even on a Saturday night. So I decided to leave early. Midnight, or maybe it was one or two a.m."

"Did you walk? Going through those dark alleys at two in the morning — it's asking for trouble. I never go out by myself after nine or ten."

"You don't do a lot of things, Sarah. But anyway, I didn't walk. I was going to call a taxi — I always get Joe Kowalski at night, he's as safe as your own brother, I always say."

"Not that we ever had a brother."

"Sarah, you do say some of the dumbest things. Anyway, I was going to call Joe; but there was this man there — a Mountie, can you imagine? — I don't know where Lily picked up a Mountie. But he was nice as pie at the party; butter wouldn't melt in his mouth. He offered to drive me home — said he wasn't one for late parties either."

"So then —?"

"Well, he started off in the right direction, all right. But then it seemed to me he was going the wrong way. At first I thought he was just mixed up, not knowing where I lived, and Lily's parties might mix anyone up, though I hadn't thought he'd been drinking that much. So I said, 'Look, I'm sorry, Al (his name was Al, did I tell you?) but I think you're going the wrong way,' and he said, 'Oh, the night's young, so why don't we just take a little drive first?'"

"And what did you say then?"

"Told him I'd just as lieve go straight home, I was tired. Not that I really thought he'd do anything like he did. I just thought he really wanted a drive, maybe wanted to do a little smooching, nothing serious. Anyhow, he put on the speed and just drove on, and soon we were out in the country. I kept trying to coax him back, but he wouldn't stop until we were miles from nowhere, real prairie. And then there was no fighting him off. I tried but I couldn't. I kept thinking, 'I'm being raped by a Mountie.' How's that for the title of something in a *True Confessions* magazine?"

"How did you get back to town? Did he leave you there?"

"Oh, he drove me home afterwards. I was scared he'd kill me and leave me for dead in a ditch, but he didn't. He drove me home and just threw me out of the car."

"And then what did you do? Nothing?"

"Well, I thought of phoning you, but at that time in the morning? I didn't want to get you out of bed. But I was bleeding so hard I had to do something."

"Bleeding? I thought that only happened the first time. Somebody told me."

"Yeah. Well, that's what I thought, too. But this man was —well, I think he was a Monster." (There were capital letters in Leota's voice.) "You should of seen his prick, if you'll pardon the expression. I never saw one so big. No wonder it hurt. I felt sorry for his wife, having to put up with that all the time."

Sarah glanced at Leota. She must've been around, to be able to make all those comparisons. But she had been married three times and had had gentlemen friends too. Sarah felt just the faintest twinge of jeolousy towards Leota, instantly suppressed. Experience with men hadn't done much for Leota, had it? Left her stranded at forty-five, without a proper home or a decent job, nothing to show for it except those two lumps of children, Danny and Marilyn, who weren't even very likeable. And now this happened to her. Sarah was better off, by any reasonable standard.

"So you were bleeding and had to do something. What did you do, Leota?"

"Decided I'd take myself to Emergency at City Hospital. I knew about that because I'd had to go there the time I had my gall bladder operation, remember? So I phoned Joe, after all, and he took me over. Didn't get my regular doctor, got this man, a Dr. Binnie, who was on duty. He fixed me up. I told him all about it, and he said he'd be a witness all right if I wanted to charge the man with rape. Said it was obvious force had been used."

"Dr. Binnie's my doctor," Sarah said. "And so did you charge the man with rape, Leota? Are you charging him?"

"Well, that's what I wanted to ask your advice on, Sarah. On the one hand, I don't like to see him go unpunished — a Mountie, of all people, imagine! — but he's got a wife and five kids, I found that out. I don't want to cause them trouble. I found it hard to make up my mind."

"But if you were going to do something, shouldn't you have done it right away?"

"Well, in a way, I did, I saw Dr. Binnie right away. And Lily and the others at the party know he started out to drive me home. But I don't know — his being a Mountie and all — his pals would protect him, I think. I wouldn't have a chance."

She's probably right, Sarah thought. And what they wouldn't ask about her life, too. She'd heard about trials of that sort. It didn't bear thinking of. And everybody in town would know about it, Rose Dooley and the women at the Read-a-Book Club and everybody.

"If it were you, would you charge him?" Leota asked.

"Oh, if it were me —!" (but that would be different, of course. She, who had always been so cautious, and known to be cautious. And Dr.

Binnie could've said she was a virgin the last time he'd examined her, though even a fact like that could be turned against you.) "If it were me — no, definitely not. It would be too embarrassing. But it's up to you."

"Maybe not, then," Leota said, "though I'd like to teach him a lesson. I could maybe put a few fleas in some people's ears without charging him."

The soufflé had flattened and gone cold while they talked. Most of it would be thrown out. Too bad. It had been a successful soufflé too. And Leota had no appetite for the lemon pudding. Sarah would be eating it for the next three or four days.

Sarah sighed. "Have some more coffee, Leota," she offered. "Tell me more about it. Get it off your chest." She felt there was something more she should be able to say, something comforting, but couldn't think what it might be.

Leota passed her cup over, took another cigarette out of the now nearly empty package. Sarah refrained from asking, as she usually did, "Why don't you cut these out?" Leota was entitled to special consideration today.

Taking a deep puff and inhaling, Leota coughed. "The bastard!" she exclaimed. "When I think of that bastard! He must really have done for me. That Dr. Binnie told me I might have to lay off sex for good. He didn't use those exact words, but that's what he meant."

"Oh —?" Sarah asked. She wondered if Dr. Binnie's advice had been medical, moral, or cautionary. Anyhow, Leota didn't always understand advice.

"But I wouldn't think you'd feel like it for a while, anyhow, Leota," she said. She wished she had something she could do while Leota smoked, other than crack her knuckles or eat after-dinner mints.

"Oh, for a while — that's for sure. I hate men. What a bunch of brutes." And suddenly, after all this talking in relative calm, she began to cry. Sarah got up and put her arms around Leota's shaking shoulders. More coffee herself, she thought. It was going to be a long, wet afternoon.

145

So Leota didn't lay charges against the Mountie, though perhaps it mightn't have been Sarah's advice that decided her. She told Sarah, a week or so later, that she had been talking to a friend who was a lawyer. Someone she had met when she was working at the lunch counter before the last. (Leota did have a lot of different friends, Sarah thought). He also, it had seemed, had advised against laying charges. But the Mountie disappeared; he had been posted somewhere else, perhaps. Leota speculated that the lawyer had known someone who knew someone, that They — people higher up out there — were keeping an eye on the Mountie, had warned him to be careful. Next time, they might have told him, he mightn't be so lucky.

Leota appeared to be relieved that the Mountie had left town. Nevertheless, she did not rapidly recover her old spirits. She gave up colouring her hair, and gray gradually took over, working upward from the roots. A permanent frown, as though of puzzlement, appeared directly over her eyes. Although she kept her orange uniforms clean and pressed, they seemed to sag and wilt in sympathy with some sagging and wilting of her own spirit. Her walk, which had always had a lively spring to it, was now plodding and heavy. Nobody now would have thought she was younger than Sarah. But Sarah was not altogether happy, after all, to have the comparison established in her favour. She was worried about her sister, and wondered guiltily if she had been wrong that time to suggest — at any rate to agree — that Leota should not press charges. Although Goodness knew what good it would have done Leota to have any revenge. The damage had been done, and how would a trial have helped Leota's depression, her nervous suspicions of strangers, the fading of her interest in life?

Several months later, in the autumn, when Leota was visiting Sarah for Sunday lunch again (a regular custom since what Sarah thought of as Leota's illness), Leota said, "Well, I heard news of that Al — the Mountie, remember?"

"Could I forget?" Sarah asked. "What news have you heard?"

"He got caught this time. A sixteen year old girl. In Regina."

"A sixteen year old girl! Oh, no." (We should have prevented him, she thought. But what do I mean we?)

"Oh, don't sound so shocked. She probably wasn't Sweet Sixteen and Never Been Kissed, like you were at that age. Anyhow, she wasn't in as lonely a place as I was. She kept him off and screamed bloody murder. So no harm done, and I guess he's out of the Force for good. Serves him right too."

Sarah could only agree.

Fall went by. December came, with the first snow, and temperatures dropped far below freezing. Sarah thought of taking a week at Christmas to visit the aunt in Toronto, and wondered if she might persuade Leota to go with her this time. Good for her to have a change of scene this year. Six months, and Leota was still not herself, though certainly the news about the Mountie had helped.

In the midst of Christmas shopping, she needed a cup of coffee. Leota had moved to the cafeteria in the Hudson's Bay store, where she was now cashier. Sarah, with her coffee and blueberry muffin (the Bay had good blueberry muffins) paid Leota at the checkpoint. "Why Leota," she exclaimed. "Your hair's red again."

"Yes, Sarah, you don't need to tell the world. Only her hairdresser knows for sure, remember."

"Well — see you on Sunday, then. At my place?"

"How about going home with me for supper tonight instead? I'm free at five this aft. Nearly time now."

Leota's housekeeping room seemed as tiny and crowded as ever, perhaps even tinier and more crowded than usual. She was beginning to put up Christmas decorations. A little tree, not yet trimmed, stood in one corner, on a small stand, with a few parcels under it. There were wreaths at each of the two small windows, each wreath centred by a red and green paper bell. Goodness, I don't go to all this trouble, Sarah thought. She must be feeling better again.

Leota, humming to herself, cooked hamburger and onions in a frying-pan on top of the hot plate. She sliced tomatoes and cucumbers in large chunks.

"Toast or fried potatoes, Sarah?" she asked, wiping her hands on her apron.

"Toast, please, Leota. My, you're looking well. I haven't seen you looking so well in a long time."

"That so? Well, I went to see the doctor earlier this week. Not that Dr. Binnie, but my old doctor, Dr. Sharp. And you know what he told me?"

"No. Tell me."

"Well, I told him all about what Dr. Binnie had said, about me not having sex again, and he just laughed and laughed. He asked me if I wanted to, and I said Yes I did; and he said, 'Leota, there's nothing wrong with you. You probably didn't understand something Dr. Binnie's said. You just do what you want. Go out and have fun.' Now what do you think of that?"

Now she would have been furious with Dr. Sharp for laughing, but not Leota. And of course she mightn't have told him the whole story, or he mightn't have put it quite that way. You never knew with Leota.

"I think you've got the advice you wanted, Leota," she said. Well, what do you know? she thought. So that was what was worrying her most all along. Or was it? Not really. Not for a long time, anyway. But thank goodness she was all right now.

The telephone rang while they were eating their supper. "Oh, Lily," Leota said. "Yeah, Yeah . . . Well, my sister's here . . . You're having a party? Wednesday night? I guess I could, if I can bring someone with me . . . Of course, a man. What do you think? . . . No, I wouldn't even ask her . . . She doesn't care for that sort of party . . . Well, it takes all sorts, doesn't it? Look, we're eating supper. I gotta go."

Coming back to the table, she said, unnecessarily, "That was Lily Boyd. She's having a party."

"And you're going? You'd better be careful. Don't take any drives with strange men."

"No, I won't. I'm taking a friend with me this time. Joe Kowalski.

"Joe —? Oh, the one who's safe as your brother."

"Yes, that's Joe. Say, if you need a taxi home tonight, he's the one to take."

"Mm. If I leave early enough I can get a bus that'll take me right to my door."

"Oh, Sarah — you early bird. Say, Sarah, if I were you I'd get my hair coloured; not red, maybe, but a pretty dark brown. Or did you ever consider a wig?"

Sarah smiled. Thank goodness, she and Leota almost never took each other's advice.

She herself, she knew, would never have trusted Joe Kowalski or any other man again. But Leota was different. Leota was a survivor. She hoped.

The Detachable Appendage

Beth Goobie

O ne day, as Kurt was playing soccer with the guys from work, he felt something slither down one leg of his shorts. It was an odd sensation, and Kurt felt different, though he could not pinpoint how. Looking down, Kurt saw the wrinkled, flesh coloured appendage lying in the grass. This was a startling moment, and Kurt was not at all sure what to do. He had not heard of this sort of thing happening before, not even in leprosy cases or on science fiction radio programs.

He looked around. Fortunately, his team had just scored and were busy jumping, hugging and slapping hands. Quickly he reached down and scooped up the appendage. He had no pockets in his tee-shirt or shorts, so he pulled open the elasticized waist of his shorts and dropped the appendage in, hoping for the best. It meandered down to its original position and attached itself. Kurt decided things must be back to normal, and went on playing soccer.

Kurt did not go to see his doctor about the incident. He preferred to see it as an "incident" rather than a "tendency," and at any rate, it had happened only once. He did not see the point in asking a doctor whether body parts commonly detached and reattached themselves at will. He had a feeling they did not. He had no interest in spending the rest of his life as an object of scientific experiments or articles in medical journals. He had never wanted to be in the *Guinness Book of World Records*.

Kurt figured the matter must be psychological. These sorts of things usually were. He wondered, briefly, if the applicable term was "psychological" or "psychotic," but could not remember the difference. At any rate, he did not want to lie on a couch and talk to someone with a foreign accent and bifocals. Kurt was the kind of man who stood up to talk to waiters. He found that being physically lower than someone else made him sweat.

Kurt decided to forget the whole thing. And for a while, the appendage cooperated. Kurt stopped ducking into bathroom cubicles to check and confirm status. He relaxed.

Kurt worked in the produce section of the Whyte Avenue Safeway store. His main interests in life were hockey, basketball, football, soccer, baseball, wrestling, archery, stock car racing, golf, and fly fishing. He had recently married.

The next time the appendage detached itself, Kurt was in a mall, watching a pottery demonstration. Having just purchased an Oilers sweater, Kurt had been walking along, minding his own business. Then he saw the woman sitting at the potter's wheel, her hands at work with a lump of clay. She was forming a cylinder. Kurt found himself fascinated as the shape formed around space. He went into a mild hypnotic trance.

And then it fell off again. Feeling something wander down his inner thigh, Kurt's eyes bugged. Quickly, he crooked his ankle, so the appendage was caught between the inside of his pant leg and foot. Then he bent over and casually slipped it into the folds of the Oilers sweater.

Kurt beat a disconcerted retreat to the nearest men's washroom. He went into a cubicle and unzipped his pants. There was no indication as to the exact location for reattachment, no small red circle or an X to mark the spot. Kurt made a guess and pushed the correct end of the appendage against his body. It stuck. Poking around with his fingers, he could not find a seam or a crack. Everything seemed to be normal.

Still, Kurt was worried. He was beginning to think this could be considered a "tendency." As he urinated, he came up with what he thought might be a viable solution. He would wear a jock strap at all times. He nodded, tucking the appendage away.

The next time the appendage went its own way, Mirabella, Kurt's wife, was out for the evening at her French literature class. Kurt, on his way to get another beer during a TV ad in the Oilers/Kings game, passed her studio. The door was open. He flicked on the light.

On the easel was a partially finished watercolour of an iris. Mirabella, working from the outside in, had left the centre of the iris incomplete, an unpainted space. Kurt found himself attracted to the unfinished nature of the iris's centre. He watched it, thinking it might shift, move. At this point, the appendage, once again, detached itself.

Kurt was not wearing a jock strap, since it had been months since the last mishap. The appendage landed in an ungraceful flop on the carpet between his feet.

"Shit," he said.

He picked it up. He was about to attempt the reattachment process, when he noticed that his fingers left slight indentations in the surface of the appendage. He poked at it. Again, his fingers left an impression.

Kurt found that touching the appendage in its detached state produced sensations in his body —not sexual, exactly. Kurt did not recall feeling this way before. It was not painful but pleasurable, in a mind-bending sort of way . . . inside, somewhere. He poked at the appendage again. This was interesting. He felt as if something moved around . . . inside.

Kurt decided to experiment. He rolled the appendage between his palms, enjoying the sensation. He watched as the shape in his hands became thinner and longer, like plasticine. He rounded the tip so that it resembled one of Mirabella's brushes, in a fleshy sort of way.

Kurt carefully removed the iris from the easel so that he faced a fresh white surface. Mirabella had wrapped the paints in a plastic bag to keep them from drying out. Kurt unwrapped them, then dipped the tip of the appendage into a deep blue. He applied the blue to the paper.

As Kurt moved the blue paint across the paper in broad sweeps, he felt a correlating interior sensation — a soft, light stroke. He relaxed slightly and took a deep breath. It was as if a hand had moved around, gently sweeping things aside —things Kurt had not known were there. As a matter of fact, or fancy, Kurt had not thought much about inside stuff, and he did not really ponder it now. He just enjoyed the sensation of breathing deeply. He washed off the tip of the appendage and dipped it into the yellow.

Kurt worked in a series of broad strokes, and when he was finished, he thought the picture might be construed as an abstract sunset. He felt very light, a shell around broad blending sweeps of colour. The paint on the canvas began to run together.

He heard Mirabella come in. Quickly, he washed off the appendage, shook it so that it flopped back into its original shape, and dropped it into his pants. It reconnected in an appropriate manner.

Kurt realized he must have missed the end of the Oilers game. As Mirabella entered the studio, he felt suddenly shy, expecting ridicule. He crossed his arms over his chest and looked at the floor.

Mirabella set down her French books. She saw his dribbling abstract. Her face lit up and she smiled.

"Kurt!" she said. "I love the colours. I like the motion — the sweep of the stroke."

Kurt felt the colours sigh and settle, expand slightly. That night, as he and Mirabella made love, the colours shifted, like the Northern Lights. He did not realize this sounded very much like adolescent poetry. He had never written poetry, even as an adolescent. He concentrated on one colour after another, finding Mirabella responded most to the deep indigo motion, its slow broad curve.

The Safeway shelves were often depleted after long weekends. Kurt worked, shoving canned goods onto the shelves. Boxes of products stood in the aisle, awaiting placement. Suddenly, he stopped. He looked at the empty spaces on the shelves, the way the cans of stewed tomatoes were stacked around them. There was something pleasing about the space, something that drew his eye.

Kurt studied the space, considering. It made the surrounding cans look almost pleasant. Why not, thought Kurt, leave a space between the stacks of canned tomatoes, in order to make the cans look more attractive? This would please the customer, who would buy more stewed tomatoes, and Safeway would make a greater profit.

Kurt's supervisor came by and yelled at Kurt for standing around doing nothing. He told Kurt to get back to filling the shelves. Kurt watched the supervisor leave with narrowed eyes. Supervisors were blockheads, he thought —just there to make sure all the spaces were shoved full of canned tomatoes . . . there to shove all the time in an employee's day full of work. Supervisors had lost their sense of a day's internal space.

Kurt was pleased with his concept. He shook his head, feeling sorry for the supervisor, his limitations, his so obviously unhappy life.

A month or so later, Kurt turned on the stereo and discovered Mirabella had left it on CBC FM. He was about to flip it to 630 CHED, when a choral piece came on. There was something about it, some sort of inner space to the music that made Kurt leave it on, give it a try.

The announcer said something about Vaughan Williams. Kurt lay on his back and closed his eyes. There was a hollow shape to the music. As Kurt listened, he began to sense shapes between the notes, the movement of the notes around silence.

Once again, the appendage let go. Kurt stood up and shook his pant leg, watching as the appendage slid out onto the floor. He picked it up.

The music continued. Kurt grinned. He would have his way with this appendage.

Gently, he stuck a finger down the middle, creating a tunnel through the centre of the appendage. The internal sensation was immediate —a great opening up, a sense of arctic space. Along the outside, he introduced a series of holes. It was as if a sequence of windows opened, connecting internal and external spaces. Kurt threw back his head and laughed.

He had molded a flesh coloured flute. Kurt was glad no one could see him — he probably looked like some kind of pervert. He placed the flesh-coloured mouthpiece section against his lips. Moving his fingers over the holes, he found he was able to produce different pitches. He turned off the stereo; it was difficult to play along with Vaughan Williams.

Thinking this probably qualified as a mystical experience, Kurt decided to approach it in a Buddhistic mode. He sat cross-legged on the floor, piping out odd, disconnected intervals and rhythms. He was not sure whether the notes could be heard by the ear — if, for example, Mirabella could have heard them. Each note seemed to take place inside, centering and then spreading out slowly, not as sound, but as space. Each note expanded gently, formed its own lingering shimmering sense of space. Then it faded and the next note created a presence . . . or absence. Kurt could not determine which. He settled into a slow, dreamy blues melody and replayed this for hours.

Then Kurt realized he had to relieve himself. He went to the bathroom, attached the appendage and began to urinate. At this point, he saw he had forgotten to shake the appendage back into shape. It was still full of holes. Urine began to splash all over the toilet, the walls, his pants.

"Shit," said Kurt.

He tried to pull the appendage off but this hurt, and the appendage remained firmly attached. There was a smug look to it and Kurt recalled, with a growing dismay, his naive decision to have his way with the appendage. This was probably the revenge of the appendage.

"Please," he hissed, pulling at it. It did not budge.

The appendage was losing the shape Kurt had given it and the holes had become indistinguishable, but Kurt continued to worry. Mirabella must not know about his. She would think him some sort of freak. She would call the doctor, the psychiatrist, the *Guinness Book of World Records*. She would leave him. Kurt loved Mirabella. She must not know about this.

That night, when Mirabella began to kiss him, Kurt made sure they made love in the dark. As he moved inside her, he felt the holes he had inserted into the appendage enlarge, the inner line of space spread out. The afternoon's notes were widening.

Through the windows on the surface of the appendage, Kurt felt Mirabella's movement around him as never before. A new awareness of Mirabella — her shape, her form — filled him. He wanted more, something more from her, the definition of which escaped him. Kurt lost himself in space and melody and Mirabella.

Kurt was growing philosophical. He began to watch to determine whether shape moulded space, or space kept shapes apart. He studied Tupperware, margarine containers, water in tea cups.

In this way, Kurt discovered the process of thought. He wondered if meditation, in the Buddhistic mode, dealt with thought as space rather than word. He remembered Mirabella had once said art portrayed thought as shape. She had gone on to say that the female psyche differed from the male in the way it conceived and nurtured identity within space. This, she had stated, was a psychological side effect of the biological womb.

Kurt had laughed, then. Now, he was not so sure. He was beginning to enjoy his experimentation with the detachable appendage. Still, he hoped this psychic restructuring, this creation of inner space, would not interact with his biological identity to too great an extent. He did not want to get pregnant.

Even with all the psychic structural leaps Kurt was making, the appendage did not detach itself again for months. Kurt had learned to cope with the messy urinating process, and always urinated alone. And then, Kurt and Mirabella attended a wedding.

The best man rose to make the toast to the bride. He raised the glass, so that the red wine swirled in a gentle motion. Kurt started, watching the liquid move within form. The appendage detached.

Kurt caught it at his ankle hem with his serviette before it hit the floor, then slid it into his pocket. He excused himself from helping to clean up, telling Mirabella something unforseen had come up, or come off, as the case happened to be. He hurried home.

Feeling like an explorer, Kurt pulled the appendage from his pocket. He kept the memory of the potter's hands in mind, carefully shaping the appendage so that the holes were eliminated. It became a receptacle, delicately shaped and fluted. He cupped it in his palm, smiling.

Inside, the world had opened up, generous in boundaries. Kurt went to the wine cupboard, pulled out the Beaujolais Nouveau. He uncorked it and poured slowly into the bowl-shaped appendage. Within the round form, the liquid moved in regular rich red movement. A smooth quiet ocean bellied out, spreading under the arctic sky. Holding the appendage up, Kurt swirled the wine gently. To contain so much . . . Place, he thought. To be between horizons like this.

Mirabella walked in. Startled, Kurt jerked his arm behind himself so the appendage lost the wine. The red liquid splashed all over the kitchen floor.

"Oh my god — are you all right?" cried Mirabella, thinking it was blood.

Kurt was lightly shaking the appendage into shape behind his back. "Yes," he said, smiling. He turned his back and dropped the appendage into his pants, felt it reassert itself in the normal fashion. "Sorry, love," he said, going over to her.

He placed his arms around her. They enclosed Mirabella's body as if the arms themselves had acquired a new awareness of space and shape. "I love you," he said.

Kurt kissed her, opening his mouth and waiting for her tongue, helping his clothing slide off before her hands. Spreading out on the bed, he cupped himself to receive her, felt within this motion, Mirabella — fluid, moving.

Kurt was visited with a strange momentary vision of himself on the Oprah Winfrey show, discussing his autobiography, which he had entitled *Self Help To Self Space And Other Inner Vaguenesses*. But the appendage did not seem to like the image of Oprah with her mike, hovering between ocean and sky. It threatened to close down.

Not even under a pseudonym?

Kurt lost Oprah and the thought of future fame under the circles of Mirabella's intent and a sudden surge of ocean current toward sky.

The Sound He Made

Richard Cumyn

This dope addict friend of mine, I had not seen him since the fall, heard that I had a kid and got hold of my phone number from my mother. Gayle and I were in a one-bedroom apartment in Lowertown then, subletting off a guy who moved back into his old house while his father wintered in Florida. Gayle was using the electric breast pump we were renting because the baby was not latching on properly. The first thing he said when I picked up the phone, he could hear the machine sucking in the background, was, "What is this Hill, I dial into an obscene call?"

I knew it was him right off. We had not seen each other for about eight months, not since the time he showed up at Miller House on a Thursday pub night and shared a cigarette with Gayle as we sat together at a table and watched student teachers dance to the Village People. The music was pretty lame. That was before I got Gayle to quit smoking.

Bam was what we called him from the time he collided with this white Citröen while riding his bike. It was the sound he made, like a gun going off, as he bounced off the hood. He didn't ask for his own cig, just kept sharing with Gayle like they were doing a private number together. He explained his nickname for her, rolled up his pant leg to show her the L-shaped scar in his calf where his front mud guard had gouged out enough meat to make a Big Mac. His words. I don't know what I did. I think I just looked away.

His real name is Mitchell O'Day. We met the summer we were twelve years old and going to the same summer day camp, the one run by the civil service recreational association down on Riverside Drive. His father and my mother both worked at Supply and Services but didn't know each other. Due to the accident, Bam missed the middle session of the camp. When he started going again, he was supposed to be using a crutch but he always ditched it in this hollow tree in Vincent Massey park first thing in the morning.

Early August sometime and we had been riding our bikes after dark, a bunch of us. Only one guy had a headlight, the kind that generates its own power against the front tire, but he never used it because he said it only slowed him down. Bam hit that Citröen like a gun going off. The driver didn't even stick around to see if he was all right. The guy with the headlight and I ran to get Bam's father. We were on his street, a dead end, just a couple of houses away, actually.

Last time we saw each other I had told him to find the nearest slimy rock and climb back under it. I guess that's what happens. A crowd of student teachers were doing the body language to "YMCA." It was a real education living there in residence that year with those teachers-to-be. It made me think seriously about home schooling but only in the abstract, though. Gayle and I had only made love the once. Bam didn't even know we were interested in each other and we had no idea how quickly things would progress. He must have had a feeling about us, though. It's not something you can hide very well. It just wasn't anything we had told anyone yet. As far as he was concerned, Gayle was just this very self-assured, sophisticated-acting honey sitting at the same table as he was. She was somebody to share a smoke with, bounce a few of his moves off of. I sat there smiling at his whole act.

He bled one bucket of blood. The bike had been run over, that was obvious from the way the frame was now operating in two planes instead of just one. Bam's father came running out with this sofa cushion in his hand, the first thing he had grabbed. Bam was sitting up hugging his knee to his chest. The whole pant leg of his jeans was soaked. Mr. O'Day stood there with this puzzled look on his face, turning the cushion over and over in his hands like he was trying to figure out some way to use it on the leg to stop the bleeding. Then he saw the wrecked bike in the middle of the street and he started yelling at the rest of us. That was how he dealt with it. His son had totalled his new BMX that had cost about two hundred dollars.

They were playing "Macho Man" for about the fifth time when one of the real idiots in our building, this nut who had decided to become a teacher after eighteen years of being an appliance salesman at Sear's, brought his Volkswagen into the building. He must have got all his buddies to help lift it up the stairs. We heard the motor running and turned around to look where people were pointing at the cafeteria windows behind us and there he was driving backward and forward in the hallway. Two student constables went out to try to stop him but couldn't really do anything except look stern and shake their heads the way their parents might in the same situation.

This was too much for Bam. He'd been working in the mail room of the Empire Life Insurance Company since high school and I could tell it was getting to him, draining him somehow. He wasn't even supposed to be with us. He'd just taken off at noon, driven all the way down, about a two hour drive, with no intention of making it back in time for work in the morning. "You got me for the whole fucking *fin de siècle*, Hill," he said. He meant the weekend but he actually went back home that same night.

Gayle was being too cool about him being there. I wanted her to give me a sign that it was time to head up for the night but she kept touching his arm when she spoke to him. When Bam saw the VW Bug outside the pub doors, he downed the last of his beer and Gayle's, too, and grabbed her by the hand. She laughed and almost stumbled trying to keep up. They ran out the door together and I went out behind them along with most of the rest of the pub.

We heard that the ex-salesman killed himself just before graduation. Not many people knew about it. They were all out trying to get hired. He was making this show of weaving close to the people in line who were waiting to get into the pub, making them think he was going to hit them. He skidded to a stop in front of Gayle and Bam. She was still holding onto his hand. In reflex she turned and buried her face into his chest.

It's hard to know what made Bam do what he did next. He has this streak in him. It made me think about him getting that Citröen driver back only a week after the accident. I don't even remember the asshole's name, only that he lived on Bam's street right where it ended, owned a chain of drycleaning outlets, and drove the only car of its make in the neighbourhood. Someone we knew said it was considered France's Rolls Royce. The guy wasn't really that old, forty maybe. He lived all alone in this huge house. Every Sunday morning he washed his car. He loved that funny looking car, we could tell by the way he buffed it dry with a chamois before he waxed it. We played ball in the park at the other end of the street and every Sunday a stream of sudsy water ran down and soaked the area around first base. Bam would look up the street at the source of the stream and yell, "Frog Face!" He knew the guy could hear him.

The name, "Frog Face," started back in the winter. Any time we had a road hockey game going and the Citröen guy was coming home after work, instead of slowing down to give us time to move the nets over to the curb, he honked his horn impatiently to let us know that he had no intention of slowing down. The first player to see one always called, "Car!" any normal time and that meant one thing. Bam was the one who first yelled, "Frog Face!" at the Citröen and we knew that meant get out of the way as fast as humanly possible. We all began saying it. That was when it started between them. That was before Bam got his nickname.

Bam still had his stitches when he fixed that fucker's wagon but good. He never told Mr. O'Day who the driver was. He never even mentioned the car. The story he told his father, the one he made me and the other guys swear we'd stick to, was that old lady Billingham's yappy terrier had run out in front of him and he had to stop so quickly that he went right up over the handlebars. The next question was how had he bent the frame all to rat shit if all he had done was flip over the

Richard Cumyn

bars and how'd his leg get so cut up by the fender? Bam said it just did, he didn't know exactly how. It just did. His father let it be.

The phrase, "Frog Face," was all Bam, even when we started saying it and fitting it into dirty songs. He had nothing against the French but he had a powerful hate on for that drycleaner who washed his car so devotedly every Sunday. Even after we stopped playing road hockey and took to the ball diamond round about the first of June, whenever he saw the Citröen he yelled the insult loud enough the guy would have had to be deaf not to hear. When he drove past, he looked straight at us like he was trying to burn a hole right through our eyes. He would have killed us if he'd been able to get away with it, that was the message. He would have killed us, not despite but because we were children. He was an adult who lived across a gulf none of us could conceive of spanning. Ever.

The guy knew us to see us, we'd yelled, "Frog Face" and splattered his car with dirty salt slush enough as he drove by. But he didn't know Bam's cousin, Henry, who was our age and lived on the other side of the city. Henry was over visiting with his little brother, Justin, the Sunday Bam got the guy back for running over his bike. I was in on it but never told anyone I knew a thing about it, not even after the shit called the police and made our fathers bring us down to the station to answer questions about it. Bam shouldn't even have been walking around, the risk of popping his stitches was still too great. But Henry's family was over visiting and it was this lush midsummer morning that made me think that it had to have always been that bright. At no time could it have been dark night. Bam had money from his paper route, five dollars, which Henry said he would split with Justin but we knew otherwise. We wouldn't have shared it either.

I would have done exactly what Bam did if I'd had the guts. It's what I was thinking when Bam lifted Gayle onto the roof of that Volkswagen: I wish I had thought of doing it first. It was such a commanding gesture. He put his two hands around her waist that she had been so proud of, barely 22 inches before I got her pregnant. She used to be proud of the fact that I could almost encircle her waist with my two hands. He boosted her up onto the roof of that car as if she was queen of the parade and he was king and this wasn't a car being driven inside a college residence by a drunken student teacher but the lead car in a grand football parade. Bam looked up at her, at his handiwork, this queen enthroned, and beamed. He opened himself all the way up smiling.

Gayle didn't know what to think, that was clear from her face. She gave me this pleading look as if to say, Who is this person you say is your best friend since you were kids? Who is he that he looks so pleased with himself? Not, Get me down from here. She was fully capable of sliding off quickly without much problem, although sometimes I think about her being up there and four weeks pregnant and neither of us knowing a thing about it. That was how green we were.

No, she stayed up there of her own volition but her look was full of these questions I knew she was demanding I answer. Explain Bam before another second passes, for one thing. That would have been something if I'd been able to do it. Explain Bam. That's a good one.

The guy who drove the Citröen, he might have been thinking the same kind of thing. He had no proof it was Bam who did that number on his baby, but a person would have to be a moron not to make the connection. You try to run over a kid out riding his bike at night and a week later the paint on one side of your car is burned off? It doesn't take genius.

Little Justin set up the distraction which wasn't difficult because he had no clue what was going on. I mean the kid was all of three years old. He loved to do just about anything there was to do with Henry and the little squirt loved to draw on things most of all. Bam gave Henry the fiver and a Coke bottle full of sulphuric acid that he'd funnelled from Mr. O'Day's basement workshop where he did plate metal etchings as a hobby.

"Don't get it on your skin," he told Henry, "and don't let Justin drink any."

Henry tapped his shoe in the stream of soapy water coming down the street and said, "What do you think I am, a moron?" Then he and

Justin started hand-in-hand up toward the big house at the top of the street. Bam and I hid in Mrs. Billingham's cedar hedge where we took turns peeking through my father's field glasses.

I saw Henry bend down and whisper something in Justin's ear. If the guy saw them, he wasn't paying an attention to them. The little pecker scooted around to the side the man wasn't washing and began to go at the car with his coloured sidewalk chalk. Bam kept grabbing the binoculars from me. When I looked again, Henry had walked a way back down the street and doubled back, giving Justin time to draw one hell of a surreal mural on the driver's door, the wet colours smeared all over the place.

Then Henry walked up behind the guy, who was down in a crouch doing a hubcap. We got the full report.

He said, "Hey mister, have you seen my little brother around here?"

"No, I haven't," said the man without looking up. I imagine him thinking, Leave me alone, you little peckerhead, this is the only day of the week I have to relax.

Then he noticed the little pair of feet under the car and the sound of creative humming. "What the?"

I saw him come around the front of the car, where he saw Justin making his masterpiece, and bring his hand up to his forehead. Next thing, he hauled the garden hose around to that side and started hosing the colours off. Justin began to cry. The guy finished spraying, then crouched down so that he was level with the boy, trying to console him but that only made Justin cry harder. We couldn't see Henry who was around the other side of the car but we knew what he was doing.

What was it about Bam and cars? The guy driving the Volkswagen, the drunk, reached one hand up through his open window and grabbed hold of Gayle's leg, at the same time throwing the car into reverse. This was getting to be too much. I yelled for him to stop. Gayle was screaming at me. I looked at Bam who was laughing while he unbuttoned his shirt. The car shot forward, toward us again and Bam stepped into its path, waving his shirt in front of it. The guy slammed the brakes on hard, leaving rubber a good thirty feet past where Bam sidestepped it. When the car stopped, Gayle kept going, rolling down the windshield and hood and onto the floor like some crash test dummy without its seatbelt. Bam was still laughing. I ran to Gayle, got her to her feet. She was shaken and crying but unhurt.

Bam said to Gayle, "You have just experienced the ultimate rush, my dear."

I told him to shut the fuck up. Then I walked back to the car and kicked the guy's door in, I was so mad. When he heard the sound he roused himself and hung his head out the window. I'd put a sizeable dent in the middle of the door panel. He got out to inspect it. Someone said later that he had been drinking since early that morning. He'd got his first practice teaching report back and had received unsatisfactory ratings in all five evaluation criteria. The third day in the school he had put some punk up against a locker and started cuffing him in the head. The principal had advised him not to come back to that particular high school to teach.

He ran his fingers along the dent where I'd cracked the paint. I was ready for him to come over and pound me out. The engine was still running, it sounded like a rattling little tank. Someone told him to turn it the fuck off, he was going to asphyxiate us all, but he left it running. He walked around to the other side and hauled back and kicked the passenger door with the flat of his foot.

"There," he managed to say. "Equilibrium."

He actually stayed at the college longer than we did although, like us, he didn't graduate. He was directing the annual drama department production that year, Agatha Christie's *Mousetrap*. He put so much time into the play that he did nothing else. None of his media labs got done, none of his lessons were prepared. We heard that the play was a big hit, though.

Slowly and deliberately, the way people will when they are trying to sound sober, he said, "If someone will help me, I will remove this vehicle from the premises," as if the whole lot of us had just finished a dress rehearsal and he was putting the wraps on it, the final word.

"If some of you would step forward . . . " He was swaying forward and back. "If someone could just . . . " dropping off, losing his thought.

"It's all right, Bud," said Bam. "Don't worry. We'll help you."

About twenty of them lifted the Volkswagen down the stairs and out of the building for him. Though he hadn't damaged anything, he had to pay a fine for the violation. I was still angry at Bam for the way he scared Gayle and I told him so when he came back inside. He looked at me like I was crazy.

"You haven't got the hots for that one, do you? Her ass is too big. She's a cow."

I told him to find the rock he'd crawled out from and slide back under. I told him I never wanted to see his ugly face again. I could have killed the son of a bitch. Gayle never knew what he said.

"He's just like that," I said after he'd gone. "One minute he has plans with you and the next he's out thumbing his way across the country."

Gayle said, "I noticed he limps. Is that from the accident?" Jesus, after terrifying her half to death, he still had her conned! I could have killed him.

The Citröen guy lost skin off his right hand up to the middle of the arm and paint off the driver's side of his car. By the time he realized what had happened, Henry and Justin were gone and we made sure they stayed out of sight until it was time for them to leave. He came around that evening, his hand bandaged, asking if we'd seen two boys that fit their description. He let us know by the way he looked at us that he knew what was going on. In September he put his house on the market and moved away.

He was out to kill Bam that midsummer night, though. The car's got those headlights that wrap around flush with the nose of the car. Bam knew it right away, even in the dark.

"Look," he said, "it's old Frog Face."

He stopped his bike smack in the middle of the street.

"Car!" he called, the way we did it in winter.

Instead of swerving around him, the guy stopped inches from Bam's wheel.

"Get out of the way, please," said the driver in this voice, this fatigued, condescending, hateful voice.

"Go around, Frog Face," Bam said. I couldn't believe it.

"Move your ass, kid, or I'll run it over."

"Go ahead."

The guy considered this for a minute and then backed down the street all the way to the park where we played ball. At first I though he was going to turn around and go another way but he stopped, still pointed toward us.

"What's he doing? What's Frog Face doing, Hill?"

I said, "How should I know?"

Then the Citröen's high beams flipped on and he started cruising up toward us, not really giving it much gas, just letting the car find its own way up.

"He's not stopping," I said, squinting, from the curb. "Better get out of the way, Mitch." What did I know?

He stood up on his pedals, balancing, waiting. Then he released his brake and, still standing, began to roll down toward the car. Though he didn't pedal, he was picking up momentum faster than the car. The collision was stupid, just a stupid avoidable thing. When Bam hit, he had lifted his front wheel right off the ground. I couldn't see all that well in the dark but the way it looked, he was as bent on attacking the Citröen as Frog Face was determined to roll unimpeded up that hill into his own driveway. It sounded like a gunshot. Bam hit, slicing his leg open on his own fender, and somersaulted the length of the car over its roof. The car kept on going straight, running over the bike on its slow, relentless march home.

When Bam arrived, Gayle was having a bath and the baby was asleep. He had three studs in his ear, big deliberate holes in the knees of his jeans. His Converse sneakers were two different colours, one red, one green. Port and starboard, he said. He was drunk. He dangled a champagne bottle by its neck.

"Where's this kid?" he said.

I told him the baby was in its cradle in the bedroom.

When he opened the bottle, the cork flew across the room and hit our one and only print, a Bateman cougar, cracking the glass. I came back from the kitchen with two juice glasses. He filled mine to overflowing and took a chug from the bottle. Some of the carbonation backfired through his nose and he started laughing and sputtering.

He talked about what he was doing, working for a record distributor now. He had a company car, free concert tickets any time he wanted them, an expense account. He was making more money than his father.

"Most of it goes up my nose," he said.

For some reason he got to talking about this story his father had told him. Mr. O'Day used to work for a mining exploration company. Much of the electromagnetic work was done in the winter when they could get out onto the frozen lakes. It was tricky, though, getting up there. They had to wait until freeze-up to be sure it was safe enough to land the planes on the ice. Mr. O'Day was the leader of a group of eight men prepared to establish a base and run tests right through until spring thaw. His men were eager to get in there and start banking their isolation pay which would begin to be deposited the day they set up camp. The problem was that there had been a series of short freezes and thaws that fall and the ice was what they called candling. Mr. O'Day thought it wouldn't hold a plane. He stepped out onto the ice and showed them by ramming his axe handle down through the first crust. He wanted to wait another week.

The other men were not willing to wait. Mr. O'Day was replaced as leader. He was told that the plane was flying that day. He could come with them or stay. He thought about his wife and new baby that he had left so far away at home. If he had been single, he told his son, he would have risked it. They could probably run the plane on its skis as close to the shore as possible. If it started to go through the ice, the worst that would happen would be that they'd get wet and cold wading through the shallows. The balance was tipped, though, by the fact that he had two people back home depending on him. He decided to forfeit the isolation pay and stay put. There was nothing for him to do up there and so they shipped him home.

The plane landed safely and the crew had a successful winter. Their tests indicated the presence of substantial ore body beneath the lake, what would become a lucrative mine. The man who took over from Mr. O'Day as crew foreman that winter went on to become a vice-president of the company.

"He said to me, he said, 'Mitchell, the night I drove you to the hospital, I was as frightened and angry as I have ever been in my life. I sat in that waiting room with your mother for five hours while they reattached the muscles and nerves in your leg and I wept. Like a little baby. Boy, it was as much for me as it was for you that I cried.' Doesn't that beat all, Hill?" said Bam.

I could hear Gayle's light splashing sounds coming from the bathroom and I knew she could hear us. When she takes a bath, she likes to let hot water from the sponge dribble down onto her face and chest. Bam talked and drank until the bottle was empty. I had the one glassful. Then the baby woke up hungry.

"I just fed him twenty minutes ago," I said.

I got a bottle of breast milk from the fridge and heated it up in a pan of water. Bam stood in the doorway of the kitchen and watched.

"You got it under control, don't you, Bud?" he said.

I had the kid on one shoulder and I was swaying from side to side, trying to calm him down while the milk warmed.

"I'll be on my way, then," he said.

"Thanks for dropping by," I said.

"Is that all, Hill?"

"I guess it is,"

"So you went ahead and married her."

"That's what people do."

"Frog Face," he said.

When she heard the door close, Gayle said, "Come in here. You have to see this."

I opened the bathroom door. The water was level with the top of the tub. Her breasts floated on the surface.

"Watch this," she said. The baby had stopped crying for the moment and was rooting at my shoulder. Gayle lifted her breasts and twin jets of milk spurted out. "As soon as your friend came in, this started to happen. I was listening to you talk and these started going crazy. Look at this water now." It was all cloudy.

"I thought you were going to say, 'As soon as the baby started crying.' "

"No, it was as soon as I heard his voice."

"Why didn't you get out and say hello?"

"I don't know why. I was starting to flow. It was nice. I didn't want to move."

"He drank an entire bottle of champagne himself. He looks . . . not so great."

"Then I'm glad I didn't get out. Here, hand him to me," she said.

"In the bath?"

"It's warm. Take his sleeper and diaper off." I undressed him and passed him down to her. "There. It's nice," she said.

It took a while for him to stop crying again. On the best of days he doesn't enjoy his bath in the little plastic tub we fill up on the kitchen table. Gayle played with him until he got used to the feel of the water. She held him so that he was half-floating, half-lying on her stomach. Her milk was flowing so freely now that it was no effort at all for him to suck. They looked like sea mammals lying in the shallows, all sleek and pink.

"I'm glad I only listened and didn't come out," she said. "He is your best friend. I like to think about you having a best friend. Does it make you sad?"

I said, "Yes. Yes, I guess it does. He came over because he had heard about the baby."

"We'll see him again," she said. "What was that bang I heard earlier?" I told her about the picture.

When he had drunk his fill the baby fell asleep. The three of us stayed like that for a long time, me on the toilet seat, Gayle and the baby floating together in the steamy water. I didn't want to move.

The Cock's Egg

Rosemary Nixon

C itoyen Mwanza hugs his titulaire folder to his chest and hurries along the pathway to his classroom. His fingers stick together. Two hours he spent in the forest last evening retrieving glue from the frangipani tree, cutting vines open to try to catch a weaver bird. Citoyen Mwanza is hungry. The Zairian teachers have not received a paycheque in three months and his stomach groans emptily when he stands before his classes explaining the stems and nodules of perennials. He caught no weaver bird last night, his stomach's hollow, and now he has stuck-together fingers.

A dog barks by a distant fire. The British Baptist Biology teacher, Mademoiselle Emma, crosses the path from her house. A moth with white half-mooned wings flutters behind her.

Last night the lights from Mademoiselle Emma's jeep washed Mwanza's window, caressed him into wakefulness, and Mwanza rose from his sleeping mat and stepped through his doorway. Outside, the land was purple darkness. The heavens, hot and in motion, like a woman changing trains.

She is the kindest of the three white women here. They are so stingy, these whites, nothing gratuit. They move in a tight huddle, shop, pray, eat their evening meal together. Charge each other for their meals. They wear their rules like clothing. These British remind him of the weaver birds, weaving careful nests on neighbouring branches of one acacia tree, haughty, squabbling, fighting over food. When Citoyen Mwanza looks at Mademoiselle Emma, he thinks of food. She is the largest of the three, well-fed, she looks the best, although the village people say she eats only *fufu* and *saka-saka* at her house.

The headlights swooped backwards. He heard her laugh in darkness. They swept the football field, and whisked Mademoiselle to her house at the far end of the compound. Mwanza's mouth was bitter with kola nut. The night dark as kola nut. He could hear his neighbour, Citoyen Tukeba, and some students playing Scrabble by the light of Tukeba's cooking fire. Disturbed guinea fowl clucked in the trees. The headlights died.

His dreams. Citoyen Mwanza is bothered by his dreams. He dreams of food, of Mademoiselle Emma eating: plantains, corn, groundnuts, papaya. Night after night he's forced to watch her broad arms lifting, food falling to her open lips while he, Mwanza, shadowing dream's edge, slinks like a wily snake, watching for fallen crumbs.

Last week, Mademoiselle Emma's rooster laid a cock's egg. Citoyen Mwanza picked it up in the dirt outside her door. He feared she might be watching through her thick, brown curtains so he called, "Ko-Ko," and when she appeared, he extended both his palms and said, "Mademoiselle, for you," the small brown oval warm within his hands.

"Oh, what a small egg," Mademoiselle Emma said, "my hen has started laying."

"Oh, no Mademoiselle," Citoyen Mwanza said. "This is a cock's egg."

Mademoiselle Emma seemed not to understand.

"The cock's egg," Citoyen Mwanza said more loudly. "The village rooster has shown your young hen how to lay an egg. Now you will certainly be blessed with many eggs to fill your stomach in the days to come."

Mademoiselle Emma stared at Mwanza. "Citoyen Mwanza!" she said, "that a modern young man such as yourself, tutored at the university, would continue to hold such ancient and ridiculous perceptions about the world! In the name of heaven, Citoyen Mwanza, you teach Biology. What apparatus is there in a rooster that allows him to lay an egg?" Then the mademoiselle laughed. She laughed until she had to blow her nose, and Citoyen Mwanza, still holding the egg, backed off her steps.

Citoyen Mwanza nearly bumps into Mademoiselle Emma now bent over on the path, and when he trips against her she looks up and says, "Be still."

"Excusez-moi," Citoyen Mwanza says. The rudeness of these foreigners. But the woman laughs up at him and says, "No, Be Still. This flower. It's a Be Still flower. See, Citoyen Mwanza?" and Citoyen Mwanza has no choice but to kneel down beside her in the compound dirt and look into her pale hand which cups a little yellow trumpet-shaped flower with a fine leaf and a green three-segment pod. She rocks on her heels, wide and flat as a market woman's.

"I'm taking one to class this morning," Mademoiselle Emma says, "along with this," and she holds up a baobab flower, white with yellow tips, the big white petal turned almost inside out. Today she wears a red and gold *nlele* like a village woman. It loops around her heavy breasts and ties below her hip. Citoyen Mwanza needs a large wife. A wife to fetch his water, find his wood, tend a garden, pound his manioc and beans. He sleeps with high school girls, those eager to see his eraser rub out their failing mark, but they move on to pre-arranged marriages with men rich as their parents can afford. Citoyen Mwanza is already twenty-six years old. Losing respect. He sees this loss in his students' eyes. Yet how can he take a wife when he has no money to pay the bride price?

A noisy clutch of elementary children race up the path, Citoyen Mwanza looks at the mademoiselle, sunlight pulsing her hair, large, frivolous and silly kneeling there on the path, and he jumps quickly to his feet, not wishing to be caught in so undignified a stance.

"You do the hokey-pokey and you turn yourself about," the children sing, and do a jump-turn on the path. They carry a collection of instruments, a cowbell and a stick, beans in a jar, pebbles in a tin can, sand in a calabash, forming an orchestra as they run. Shesha–shesha shesh sh sh sh.

"And that's what it's all about!" Mademoiselle Emma sings, and greets the children with her happy laugh, as if a large white woman crouched on her hands and knees on a public path at sunrise is an everyday occurrence in an African village.

"Citoyen Mwanza, I've been teaching the small children some English songs," she says and staggers to her feet. The children swerve by, and there is stillness save for the buzzing of the flies. The heat rises and the wind dies and Citoyen Mwanza looks up at the sun, so big and round and hazy. The ancestors do not breathe. The compound smells of latrines and blossoms. He marches into the office of the titulaire for his ration of chalk.

Already before class begins, under the orange tree, the student Bilo, a surly sixth-form boy with bad teeth and no understanding of Biology, punches another for stealing his girl. Citoyen Mwanza has to separate the students and this makes him dishevelled and late for class. When he enters the classroom he hears the pastor's daughter complain that the fried goat meat she bought at market had a tuft of hair on it. His students can afford goat meat? A staff meeting called at ten o'clock, in the middle of Citoyen Mwanza's Biology quiz, forces him to collect the papers quickly and all the students shout that therefore the test should not count. On his return, to punish them, Citoyen Mwanza orders the students to sweep the classroom with palm branches, and in their frenzy of slapping walls and desks and floor, the students stir up such a choking dust it drives them from the classroom. They run off into the bush making great shows of coughing, pretending not to hear his enraged orders to return. Mademoiselle Cynthia, the angry, scrawny British Baptist, watches from her classroom doorway, glances sharp as a machete blade. Somewhere, he hears the smush smush smush of mortar and pestle in corn. Mwanza longs to sleep through the heavy heat of his hunger pangs.

When Mwanza cuts through the grass down toward the stream to bathe in the early evening heat, he sees the bowed heads of the three

British Baptist women through Mademoiselle Emma's screen door. Letters, maps, compasses. These women are always measuring their way. Mademoiselle Emma rises, then squats just inside the door, lighting a mosquito coil. Light shines through her. There is a smell in the air as old as Africa. The smell of bees in honey. A half-mooned moth floats above the mademoiselle. A tall woman with a growth on her ear runs by chasing an orange lizard. For a moment she obscures Citoyen Mwanza's view of the mademoiselle, glowing large in her bleached Matadi floursack dress. "Minoterie de Matadi" her shoulders read in large black print. "Qualité supérieure" read the great buttocks in small blue letters. "Poids net 4536 kilos." At her hem line: "Produit de la Republique du Zaire." The moth alights on Mademoiselle's forehead. The evening light turns green and Citoyen Mwanza leaves the village compound. He passes a group of village wives, climbing back up from the stream. The right side of the road gapes in an extended hole from last night's rain, so the women come barely to Mwanza's loins as he passes. Mornings Citoyen Mwanza sees these women heading for their fields, sour mouths, backs bent beneath their hoes. They avert their eyes as Citoyen Mwanza, the teacher, passes. Afternoons these same women lean into the river, washing clothes. They scrub pants and *nleles*, flap the clothes between them. Sometimes the wet cloth descends over their heads. Then they fight their way out, laughing, their own *nleles* wet and heavy against their arching bodies.

Citoyen Mwanza sheds his clothes and sinks into the bathing hole. The water, deliciously cool and flowing, laps around his privates. The ancestors' breath is on the evening wind.

Next morning at sunrise Citoyen Mwanza kneels in a patch of *ntundulu*, swallowing the citrus-tasting berries. Speak to me, oh ancestors, he prays to the morning wind. Bring me a wife. Before the students crowd into the church for morning prayers, Citoyen Mwanza heads down to the river to check the fishtraps he set overnight. Touch me with good fortune, he prays. Empty. All is quiet on the river. The wind flutters the palm trees, the sun rises like a great fire. Mwanza feels

Rosemary Nixon

weak with vertigo. He longs for honey. Milundu compound is thick
with the buzz of flies.

Saturday, after morning classes, Citoyen Mwanza walks the road
to market. He stops first at the doughnut seller, caught by the delicious
aroma of hot fat in the huge cast iron wok. He wanders through the
market place, skirts a small boy balancing a chameleon on a stick,
ignores his students who barter for a bit of sugar in a paper cone, boiled
chikwanga wrapped in banana leaves, a piece of salted fish, a half-glass
of peanuts. He ignores the village men who gather to chew lobes of kola
nut and spit their rich red juices in the market dirt, ignores the bright-
eyed goats that leap sideways and butt without warning, ignores stray
dogs. If he could just afford himself a small packet of *chikwanga*. A pile
of fine Western shirts lies heaped at a vendeur's stall, straight from a
missionary barrel. Beside them hangs a row of used tea bags. The
caterpillar vendeur pours tasty green roasted caterpillars from one
hand to the other; smoke blows in Mwanza's eyes. Citoyen Mwanza
is examining a stick of roasted bats when he sees the three British
mademoiselles weaving their bicycles slowly down the rutted hill,
shopping baskets balanced on their handlebars. Citoyen Mwanza drops
the bat stick and waves. The women reach the abandoned railroad
track. The two thin mademoiselles ignore his greeting. Elbows out,
they steer carefully their bikes across the ties. But Mademoiselle Emma
grins, shouts, "Bonjour, Citoyen!" raises her arm, and drives her bike
against the iron rail. The bike skids sideways. She tips slow motion,
raised arm veering, leg lifting high. She sprawls on the railway ties,
skirt billowing and caught above her knees, her glasses hanging
sideways off her face. A jostle of women, market vendeurs and students close a circle round her, mocking, slapping knees, gyrating to
reenact her fall. Small children, unable to see the object of derision, run
to collect stones in the hopes a crazy man is caught within their circle.

Citoyen Mwanza, frenzied, stuffs a roasted bat down the loose folds
of his floursack shirt in a desperate throw of caution to the winds. Then,
seizing the opportunity, he leaps. Three manly skips and he reaches
Mademoiselle Emma's side, brushes off her shoulders, offers his arm.

Mademoiselle Cynthia hops off her bike like a scrawny chicken, and yanks down Emma's floating blouse. Surprised, Mademoiselle Emma smiles cheerily, flaps at her skinned knees, and puffs to her feet.

The crowd, caught in this hiatus, stares at Citoyen Mwanza who stands gallantly beside the white woman, left arm squashed against his stolen bat. "The show is over," Citoyen Mwanza says in careful English. He read that line in an American Western he borrowed from the school library.

"Yes. Go on with you," the mademoiselle laughs, flinging her arms. "The market vendeurs await your business." The crowd hesitates, splinters and streams back to the stalls.

"Thank you most kindly, Citoyen Mwanza," Mademoiselle Emma says. She extends her hand. Citoyen Mwanza takes it. Her warm fingers, mottled with dirt, curl large around his.

Citoyen Mwanza nods to the women, ignoring the frowns of Mademoiselle's two friends, and strolls through the crowd, head high, past the mademoiselle's bike (ah, what he would give for such a bike), steps over the railway tracks, elbow clenching his squashed bat as tightly as one would parade a school textbook or a new bride in one's home village. His knees shake with relief. Bees moan. A half-mooned moth takes flight. Citoyen Mwanza puffs up the last muddy stretch of road and turns toward CECO compound.

By morning the news has flashed over the school compound. When Citoyen Mwanza breaks a twig from the lemon tree to brush his teeth, he hears the teachers' wives gossiping over their cooking fires. "Mademoiselle Emma favours Citoyen Mwanza." When he emerges from the bushes, wiping his hands on grass, he hears the students' chatter. "Citoyen Mwanza yearns for the mundele Emma. For her, he has performed an act of kindness." Early afternoon he hears the whispers as he strips the silky fluff from a kapoc tree to restuff his mattress. "Mademoiselle Emma sees in Citoyen Mwanza a husband."

Citoyen Mwanza drags home his kapoc fluff and lifts the cock's egg from the tin against his window. He holds the small hot egg between the fingers of his right hand and passes it over his body, head to toe. He will draw the mischievous spirit that has been causing his ill-luck into this egg. The ancestors have spoken. His fortunes include a mundele. Citoyen Mwanza lays the egg tenderly back in the tin, digs a small hole, breaks open the fragile shell, and disappears the black yolk into the ground. Then he lies on his sleeping mat and lusts for food.

Citoyen Mwanza, circling the hydrangea bushes at the sidewalk's end, sees his wife step out of the staff room at TASOK International School. Her green Western sundress swings about her thick white legs. She shifts her school books in her haversack and wiggles her toes in her Birkenstock sandals, a habit that indicates she's satisfied. Then she heads through thick sunlight to her classroom door.

A few short years ago, Mwanza could only dream of entering TASOK school grounds, could only dream of affording a wife to fetch his water, pound his manioc and beans. Now his servants, not his wife, bake his bread, wash his trousers. Now each day Citoyen Mwanza satiates himself on tender chicken, roast cow, canned pig, pineapple pie, and chocolate bars. Now he drinks all the tea he wants, thick English tea from tea leaves Emma's mother sends. Tea golden syrupy with milk and sugar, the colour of bees and honey. The day following his marriage, Citoyen Mwanza announced to Emma that she must give away her nleles and dress in Western fashion. He has insisted their sons have British names. Even now he will not listen to Emma lament the boys know no Kikongo. He is a modern Kinshasa man. Emma calls him her Congo man.

" 'The Congo.' A poem by Vachel Lindsay, 1879 to 1931," Citoyen Mwanza hears his wife say through an open window. Pages rustle. "A memorial to Ray Eldred, a missionary of the Disciples of Christ, who perished while swimming a treacherous branch of the Congo." Her legs will be planted wide. Her voice will rise as she rolls into the poem.

"Their Basic Savagery. Fat black bucks in a wine-barrel room . . . "

Citoyen Mwanza looks at his watch. Tea break. He can hardly believe, even after three years, that he owns a watch. A Seiko. And his watch wasn't bought from a tray of watches at Kimpese market either. Why, the Kimpese market would not offer such a watch as this. Citoyen Mwanza made a list, right after his marriage, of the things he would need. One must dress, eat, live according to one's status: a penknife, a bicycle, a watch, a tape recorder,

"Pounded on the table," his wife recites in a voice shrill with excitement,

"Beat an empty barrel with the handle of a broom,

Hard as they were able, Boom, boom BOOM,"

So now he listens evenings under electric lights to the tape of Kenny Rogers bought from a Peace Corps man. This morning he will visit his good friend Kapalata at his store. Since his marriage, Mwanza does not work at all. Emma's salary keeps them rich. Kapalata is impressed with Mwanza's wealth. He jokes that Mwanza should find for Kapalata a *mundele* wife also. But Kapalata has three Zairian wives already and both men know that he is jesting only.

"Then I heard the boom of the blood lust song

And a thigh bone beating on a tin pan gong," Emma cries.

Emma never comes along to visit Kapalata who she says stares at her; also she has heard Kapalata brag of his sexual prowess. Such talk annoys her; she grows damp-skinned and fidgety in its presence.

Sometimes Citoyen Kapalata hints that Mwanza take a second young wife, but on this point *mundele* women become difficult.

Citoyen Mwanza struts past his wife's classroom looking neither left nor right, as befits his status.

Citoyen Mwanza laughs when he remembers Kimpese compound. He sends fifty zaires monthly to his family. His five young brothers attend school. Mwanza's parents have put a tin roof on their hut. Even Emma's broad smiles on their wedding day, which struck fear into the wedding guests, did not bring bad luck. The ancestors surely are watching over him. Did he not once harbour a cock's egg?

Mwanza slips the tape into the tape deck in the Kombi and pulls out onto the potholed road leading to Kapalata's cloth store.

"Mumbo-Jumbo will hoo-doo you!" chants Emma in his ears, drowning out the man's voice on the machine. It emerges lower, slower, as if his voice box is askew with emotion, ripe with silver-tongued devils.

"*Songonene*! What news?" Kapalata calls when Mwanza arrives at the store. His friend gives orders to a clerk and conducts Mwanza to his living quarters at the back where he opens two Fanta bottles filled with lime juice, and sets out *Kwanga* and green mottled passion fruit.

"With life, everything is well," Citoyen Mwanza says. He leans back in his chair to gulp his juice but stops when he hears rustling behind the door adjacent, just down the hall.

"You have guests waiting perhaps?" Citoyen Mwanza says to his friend. Kapalata is becoming very stout. The favour of the ancestors surely rests on him.

"No, no one, my friend," says Kapalata. He goes to his cooler and brings out a small tray of salted fish. "How is life on the great compound at TASOK International School?"

"I have no worries on that subject," Citoyen Mwanza says. "And of your own life?"

"Ah," Citoyen Kapalata sighs. "My third wife is sexually undisciplined. A woman who longs to be swallowed whole. She has conceived a fourth child before the end of the breastfeeding period of our third, and so I fear my next son will be deformed. She is too young, too active."

"Ah yes," sighs Citoyen Mwanza in sympathy, and grows restless, as if insects were burrowing beneath his skin, imagines Citoyen Kapalata's round-cheeked young wife with eyes like tigers-eye stone, imagines Emma, fierce-eyed and sweating. Boomlay, boomlay, boomlay, BOOM.

Citoyen Kapalata sits down, and they discuss the crops, the rains, and Kapalata's recent business trip to Europe for new cloth. A light breeze stirs the palms. A bee drones in the compound.

"Citoyen Kapalata," the young clerk calls down the hall. "One needs your assistance. A young man cannot decide which cloth to buy for his wife and values your opinion."

"Always the job," Citoyen Kapalata grumbles proudly, and disappears down the hall.

Kapalata's voice fades. Citoyen Mwanza drinks more juice and eats two pieces of salted fish. Licks his salty fingers. The sound of footsteps. A closing door. Citoyen Mwanza hears wheezy breathing from the room adjacent. He eats more *kwanga*. His head grows heavy in the heat. He dreams of a field of flitting moths, of baobab blossoms, smells rich honey-bitter smells. A breathless cry springs from the room adjacent. Mwanza rises and tries the door handle.

Mwanza sees:

The top half of a woman sticking out of the thick brown jaws of a snake. The huge snake gulps, is still, then spasms once again. The woman struggles, her torso wet with sweat; another cry escapes her; she breathes with difficulty. Head thrown back, her eyes are closed and moist. She shudders in the heat. Her hands rest on either side of the snake's wide jaw. Citoyen Mwanza pulls the door shut with trembling fingers. The woman is Citoyen Kapalata's youngest wife.

Fifteen minutes later Citoyen Kapalata re-enters the back room. He is jovial, sweating profusely, running his hands over his western shirt.

"The room grows warm, my old friend," Citoyen Kapalata says. "My apologies for the delay. Me, I work always. Three wives cost time and money. What I need is a *mundele* wife like yours to do the business for me. Let us perhaps move outdoors into a small patch of shade. More refreshments?" He scratches his wide stomach and goes to the cooler for two cokes in Fanta bottles. Citoyen Mwanza sees now on the table four fetishes: a rag, an old picture frame, three rat hairs and a small bottle of *malafu*. He memorizes them. His throat is thick. The fetishes will give him powers. Emma will tremble at his manhood. He gulps his coke too quickly, coughs. Citoyen Kapalata laughs, pounds him on the back. Citoyen Mwanza feels like a small lizard peering against glass. Somewhere, a long way off, a monkey screeches. They move outdoors where a light breeze softens the hard sunlight. The scent of baobab flowers and bougainvillea is strong. It mixes with the thick rich scent of yellow cassia. Insects buzz. Kapalata sneezes.

"I believe your wives are well?" Citoyen Mwanza whispers.

"So they are. Luvualu, are you being lazy?"

Citoyen Kapalata's youngest wife enters the courtyard with a palm frond broom. She bends and sweeps swishing patterns in the settled dust. Her hips sway with each brush. She smiles. Her throat sparkles copper in the sunlight, becomes the colour of the earth she sweeps.

"And you?" Citoyen Kapalata asks. "You have all your essential powers?"

"I am thinking, with life — which is very good — " Citoyen Mwanza says quickly, "one's fortune might always be better." He glances furtively at Citoyen Kapalata who bites into a passion fruit. Green juice squirts down his chin. Citoyen Kapalata nods.

"So I have found."

They sit in silence in the fragrant noonday heat.

Late afternoon Citoyen Mwanza climbs into his Kombi. His fingers stick with sweat. A rag, an old picture frame, three rat hairs, a vial of *malafu*. A rag, an old picture frame, three rat hairs, a vial of *malafu*. He snakes down the window and starts the engine. Boomlay boomlay boomlay boom. He slips in the Kenny Rogers tape. He's a silver-tongued devil. He's got nothing to lose. Sunlight bursts beneath Citoyen Mwanza's eyelids. He pulls onto the potted road. The tires hum. Boomlay boomlay boomlay boom. He'll lay a cock's egg for Emma. Her toes will cramp with all their wiggling. A rag, an old picture frame, three rat hairs, a vial of malafu. His baobab petal, he will call her. He'll be her trumpet. He'll turn her inside out. His ears fill with an orchestra of bees.

Mumbo-Jumbo will hoo-doo you

Mumbo-Jumbo will hoo-doo you

And Citoyen Mwanza, dizzy with lust, imagines all the Kimpese girls who lifted their skirts for him in the forest, laughing.

Fall River

Tonja Gunvaldsen Klaassen

This is not the first time I dreamt of fire. Running and running to the west field. The moon was there — it was close to morning. The headaches come, as they always do after a night of running and fire, banging their strange noises even in this quiet room.

There are many silences in a house of fleshy women. We carry it heavily up the stairs to our rooms and lock the doors. Late at night when the curtains were closed and my shadow was huge on the wall, I listened for Abby's breathing, her bed moaning under the weight. None of us said good-night or commented on the morning, as though time and the seasons were distasteful and therefore did not exist. Ours was not a house built for idle chatter.

I wish he had never married Abby, it was she who brought this heaviness to the house. Even Emma, who was thin like our own mother, became fat and her features distorted. She loved me, we had no need for Abby. Emma smoothed my hair and told stories of wild-haired women who came from the sea, women with hair red as my own.

I turned Emma's stories like stones over and over in my mind until they were smooth, changing my father's wife and his house into something I could love. I added hallways between rooms and rearranged the furniture until the house resembled the grand, orderly homes on The Hill. It soothed me at first, a child's game to fall asleep, but it always went too far, waking in me a fevered restlessness.

This was the beginning of the fire dreams. Trapped in the house, choking in smoke, room after room of doors and stairs. Or sometimes just standing in the parlour in my nightgown, watching Father sleep on the sofa, the red flowered wallpaper climbing around him, as though I was haunting him and the house.

In daylight, the house never changed. Emma and I had our side and they had theirs. Abby used to come tapping at my door with her plates of cookies and sweets, but I sent her away.

My room is the larger on our side of the house. After the fight that woke the fear of Hysteria in us all, Emma moved to the smaller room and locked the door.

In the morning, Father left by half-past nine.

The following quiet covered us in a thin layer of dust. We didn't come out of our rooms, except to eat.

I was happy to have more space and for a while the dreams of running fire and falling water stopped. But the doors were more than I expected. Four of them: only one leading out. Emma's frequent invasion, passing through my room to get to her own, bothered me less than the door by the head of the bed. It broke the wall separating my room from Father and Abby. That door allowed their presence in my room. I could hear their rhythms —no loving, the thought sickens me —but their breath, the movement of the bed, their shoes falling.

Emma shut herself in the smaller room where sometimes I heard her nights of wordless rage, when her body banged about like a long dark fish out of water. One night I heard her cry out and then the banging stopped. When I tapped at her door she didn't answer, but I slept there on the floor in case she needed me.

We don't know these heavy bodies that keep us here, moving us up and down stairs. Although something inside me demands extremes —a burning and melting, falling water and bleeding —my body adds another layer of flesh and keeps that other inside.

I don't feel at home here in this room with its locked door, its barred windows. It is not the room or the lock which are so unfamiliar to me, but the questions. I am not used to the noise, to the assumption that I have the answers.

I tell them I remember being in the kitchen at eleven o'clock and on the stairs before that, returning pressed handkerchiefs to my room. But I may have been in the loft late in the morning. I meant to go fishing, to get out of the heat. I was searching for sinkers.

I depend on the river. Once, when we lived in poverty and my father was working to find what his father had lost, he too was dependent on the river: for the fish we ate and the money they brought.

The Quequechan gathers itself up into spectacular falls before it runs on to find the sea. I have lived at the bottom of these falls for thirty years. Only once has that water stopped falling —some fourteen years ago — the winter the river froze, the winter Uncle John brought his horses over the ice.

The falling is no mystery to me. I need to gather myself up, to find what my father has lost, what part of myself was left behind when my mother died.

She was thin: fine boned and lovely. I watched her fall, her wrists pounding the floor —almost as though she was angry. Doctor Bowen told Father the illness runs in families from mothers to daughters. He guards against it, watching Emma and me.

Sometimes I feel it well up in me and I let it, to feel close to her, my mother.

It's been a long time since I was a girl. I've never felt like a woman. The bleeding makes me long for water, for these cow-heavy hips to turn to fish. I carry pails of water down the steps to the cellar to wash away

185

the scent and stains. With no bath, no running water, I eat salt and wait for the sea.

It was Father who taught me how to fish. Of necessity, I suppose. After mother died and Emma still in school, he had to do something with me while he earned his name and fortune back. I imagined that I might fish with him forever. I carried his makeshift sinkers and listened to the whirr of his line.

We never fished together.

I watched every move he made, from the first great whirr to the fish's head smacking against a stone. Some things change and some things don't. Our mother died and Abby came to live with us, but after that no one ever left. Emma finished school and I started. Neither of us ever married, he wouldn't have it and no one would have us, living at the bottom of The Hill as we do.

It is Father who wears my ring.

Yes, I love him, he is my father. But more than that, I am his daughter. He wanted a son, but when I arrived, another daughter and his wife so ill, he gave me his name — Lizzie Andrew Borden — and this one thing above any other is the tie that binds us. Our name.

The name his father once lost along with his fortune.

I knew he had money, though that was a subject he refused to entertain, even with me. He never shared, never borrowed — that was his victory.

He was well known for his thrift. His marriage to Abby was convenient but respectable, she a Durfee, her forbears like my father's founded Fall River. In procuring a housekeeper and mother for his children, he had unintentionally rescued her — a penniless spinster. He wasn't about to pamper her with his hard earned money. The house he bought was modest.

But Emma found an upstairs faucet.

She was older and smarter, she furtively carried pitchers of water to her room, never wasting it, never running the water over her fingers and into the basin below. It was to be ours, Emma's and mine.

We couldn't keep it from him, his whole body tensed with our secret as a twig bends toward water. A gift I think he lost in this sea of silence. I didn't believe he would take the water away from me —he was harsh with Emma, but indulgent with me.

There were to be no secrets shared between Emma and me. No secrets between me and anyone else.

He had the faucet shut off permanently.

I have touched that tap many times since then, since I was small, every time expecting water, expecting he would have turned it back on, not for Emma, but for me to find. A secret shared by Father and me.

I want a whole tub of hot water like the women on The Hill enjoy. I am filled with fury waiting for water.

The heat wave is going into its third week. This is strange weather, so close to the river and no rain. The thunderstorms have turned the milk sour, paint is peeling off fences, gardens and grasses are turning to straw. The heat is oppressive and crazy-making. Fall River is standing still and boiling over at the same time.

Every day they come with their questions. I've asked them for a pitcher of water, my mouth is dry. Emma brings me pears and sits with me while I wait. It is too hot to talk.

There are things I do not remember. No one's memory is perfect, of course, but I forget the strangest things.

It's funny I don't remember the horses that night they were taken away. It wasn't so long ago. Father wouldn't have them anymore, said they were an extravagance he couldn't afford. Afterwards, the emptiness of the barn and the tension in the house wouldn't be stamped out. My father was kinder when I was a child. He wasn't gentle, never gentle, but he was protective.

They were gentle, the horses. Strange that an animal so heavy can be so graceful. Strange that an animal so graceful can be bought or sold.

Emma told me I was there when they were taken away. I have no memory of that night, but on other nights I dream myself a young girl with red hair and stamping feet, running between their long legs.

Now the barn is tangled in fishing wire, odds and ends, nails and broken locks so that it is hard to imagine horses there at all. The loft holds another kind of disorder: fallen dust, feathers, straw in the corners. There are no doors, just a hole in the floor. I could sit in the straw and watch the birds or read.

The birds. I remember the birds.

Not long ago, they filled the loft with the sounds of their day, their gossip and loving, feeding their young. Father had been calling me in the house until my name rattled the window panes. I came when I heard, but by that time he'd forgotten what he wanted except to know where I'd been. He was furious I'd been feeding the pigeons, said he'd have one for his dinner. "You do not feed animals that do not feed you." The house filled with the noise of his cutlery and their fine bones on the china plates.

Afterwards, his brooding, the *oo-oo-ooo* and noisy flight of it. He never mentioned them again, never called me in from the loft. He was sorry. When I discovered the green bands left out on the straw and two of the smaller birds missing, I knew he had not taken them. Someone had broken into the barn.

This was the second time in many many months. Earlier in the summer, a piece of Abby's jewellery which had been secretly removed from her dressing room showed up in a small wooden box left by the door of the barn. Such small threats bring families closer together, don't they?

Uncle John came the night after my pigeons were stolen. I never saw him, I stayed in my room. I can't say what he might have said about the birds. Father went out and throttled the others. We didn't eat them. He left them there by the ladder to the loft, a message: the birds' heads twisted off, their breasts so heavy with it.

Do most people remember the generalities or the specifics of their parents' deaths when they die on a day like any other? I tell them I may have been out in the loft late in the morning. I was in the kitchen at eleven o'clock.

Sometimes I iron or bake or reheat the mutton and gravy we've had for our breakfast, leftover from the night before, and serve it up with biscuits for our dinner.

I don't remember.

I can imagine standing over him, my father, like looking down from the top of a staircase. I am so light and he so old, that red flowered wallpaper climbing around him. It seems so clear to me and yet makes no sense. Who would have warmed the mutton and fixed our dinner?

When I try to fit these pieces together — too many pieces for so short a morning — the panic flies in my throat and runs along my arms like the night the pigeons were stolen.

Did my father have any enemies? Had I any hard words with my step-mother? What did we eat for breakfast? Were my father and his wife happily united? Did he seem affectionate?

My father still wears my ring.

I should think he left by half-past nine, already it was warm. He always left by half-past nine. None of us said good morning or commented on the heat so early in the day.

I don't remember eating breakfast with him. I may have eaten a cookie. Late in the morning I ate some pears. It was the beginning of the heat wave, I ate three pears.

I can't say where I was when I ate them. I picked them up from the ground where they'd fallen off the tree. I was in the kitchen at eleven o'clock. The screen door was unlatched. It's funny, I can't think where I ate them. I forget the strangest things.

The Wedding I Never Attended

Ed Kleiman

S ome people like to learn about their future by having their palms read or having tea leaves deciphered. Some like examining the entrails of slaughtered enemies. I prefer wedding photos. They seem to me foolproof. Take my brother Barry's wedding photo, for example. His wedding took place in Lethbridge, back in 1957, and I've always regretted not having attended. Not that I'm overly fond of family functions. Too often they're dominated by a sense of duty that just leaves me feeling dull and tired. You must come and smile and stay — whether you like it or not. But the photograph I have of my brother's wedding — all those impossible people collected together at that impossible event —looks as if it has totally vanquished the fates that, till then, had held sway over our family from Day One.

Marriages in our family have always been revealing events. Take my parents, for example. Their matchmaker was the Russian Revolution. An extraordinary claim, you might say. But not really. My mother's family lived in an immense two-storey house in the south end of a Russian village called Balta — near the Black Sea — and my father's family lived in little more than a hovel in the north end of that same village. With the coming of the Russian Revolution, a radical redistribution of wealth took place, with all the local Red commissars pocketing everything that hadn't been hidden away. The hovel was used to house

Red cavalrymen, and my father's family was billetted in the second floor of my mother's home. So my father and mother met.

"I didn't even know he existed before the Revolution," my mother says with a note of astonishment still in her voice. "Then one day they moved in upstairs as if they'd always been part of the family. And not just one person —my future mother- and father-in-law, their sons and daughters and a son-in-law, as well."

"It was a surprise, for sure," my father says. "But later when the Communists got us marching through the village with wooden rifles, I knew it was time for our family to leave. I would send for your mother later. The next day we were gone."

"With all *our* sheets," my mother adds testily.

"We needed those for crossing the Prut River into Roumania."

"You *flew* on them, I suppose, across the water like on a magic carpet?"

"No, no. I've told you before. The river was covered with ice and snow, and we crawled across under the sheets so the border guards could not see us."

"And *we* had to sleep on bare mattresses," my mother concludes.

Three years later, after my father's family fled Roumania and set sail for the Canadian prairies, my mother's long-held hopes were fulfilled when she received a letter one day — all the way from Winnipeg — proposing marriage, along with a Cunard ticket for the next boat to leave Riga.

There they all are, in my brother Barry's wedding photo, my father in a tuxedo and bowler hat, neither of which he's ever worn again, and my mother in a long dark evening gown that tells you, in no uncertain terms, that —despite the lack of sleeves or even shoulders —it cost a bit. But the clothes don't fool you for a minute. You look into those faces and you see the Russian Revolution there, the toughness, the determination to escape. The photographer and guests and lavish wedding hall are barely acknowledged, tolerated —but just for the moment.

Ed Kleiman

To the right of my mother is her niece, Anna, with her husband Mel. The faintly tragic air on Anna's face as she gazes at Barry is all that is left of the adolescent crush she'd held for my brother, a passion long ago forgotten by most people, but one which still means a lot to my mother Rose. She still sees Anna as Barry's best friend and, accordingly, her best friend. As a result, she would, without hesitation, do anything for Anna, except maybe dying —and would probably do that too, though she'd have to think about it for half a day first.

Anna is enormous, over two hundred pounds. Her elaborate hairdo, combed high and fluffed out, makes her look even bigger than she is. Her dress is specially made, blue taffeta over silk, and costs more than anyone there would earn in a month. On her right hand, she wears a clear blue sapphire, simply cut, that flashes out its unmistakable message for a circumference of at least thirty feet: *Money! Money! Money!* Her necklace and earrings are no less opulent. The face she turns to the world is child-like, open, radiant. In my mother's eyes, she'd be a goddess if she weren't such a scandal. All that passion combined with all that weight and jewellery leaves her puzzled.

But Anna isn't puzzled. The weight she sees as part of the Buchalter curse of clumsiness and awkwardness. Downright doltishness. She's heard it in her father's voice, that bumbling quality; whereas from her mother she gets her expensive tastes, style, critical eye, intelligence, wit. But at times they threaten to disappear, almost totally submerged in her huge frame. Anna is a battleground between grace and oafishness, and she looks upon her predicament with no small degree of amusement. Also, it is a challenge which she does not dare ignore.

Anna's mother does not care at all for this particular son-in-law, and she is not at all bashful about letting everyone know it. She will not tolerate his calling her "Mom". And so, much to her annoyance, he has taken to calling her "Frieda".

"Well, Frieda," he says as both families gather after the wedding rehearsal —one of the many events in Lethbridge described to me later — "You've got to admit, no matter what you thought of me before, that I've provided your daughter with everything a wife could hope for: a house, car, money, children . . . "

Impatiently she cuts him off. "I don't have to admit anything." Her eyes still flash with anger even though Anna and Mel were married almost ten years ago.

"But what else could Anna want?"

The anger rises in her voice: "A husband the world could respect!"

Once more Mel senses defeat, though not yet the magnitude of it. He knows his reply sounds apologetic so he makes the words boom out: "Well, Anna likes me well enough."

"That *naar*? —that fool?" Frieda translates just in case he doesn't understand, "she never did have much taste." And her eyes glower at Mel, acknowledging him to be the living proof of her statement.

Mel is even more gigantic than his wife. His mother-in-law holds even his size against him. Even? I should say especially. He sells women's underwear in Miami (another sore point), and his store there is the most successful in the whole city.

When I think of them flying all that way from Florida, I envision the plane just barely able to skim the tree tops. In Lethbridge, they rent the biggest, poshest car available: a Lincoln convertible with a purple body. Everyone in town knows the car. Hertz uses it mainly as a promotional model in TV ads, but there it is suddenly on the streets of Lethbridge and in it two *superhuman* beings.

Everything in Lethbridge becomes smaller in their presence. "Isn't there a bigger hotel?" Mel asks as he enters the lobby of the Marquis —Lethbridge's best. "A better restaurant?" "Larger stores?" Mel's voice booms through the streets and my mother Rose looks at him proudly, letting all know that he is her nephew and he owns the largest and most successful store in women's underwear in Miami.

Mel became intensely interested in that line of clothing when he was still a high school student and discovered that he had grown to such huge dimensions that his mother was forced to make his undershorts. Certainly, no underwear sized XXXL was available in the stores. And he later discovered that what was, as an adolescent, the source of both embarrassment and awe had become a lifelong passion. Underwear. But no signs of all that pent-up, teenage lechery now remain. Nor of his adolescent recklessness.

For weeks in grade ten, St. John's High School had been abuzz over what had happened one Sunday afternoon. When his best friend's parents, the Schellenbergs, were out at a Y.M.H.A. meeting, Mel and a few more friends had actually been able to convince some bold and adventurous girls to play strip poker in the Schellenberg's garage. After three frenetic and sweat-stained hours, the girls had emerged, red-faced and triumphant, not only still in possession of all their clothing, but also in possession of Mel's trousers, shirt and extra-large underwear. Wearing an oversize woman's raincoat — taken from the closet of his friend's mother — Mel had had to flee home over backyard fences and narrow back alleys.

But now no one would ever have guessed at his earlier embarrassment. He looks about him at waiters, gas pump attendants, policemen — in fact, at everyone in Lethbridge — as if he could buy the City Hall and the whole town itself and raze the whole mess to the ground if the town insisted any longer on annoying him with its smallness. "Why, a fellow could walk around this whole town in just a morning," he says with a note of astonishment in his voice. "Provided he didn't walk *too* fast."

But Anna knows how to keep his outrageous talk in check. Words never fail her in any crisis, and that gift has served her, as well as her mother, very well. In Miami she's become editor of the sales catalogues for women's clothing stores, and, in minutes, she can put a discreet-but-telling paragraph down beside the most outrageous — and transparent — article of clothing. For Mel her strategy is simple. "Just don't forget," she scolds, "who taught you how to play poker!"

But if Anna has, throughout the years, been my brother's secret admirer, then my Aunt Faigele, my father's only surviving sister, has been my brother's outright nemesis. Between my Aunt Faigele and Barry there are no devious strategies employed, cunning slights, equivocal phrases. Between them it is outright war.

THE WEDDING I NEVER ATTENDED

The day has long since passed when my aunt could forgive the things he's said about her. When she'd phone our place and was unlucky enough to get my brother Barry on the line, he'd announce loudly, "Well, if it isn't Cuckoo Bird on the phone!" And then, turning to us: "Anyone want to speak to Cuckoo Bird?"

"Barry, don't be such a pest," my mother would scream. But just let my Aunt Faigele say anything even slightly critical, and my mother prepares for the kind of war that Stalin waged against the Nazis.

Aunt Faigele is though of as a cuckoo by most of the family. Not because of what she is, but because of what she does. She's always wanted to be a millionaire, you see, and if only she could have scraped together a little more capital, with her initiative and enterprise, she'd have made the Reichmans take to the hills long before the banks forced them to. She buys and sells properties, rents out apartment blocks, opens second-hand stores, bids on condemned buildings, runs a neighbourhood newspaper, has opened a bakery, started up Jewish theatre in a cinema that folded, and has plans, eventually, first to take over the North End and then the whole city of Winnipeg — all with resources that total no more than five hundred dollars. How? By mortgaging properties she doesn't quite own yet, then getting bank loans using those mortgages as a down payment, and later moving swiftly and expertly into stocks and bonds whose volatility would frighten off even the Rothschilds. She has at times emerged from business deals owning whole blocks of the North End. Once I heard her trying to explain just one part of such an arrangement when she was outlining to my father why he should again bail her out of trouble with the banks.

"Don't be such a pussy cat, Velvel," she cried. "What's five thousand dollars when next week we can have forty thousand?"

"But Faigele . . . "

"Velvel, I'm so disappointed. What would our mother say? With your money to invest, I could be a millionaire already five times over."

The only trouble was that her business arrangements were so complicated that no one, not even she, could for long retain a firm grasp of all their complexities. And she didn't dare write them down for fear they could become evidence if she were ever tried for tax evasion. So when she forgets all the ins and outs of a business deal and all speculations collapse like a house of cards, and the banks foreclose and the bailiffs come, and the tax collectors send letters, she has only one recourse. She has a nervous breakdown. And the rest of the family has to tidy up the mess as best it can.

But Barry's jibes draw vehement attacks from her, as well. When my mother announced, as so many North End mothers announced right after their son's Bar Mitzvah, that he would one day be a doctor, Aunt Faigele attacked at once.

"You see this arm?" she cried out, pushing back the sleeve of her blouse. There the arm was — puffy, shapeless, an unhealthy white. "When grass grows on that arm, then your son will be a doctor."

But she's still not buried in the earth, and Barry is a doctor and she looks from the wedding photograph with astonishment on her face. She was determined to come to the wedding, to see for herself the bride and her family. She hadn't really believed in their existence. For that matter, she didn't believe in Lethbridge's existence. So she said to her husband, Morris, "Tell your boss, there in the C.P.R. station, that next month we go to Lethbridge."

"But, Faigele, it's not yet my vacation time."

"Vacation time, schmacation time. Tell him."

"But how will we afford the clothes? The trip?"

"You just tell him for a week to find someone else to sweep the floors in the C.P.R. station. The clothes and the trip and the hotel I'll look after."

And she is as good as her word. Clothing departments at Eaton's she had never before visited were suddenly startled into an awareness of her existence, *transfixed* you might say — and it would be months before they recovered from the shock. An evening dress, pearls, hand-bag, coat, shoes — the most expensive, the most stylish — in her they all encountered a challenge their designer had never dreamt of.

"But how will we pay?" Morris cried in astonishment that night.

"Who's to say we'll pay? Tell me, did I say we'd pay? Eaton's is Eaton's and Faigele is Faigele." And then Morris understood.

The train journey to Lethbridge was harder to arrange, as there were no trains arriving early in the morning and Faigele was determined she would not miss anything on Barry's wedding day. But there was an early freight from Calgary, and although Morris's railway pass alone might not ordinarily have got them into the caboose of that train, Faigele's presence at once vanquished all opposition. So it was in the caboose of the morning freight that they arrived in Lethbridge. And then it was on to the town's major hotel, the Marquis, to camp on the floor of a relative's rented room. The hotel did not long survive the after-effects of that visit. Before many years passed, it was torn down, to be replaced by the Royal Bank Building, which ever since has gazed warily toward the railway station for any signs of yet another freight train bringing newcomers to the town.

Aunt Faigele is more lavishly dressed than anyone in the wedding picture — except possibly for her husband Morris, who looks both uncomfortable and yet amused in his brand-new tuxedo. Perhaps that is because all the sales tags of his clothing have been folded in. They tickle his neck and stick uncomfortably into his waist, though they won't appear in the photo. But Faigele doesn't look uncomfortable. She's used to wearing clothing with the price tags still on. She doesn't even notice them anymore. And if the powers that be at Eaton's ever intend to have any more of her business, they better get used to having most of her purchases returned.

She feels no qualms at all about returning clothing to Eaton's. After all, thirty years before she'd returned her wedding dress. "What!" she'd said in astonishment, "to wear it one time and pay such a price? I have a better idea." And if she would return *that* item of sentiment and memory, she would return anything.

Why, several years after that marriage had taken place and she'd returned almost everything she'd worn, she'd adopted a brother and sister ten and eleven years old. Having her own children had been made impossible two years earlier because of the complications of a miscarriage. Adopted, did I say? Well, sort of. Bought, as a matter of fact, and smuggled across the American border. Our family is used to getting smuggled across borders. Three hundred dollars apiece, they had cost her. And a bargain at that. Or so she had initially thought.

I still remember the whole family being brought over to meet these new relatives: two blond children with hard faces looking suspiciously at all the adults dressed as if for a celebration. But they didn't last three weeks. Children, for Faigele, required just too much patience. They had reacted blindly — breaking some of her special dishes, stealing her watch and the new sweater she'd meant to return to Eaton's. So back across the border once again those children went. Not for her to cope with juvenile delinquents. It's true, there were no price tags to pin back on them, but still she got most of her money back. I sometimes think of those two — the blond brother and sister. They should have been in the wedding photo as well. How foolish for them to have created such a ruckus during those crucial first few weeks of their adoption. If only they'd been more accepting, Aunt Faigele would have made sure they survived, that they became successes. With her, they could have thrived.

So buying clothes she would later return to Eaton's and getting onto the caboose of a freight train and camping on the floor of a relative's hotel room hardly strained Aunt Faigele's nerves at all. She and Morris, in their still-to-be-returned clothing, stand to the left of my mother and stare out at the proceedings, she with astonishment that this impossible event should be occurring at all, and he with that puzzled look of amusement on his face, which — on second glance — looks to be more at this new display of her daring than at anything else.

Before they leave, in a passenger train this time, she will try to buy the hotel they are staying at and for years afterward will complain that her new Lethbridge relatives should not have intervened when the deal was all but salted away.

Now, at last, we turn to the bride and groom. Of Brenda, I can say little. She was a stranger to me then, and I see only a proud figure in white staring boldly into the camera. Is there even then, behind that look, a frozen quality to the smile that reveals her nervousness at this puzzling family she's married into?

My brother Barry is perhaps easier to describe. Perhaps. The face is dark and downcast. All the pain of the last ten years is there for everyone to see, but they do not recognize it. His troubles began with an I.Q. test in Junior High School that revealed, if I am to believe my parents and Barry, that he was brighter than anyone who'd ever taken such a test there before. That test was a curse. It made him arrogant —impossible to tolerate, in fact. The teachers giving the test had agreed not to reveal the results to their pupils, but like everyone in the history of the world who has ever administered those tests, they blabbed it all out within seconds of tabulating the results.

But nothing could blunt his interests. Those were the days when he read John Dos Passos' *U.S.A.* and couldn't find anybody but me to discuss the book's experimental nature with. And what did I know? Nothing. The book got him interested in jazz, cinematic techniques, architecture, sociology, aeronautics, astronomy, even grinding lenses for a telescope he was making.

"Look at what he's doing with the book here," he insisted. "He's using newspaper headlines in fiction. And jazz in his sentences."

"So?" I said dumbly.

Then he'd turn to the piano and play some passage from a Duke Ellington piece. "Can't you hear the same music in this paragraph?"

"What music? Which paragraph?"

But my brother's real problems began when he passed into Grade Ten and all his arrogance caught up with him. There he was mocked for all his interests, spoken of as pretentious, became the butt of teachers' jokes. And so he quit school in the middle of winter and nearly destroyed us all. He became a figure of ridicule in the neighborhood.

What's worse, he fought back with the wrong weapons. He became pompous, conceited, a name-dropper. In fact, he became the stupidest person with the I.Q. of a genius that I'd ever met.

A low point came when I was home for weeks with a broken ankle, the result of a missed vault in gym class. My brother who was reading a book on the chess masters offered to play me a game.

"I'm going to win this game," he announced, "without your taking any piece higher than a pawn."

"Let's just play."

"And if you win more than three pawns, I'll buy you a dinner at Wally's Steak Loft."

We played for hours all afternoon and into the evening, each move taking as long as half an hour. Again and again, we each worked out the consequences of the game to its conclusion. The game itself went on for three days — with my mother screaming in alarm and my father storming out of the house in disgust.

But on the fourth day, I struggled on crutches with my brother to Wally's Steak Loft. "But the food isn't even kosher," my mother screamed down the street after us.

Wally's Steak Loft was a fly-blown place with wooden benches and we were served by a surly high-school drop-out who saw in my brother someone giving himself airs, but who was in reality no different than himself.

At the end of that meal, which tasted like *dreck* —just plain old shit —my brother asked, "Now tell me, Michael, tell me, did you ever taste a better steak?"

This to his younger brother who Barry knew had never tasted steak before in his life. "Thanks a lot, Barry," I lied, and after he left a dollar tip for the contemptuous waiter, I limped out with my brother at my side. That night, after everyone had gone to sleep, I threw the chess game into the garbage.

But just when all seemed lost and beyond the point of recall, he began taking evening classes and correspondence lessons to finish high school, and then he went on to university. His grades got him through Medicine, but his pompous manner undercut his every achievement. Knowing the results of that high school I.Q. test has made him pay with pain every day of his life.

But who is the bird? Brenda, who has seen beyond the pompous tones and arrogant manner. I see her leading him out of that high school as if out of a tomb.

So the wedding for Barry is a rebirth, and his mother, standing so stalwartly beside him, is transfixed by a kind of ecstasy as he emerges at last into the light. Fleeing the Russian Revolution and setting sail for Canada has been a minor triumph compared to this. Cousin Anna, behind her in the photo, knew all along what was there, but no one would listen. And then perhaps even she doubted what her fifteen-year-old infatuation had revealed to her astonished eyes. It was an infatuation, she knows. Besides, cousins don't marry cousins anymore. But still she is pleased to have someone else share her vision of Barry.

Of course, Aunt Faigele sees only the devil who called her "Cuckoo Bird" on the phone. She *knows* this marriage will never last. Barry's pompousness, she is sure, will once more make him a figure of ridicule. So why should she pay real money for clothes to attend an unreal event. No, certainly not; she will not keep these clothes she is wearing from Eaton's. The sales tags pinching into her body are a constant reassurance and comfort that not one penny will be lost. She gazes at my brother Barry and his bride as if they are a mirage.

The look would shake even me if it weren't for the radiance in Brenda's eyes, for whom this wedding is the realest event of her life.

I gaze now at other faces in the wedding photo. At Brenda's parents. Who is to say what is in those faces? The mother wears a hat that scandalizes our family for years afterwards: a bright yellow and brown thing that would look more appropriate on a farm at the height of the harvest.

Who are they, these new relatives? Brenda's father is a clothing manufacturer who turned out thousands of military uniforms in the last war. But his is not a warrior's face. It is a round gentle face. He wears glasses which do not quite conceal some pain in his eyes. From whom? I look from face to face and then pause at Brenda's younger brother, Mortie — that smart-aleck look. Yes, here is the source, I am sure.

Ed Kleiman

Brenda's mother is looking at Anna with astonishment. That immense stone on Anna's finger, that gigantic hairdo. She'd be patronizing if she didn't recognize there a native taste and sense of style that is beyond her understanding. She has never before ever met anyone of Anna's size and obvious physical strength, and they make her aware of her own frailty: the lines on her face, the fragile lightness of her body. Anna's healthy face reveals nothing but her openness and good humour, yet Brenda's mother is just beginning to suspect just how ridiculous her hat would look in Anna's eyes.

For Anna is too good-hearted to patronize anyone. Besides, on this trip from Miami, in fact this very morning, Mel was unable to get out of bed, couldn't even see for a couple of minutes, though his eyes were open. She can remember only to well the symptoms preceding her father's final stroke for her not to guess what the future holds in store for them. So she stands there aware of Mel's bulk —and of her own —and of how all their intelligence and wit must struggle against the oafish giants they have become.

There are grandparents as well, and aunts and uncles, cousins, nieces and nephews: locked-in faces, faces with suppressed rage, faces that radiate a single note of innocence like a struck tuning fork, proud arrogant faces whose good looks will never become beautiful. They are all there, these new in-laws as well as old relatives —a curious family — some governed by powerful fates for far too long, recorded with photographic clarity, but yet not all that easy to read. There is my family that I'm getting to know better with each second more that I gaze at this photo. Do I sense my mother's perseverance in some yet unknown in-law? Or my aunt's darkness in a new cousin I have yet to meet? I gaze at this photo as if at members of a family I've known all my life. I blink and the next moment they are strangers. Yet there was one fleeting moment when I glimpsed their fates.

Have you not glimpsed that moment also when staring at this wedding photo? Do you not know this family? and I yours? This larger family at a wedding you and I have never attended? I see them all before me: the groom, the childhood sweetheart, the dark suspicious aunt, the father in a tuxedo, bowler hat and dark polished shoes that he was forced by his wife to buy. And the bride —the radiant stranger entering into our lives, wearing a gown from which all sales tags have been carefully snipped because she fully intends —despite all tradition — to be dressed in this gown once more before leaving this earth. That knowledge serves as a dark background from which she emerges in white. It serves, as well, as a centre of strength for the whole photo.

Though my new bride and I could not be at Brenda and Barry's wedding, for we were on *our* honeymoon (a brief European tour in between two years of teaching in London), I have always been glad that we were able, in the midst of busy Venice, to find a glass-blowing factory where we could buy their wedding gift: six red wine glasses with golden rims and a decanter, red as the wine it was meant to contain. A wish from the Old World following them to the New, smuggled in with the clink of glasses touching and the unspoken words of greeting, vanquishing forever the land of bitter memories — of Wally's Steak Loft and the struggles of our youth.

RUDY WIEBE first won the Governor General's Award for Fiction in 1973. He is author of seventeen publications, most recently *River of Stone* (Alfred A. Knopf, 1995) and *A Discovery of Strangers* (Alfred A. Knopf, 1994), and has worked as editor on numerous anthologies.

KEN MITCHELL lives in Moose Jaw, Saskatchewan and has written many plays, works of fiction, and poetry. He says, "My writing style continues to evolve, through the introduction of new subjects and themes. While continuing to be fascinated by the character(s) of Saskatchewan, I am looking further afield for counterpointing ideas. For example, two current projects include the stage adaptation (for the Globe Theatre) of a Saskatchewan story, 'The Great Electrical Revolution', and a novel about fratricide set in the Greek Balkans."

HELEN ROSTA lives in Edmonton, Alberta. Her short stories have appeared in various magazines and anthologies including *Kitchen Talk*, eds. Edna Alford and Claire Harris (Red Deer College Press), and *Frictions II*, ed. Rhea Tregebov (Second Story Press). A collection of her short stories, *In the Blood*, was published by NeWest Press in 1982.

FRANCES ITANI has published eight books of fiction and poetry, including *Man Without Face* (Oberon, 1994), a book of short fiction for which she won the Ottawa-Carleton Book Award, and *A Season of Mourning* (Brick, 1988), a book of poetry She has also won the Tilden Canadian Literary Award. Itani lives in Ottawa where she has taught Creative Writing for many years.

GUY VANDERHAEGHE is author of three collections of short stories: *Man Descending* (1982), which won the Governor General's Award for Fiction; *The Trouble with Heroes* (1983); and *Things As They Are?* (1992). His novel *Homesick* was co-winner of the City of Toronto Book Award, and his play "I Had A Job I Liked. Once" received the Canadian Author's Award for Drama.

DIANE SCHOEMPERLEN was born in Thunder Bay, Ontario in 1954. She has lived in Canmore, Alberta and in Kingston, Ontario since 1986. She has published six books, most recently, *In the Language of Love* (Harper Collins, 1994). She says of her writing, "I like to play with the more traditional narrative forms, always looking for new ways to tell a story. In 'This Town', as in most of my late work, I used my own experience as a launching pad for fiction and I tried to look at allegedly "ordinary life" with a clear, and often humorous eye."

EDNA ALFORD is recipient of the Marian Engel Award (1988) and co-winner of the Gerald Lampert Award. She published two collections of short fiction, *A Sleep Full of Dreams* (Oolichan Books) and *The Garden of Eloise Loon* (Oolichan Books). Her work appears in a number of anthologies and a radio play "Blue Canadian Rockies" has been broadcast on CBC Studio '95. "The Garden of Eloise Loon" was written in response to a story told to Alford. She says, "While the finished work is fiction, the story told to me was also one of alleged infanticide; the socio-economic circumstances and the abusive relationships, while depicted through fictitious detail, were also similar."

JAKE MACDONALD has published four books of fiction: *Raised By the River* (Turnstone Press); *Two Tickets To Paradise* (Oberon, 1990); *The Bridge Out of Town* (Oberon, 1986); and *Indian River* (Queenston House). He works full-time as a writer and lives, during the temperate months, on a floating wooden house in Minaki, Ontario.

SANDRA BIRDSELL is author of two novels, *The Chrome Suite* (McClelland & Stewart, 1992) and *The Missing Child* (Lester Orpen and Dennys, 1989), and several books of short fiction, including *The Two-Headed Calf*, to be published by McClelland & Stewart in 1997. Birdsell says of her writing, "Although I have been a city dweller longer than a rural person I am still, for the most part, drawn to set my fiction in a rural landscape. It seems to me that my fictional characters have a greater spiritual dimension than when I have them stumbling about in a city setting."

PER BRASK is a playright, poet and writer of short fiction. In addition to having his work published in many literary journals, he has worked as translator for several plays and books of poetry and fiction. Of his writing Brask says, "I write as a means of getting to know what happens inside myself, as a way of responding, as a way of living in the world, of coming to terms. I have no message, but I believe that the imagination is sacred and for this reason it knows both the dark and the light."

SHARON BUTALA has published five novels including *The Fourth Archangel* (Harper Collins, 1992), two short story collections and two books of non-fiction. Her recent non-fiction work *The Perfection of the Morning* (Harper Collins, 1994) was the number one bestseller on the Globe and Mail list in 1994. On writing Butala says, "I write mostly about the farming and ranching people of southwestern Saskatchewan, and about the land and its history. This is where I've made my home for the last twenty years."

LOIS SIMMIE lives in Saskatoon, Saskatchewan. Among her publishing credits are *Betty Lee Bonner Lives There* (Douglas and McIntyre, 1993), *The Secret Lives of Sgt. John Wilson* (Gouglas and McIntyre, 1995), and *Mr. Got To Go* (Red Deer College Press, 1995). Of "Mick and I and Hong Kong Heaven" Simmie says, "Some of my characters live on in my head and others don't. Mick is one who has."

BONNIE BURNARD is author of *Women of Influence* (Coteau Books, 1988), from which "Music Lessons" was taken, and *Casino and Other Stories* (Harper Collins, 1994). She says, "Recently, I've been thinking that my impetus to change life into fiction is nothing more than a need to slow life down, to bring it closer to me, and not for the purpose of cold-blooded examination but simply because I prefer it slower and closer."

SHARON MCFARLANE has had stories published in several periodicals and anthologies, including *200% Cracked Wheat* (Coteau, 1992). She writes and farms in southern Saskatchewan, where most of her stories are set.

ELIZABETH BREWSTER has published many books of poetry and fiction, most recently *Away from Home* (Oberon, 1995) and *Footnotes To the Book of Job* (Oberon, 1995). The Saskatchewan Arts Board has recently awarded her a Lifetime Award for Excellence in the Arts, to be presented in May, 1996.

BETH GOOBIE's Mission Impossible (Red Deer College Press, 1994) has been short-listed for the Governor General's Award for Children's Literature and was winner of the R. Ross Annet Award. Other recent publications include *Scars of Light* (NeWest Press, 1994), five *Series 2000* books for teens (Prentice Hall Ginn, 1992-1995), and *Could I Have My Body Back Now, Please?* (NeWest Press, 1991). She says, "Writing is the reach for balance and choice, an ongoing dialogue between dimensions, an act of making and meeting self."

RICHARD CUMYN is author of *The Limit of Delta Y Over Delta X* (Goose Lane Editions, 1994). A second collection of short fiction is scheduled for publication in the fall of 1997 by Beach Holme Publishers. He lives in Kingston, Ontario.

ROSEMARY NIXON's first book of fiction *Mostly Country* (NeWest Press, 1991) was shortlisted for the Writers Guild of Alberta Howard O'Hagen Short Fiction Book of the Year Award for 1992. Her second book, *The Cock's Egg* (NeWest Press, 1994) won the award in 1995. Nixon has published in literary magazines across Canada and her work has appeared in several anthologies. Nixon teaches creative writing through the extension programme at the University of Calgary and the Calgary Board of Education. She also works as a freelance editor and teaches summers at the Sage Hill Writing Experience in Saskatchewan.

TONJA GUNVALDSEN KLAASSEN writes in search of home and family, the journey there often revealing strange details of nature and memory. Her stories and poems have appeared in several literary journals, and her first book of poetry, *Clay Birds*, will be published by Coteau Books in spring 1996. She lives in Saskatoon.

ED KLEIMAN grew up in Winnipeg's fabled North End, a fragile, ramshackle community of immigrants from Eastern Europe that, for him, has served as a crucible of the imagination. Much of Kleiman's fiction continues to spring from that vanished source — a community that now belongs to the world. He has published two short story collections, *The Immortals* (NeWest, 1980), and *A New-Found Ecstasy* (NeWest, 1988), and his work has appeared in twelve anthologies in Canada and the United States.

PAUL DENHAM teaches Canadian Literature in English at the University of Saskatchewan. He has co-edited various anthologies, and has written on Raymond Knister, Sinclair Ross and Dorothy Livesay. A member of *NeWest Review* since 1983, he is also a member of Amnesty International, Friends of the Broadway and the Saskatoon Opera Association, and a regular volunteer with the Saskatoon Fringe.

GAIL YOUNGBERG has been a member of the *NeWest Review* group since the magazine first moved to Saskatoon. She is a freelance writer and editor, and a member of the Saskatoon Women's Calendar Collective. She has published a history of Saskatoon (as Gail McConnell), and some of her poetry has appeared in *Grain*.

Printed in May 1996 by

in Boucherville, Quebec